I0817861

THE MARIONNETTISTE OF VERSAILLES AND OTHER ODDITIES

Adam Millard was born in Shrewsbury, England, in 1980, and grew up in Wolverhampton. He is the author of the zombie novels, *Dead Cells*, *Dead Frost*, and *Dead Line*, and the supernatural novels, *Deathdealers* and *The Susceptibles*. He can be found at www.adam-millard.com

By Adam Millard

Only in Whispers
The Ballad of Dax and Yendyll
Grimwald The Great
Dead West
Dead Cells
Dead Frost
Dead Line
Deathdealers
The Susceptibles
Olly
Skinners
Divided
Chasing Nightmares
Peter Crombie, Teenage Zombie
Peter Crombie Vs The Grampires
The Secret Diary of Peter Crombie
Hamsterdamned
Vinyl Destination
Hamsterdamned
the Human Santapede
Milk
Zoonami
The October Boys
Stuff That
Jurassic Car Park
The Village of C

The Marionnettiste Of Versailles

And
Other Oddities

Adam Millard

This Edition Published 2024 by Crowded Quarantine Publications

A CIP catalogue record for this book is available from the British Library

ISBN 978-1-7384764-2-8

Crowded Quarantine Publications
124 Dimsdale Parade West
Newcastle-under-Lyme
Staffordshire
ST5 8DU

For Theodore,
You didn't pick me, but you're stuck with me from now on.

Table of Contents

The Marionnettiste of Versailles

The woman lit a cigarette and grimaced as smoke drifted up into her eye, causing her kohl to run slightly. Her dyed hair betrayed her actual age; unfortunately, the road-map etched into her face did not.

'Monsieur Grégoire, is there nothing cheaper?' she asked, glancing around the maison funéraire as if everything was labelled with its price. She wandered across to a wicker casket, flicking her ash on the carpet, unmindful of the annoyed eyes surveying her. 'This one,' she said. 'This is made of basket. It must be the cheapest in the room.'

Arnaud Grégoire sighed. 'You would think,' he replied, biting his tongue to prevent any manner of obscenities from flowing out. 'But I believe it to still be beyond the threshold of what you would wish to pay to bury your husband.' And such a poor, poor husband, Arnaud thought, for having to put up with your trout-faced misery for so many years.

'This is simply ridiculous,' the woman spat. 'How is anyone expected to be able to afford to bury their loved ones at these prices? It's a wonder people aren't just lining the streets in sacks, slowly decomposing in front of their own houses.'

That, Arnaud thought, would make life so much easier.

'I'm afraid I don't set the prices, Madam Mauriceau,' Arnaud said, almost sneered. Her belligerence was starting to take its toll on him. He would never have guessed, when she'd entered, that she was capable of turning one man's blood to mercury, and yet here he was, wishing for her to simply choose so that he might begin proceedings, or for her to leave, go away, never darken his doorstep again, the annoying, little witch...

'Then I may have to take my money, and my dead husband, somewhere else,' she said, with a tone of finality that Arnaud found most childish.

He could ill afford to lose Madam Mauriceau's money, however little it amounted to. Brunet & Sons was on its last legs already, without people just waltzing out with their half-finished relatives. He stepped up to her, only to meet with a plume of bluey-grey smoke, exhaled from her dragonlike mouth. Blinking away the discomfort, he managed to force a smile, though it was hardly noticeable and the woman in front of him was paying no heed to him, anyway.

'Have you thought about cremation?' Arnaud asked. 'We have a special offer this week only,' - they didn't – 'and would be delighted for you to take advantage of our generosity.'

With this, she faced him. Arnaud thought he saw something – a sparkle in those long-dead eyes – though he could have been mistaken. 'What's your idea of a special offer?' she asked, glancing around the carpet, searching for a suitable place to discard her cigarette butt. Arnaud didn't waste any time; he paced across the room and returned to her with a marble ashtray.

'Well within your budget,' he told her. 'You'll even have money left over to take yourself out for a fancy meal, perhaps a makeover.'

If she heard the sarcasm in his voice, she didn't react. No, she was too busy pondering the offer, no doubt satisfied and yet willing to push her luck with a lower offer, just in case Monsieur Grégoire was as desperate as he looked...which he was.

'A hundred below the budget,' she said, 'and you can burn my husband as much as you like.'

Arnaud watched as she squashed the cigarette butt into the marble; her rheumy, spindly fingers were as inhuman as the rest of her. It was like watching a man on stilts try to dance.

He sighed before giving her his most competent, comforting smile. 'Then it is settled,' he said. 'I'll start with the paperwork, and you, Madam Mauriceau, can go about your day, as I'm sure you have a lot of pressing matters to attend to.'

'Not really,' she replied, fiercely. 'Getting rid of him was the main thing on my list.'

Arnaud began to sign papers, handing them across the desk to Madam Mauriceau in order for her to do the same. Within an hour she was gone, never to be seen again, and Arnaud Grégoire heaved a sigh of relief as he made his way through to the back room.

To the place where the magic happened.

*

He placed his favourite cylinder in the phonograph – Bach's "Air on a G-string" – and as the introduction swelled he danced across to the table upon which Monsieur Mauriceau stared lifelessly towards the ceiling.

'How did you suffer her insolence for so long?' Arnaud asked the prone body. 'You're a bigger man than I, for I would have certainly put an end to her misery a long time ago.'

The body, of course, didn't reply. At least, not really. Arnaud thought he heard Monsieur Mauriceau defend his wife's attitude, suggesting it was merely a result of losing him, that she was often very lovely, but the voice was very thin, almost incomprehensible.

'Defend her all you like, Monsieur,' Arnaud said as he began the tedious task of unpacking his tools from a leather bag. 'That's your wont, after all. But I must say, I found her most disagreeable, and would have simply lopped of her face while she slept. Just my opinion, you understand, and one that you should take with a pinch of salt.'

Monsieur Mauriceau's lips remained still, and yet his voice said, 'You are merely a mortician, not even worthy of an opinion. Abelle was a darling, a saint, and it would do you well to remember that.'

At this, Arnaud sniggered. 'A darling, indeed,' he said. 'I would never have married such an uncouth wench.' He began to sharpen a blade, running it gently across the whetstone. 'And her hair...who does she think she is fooling?'

The body on the table said, 'What do you mean by that?'

Arnaud turned, smiled. 'Did she not always dye it? Oh, is that a new thing? Of course, now that you're dead and gone she will be in search of a replacement. Silver hair – which I assume is her natural colour – would be a little off-putting to the more desirable bachelor.' He grinned once more at the motionless cadaver of Monsieur Mauriceau before continuing with his preparations.

'Well,' the voice said. 'She most probably just wants to look her best for the funeral—'

'Are you an idiot?' Arnaud interrupted. 'She will be out every night in search of a man, a man that you could never be. It's what they do. They're leeches, sucking the blood from us until...well, until we end up like you have. Would you believe that she refused to pay for a decent casket? How terrible is that?'

'Money was very tight towards the end,' the voice said, although Arnaud could hear the sorrow contained within. 'We were never very frugal as a couple. With a bit of luck she might maintain control of her finances a little better now that I'm gone.'

'Well,' Arnaud said, pulling himself into a pair of gloves. 'She's off to a great start by refusing to give you the send-off you deserve. She settled on a cremation.'

The body might have flinched with disgust on the trestle-table, though Arnaud probably imagined it. 'She wants to burn me?' the voice said, perturbed to the point of cracking. 'I don't want to be burned. I want to be buried, serenely, happily. I would live beneath the ground with my thoughts, in peace...'

Arnaud stepped across the room, cracking his knuckles. 'Would you really like to spend eternity beneath the ground like that?' he asked. 'It would be enough to drive a man insane, and from what I've seen of your wife you must already be halfway there as it is.' He laughed, perhaps a little too harshly, but Monsieur Mauriceau didn't seem to mind; he was too busy staring up at the ceiling, pondering a riposte.

There was a fly in the room; an annoying, noisy little thing that kept landing on Monsieur Mauriceau's bottom lip. Arnaud could hear the thoughts running through the mind of the corpse, thoughts of how terrible it would be to go underground, to have worms and ants and all manner of creatures crawling upon his person until there was nothing left but bone and sinew.

'Well, it's a good thing she wants to set fire to you instead,' Arnaud offered, though he didn't think it would be much of a comfort. There was a slight pause, and only the incessant drone of the excited fly to fill it.

'Is there nothing else?' the voice asked. 'No other way?'

Arnaud grinned. It was always the same question, over and over, and he never tired of hearing it. 'There might be,' he told the body. 'I have a unique skill. Some might call me morbid, but I would simply say it is a way of immortalising. Would you like to be immortal?'

The flurry of excited replies were overwhelming – as always – and Monsieur Mauriceau would have snapped Arnaud's hand off with elation had he been able to move. Arnaud moved across the room towards a cupboard; its door a deep, dark red, as of mahogany; a shiny, brass knob sat halfway down it, which the mortician reached for, turned, and pulled.

Silence, apart from the fly, and then a further torrent of pleas from the corpse upon the table. 'Monsieur Grégoire, they are beautiful!' Such detail, such wondrous detail! You are not a mortician, Monsieur, you are an artist! Oh, how wonderful you should offer me such a life! I will be forever in your debt, and forever yours to do with what you will...'

Arnaud knew the corpse was going to say that, for they always did. It wasn't growing tiresome just yet. He closed the cupboard door, turned to the cadaver on the table, and said, 'I only suggest cremation to the relatives of the ones I want to keep. I have animals that I burn in your place so that nobody is any the wiser.'

'Such a neat trick,' the voice said; once again the lips remained still.

Arnaud paced around the trestle-table, glancing down into eyes that gawked up at him. Such amazing eyes, eyes that would look even more majestic once he had converted them.

'Then we must begin,' Arnaud said. 'It is a long and arduous process, but ultimately worth every second.'

'Oh, such brilliance! Such talent! You are genius epitomised, Monsieur Grégoire!

Arnaud nodded. 'I am the Marionnettiste of Versailles,' he said, 'and we are going to get along just fine.'

*

Bach played gently along in the background, but that was all it was now: Background music. Arnaud wasn't even listening anymore, for he had a voice to speak to, and a most interesting conversation regarding Faust and Jean-Paul Sartre, and anything else he wanted to converse about.

Monsieur Mauriceau was nice and light, sitting atop his knee. Arnaud had made certain of his own comfort after suffering several early mistakes, leaving too much bone and fat within the cavity of what was once a hen-pecked man.

'So, you admit that Sartre's The Respectful Prostitute was nothing more than a racist statement to cover his own prejudices?' Arnaud asked the marionette perched upon his knee.

And now it's lips did move. Of course they did, for its mouth was controlled by the marionnettiste, though the words that came were its own, of that Arnaud was pretty sure.

'I believe that to be the truth,' Monsieur Mauriceau said, smiling as Arnaud twisted his fingers inside the cavity. 'Though I do not believe it to be anywhere near his best work.'

And so they talked, for hours, about things that had plagued Arnaud. Their audience sat circling them, the rest of the marionettes from the cupboard. Occasionally, one of them would ask a question, and Arnaud would answer, unless Monsieur Mauriceau answered first, for he was a very opinionated little puppet.

Arnaud smiled as his creations enjoyed the palaver. He was the bringer of life, the giver of second chances, and he was happier than he'd ever been before.

Your Cheatin' Heart

"Give me a glass of Coffin-Varnish, Emmet," William Jake said, leaning against the bar. He glanced around The First Chance Saloon, spotting only a few faces he recognised. "Damn quiet today, ain't it?"

Emmet, the bartender, poured the rotgut and pushed the glass towards William. "Always the same on a Tuesday, Willie," he sighed. "That new place over in Scottsbluff ain't helpin' none, either."

William knocked back the contents of his glass and gestured for a re-fill. Emmet obliged.

"Say, Willie," Emmet said as he began to wipe the countertop with a filthy towel. "You wouldn't happen to be aware of any rumours doing the rounds, would you?"

William hadn't anticipated conversation, so the bartender's question came as quite a shock. "What? About the *bar*?" he asked, pushing his glass nervously from one hand to the other. For some reason, Emmet was loath to make eye-contact with him all of a sudden.

"No, the bar's fine," Emmet said. "Hell, this place'll be here long after I'm feeding the worms, ain't no doubt about it." And yet, even as he spoke, he appeared to have the weight of the world on his shoulders. "I just heard some things, is all," he said. "Things I don't care repeating, and I told that fool he'd better be careful, running around town like that spouting all kinds of nonsense. I said you would—"

"This *nonsense*?" William said. "Ain't about *me*, is it?" He sipped from his glass, enjoying the burn in his throat; not enjoying the reluctant countenance of the man behind the bar, who knew something he didn't and looked terrified to speak out of turn.

Finally, and through gritted teeth, Emmet said, "You know Rushville, Willie. Full of people out to make a name for themselves—"

"Are you gonna tell me what the hell people have been saying, or am I going to have to start shootin' up your stock?" He meant it, too. He could feel his blood boiling; the thought of people sneaking around and yattering their mouths off vexed him immeasurably.

"It's *Lou* they've been talkin' about," Emmet said. He was still unable to make eye-contact with William, and for good reason. "They've been sayin' she's been playin' around, Willie."

It felt as if somebody had slammed a tomahawk down on the back of his head. Of all the things he was expecting to hear, Lou dancing around with another man was not one of them. He sat cradling the glass, squeezing until his knuckles turned white. It wasn't true; she knew better than that. It was just somebody's idea of a joke – a sick rumour intended to fill the awkward silences at the poker table.

"Who?" William grunted without looking up. He knew Emmet was petrified of what he might do, as if he would clean the guy's plow just for alerting him to the rumour.

"Willie, I don't want to see you in Calaboose—"

William launched his glass over the bar, where it smashed three bottles and sent a fourth rolling along the shelf. "Who?"

Surveying the damage only for a moment, Emmet said, "Jebediah Jones." It was no use trying to protect the fool; he was bound to come a cropper eventually. As far as Emmet was concerned, the sonofabitch should have kept what he'd seen (if he'd seen anything at all) to himself. "Willie, ain't no use getting' your back up. You know as well as I do Jebediah's a mudsill. Ain't nobody gonna believe a word that falls out of his mouth."

Jebediah Jones spreading scuttlebutt was one thing, but when it involved Lou – and things she couldn't possibly have been capable of – somebody had to shut him up.

"And this was this morning?" William asked. He was so balled up he could hardly speak; what he did manage was tremulous and staccato.

"Right before you came in," Emmet said. "He was full as a tick on Who-hit-John, so nobody was paying him no mind. Hey, stay, have another drink, Willie. Don't go on the shoot…"

But it was too late. William slammed his payment down on the countertop, placed his hat atop his head and headed for the batwing doors. The few patrons in the saloon avoided eye-contact with him as he left. There was going to be fuss, and they didn't want to become part of it.

Emmet sighed and began picking up shattered glass from behind the bar.

*

It was hot as a whorehouse on nickel night outside; William knew exactly where Jebediah would have gone after leaving The First Chance Saloon. He was always soaked, and after spending the little money he had on the morning he would have gone in search of cheaper, more dangerous, booze. William was aware that Jebediah was in with the Pitt brothers, and James Pitt had recently acquired a couple drums of Tarantula Juice.

It didn't take it out of William to figure out where he would find the lowdown piece of trash who'd been shooting his mouth off about Lou. He paced across town towards Pitt the elder's yard. They were coffin makers, had been since they were twelve; William had known Jack and James Pitt when they were between hay and grass, and they were a lot less dangerous back then.

He didn't have beef with the Pitts, though, and if he did everything according to Hoyle there would be no reason for them to get involved.

He arrived at the yard to find Jack Pitt shaving the bottom off a baby-crate. There was something about the miniature coffin that almost made William turn around and go back the way he came, but then he remembered Lou, and that fool Jebediah, and then all he could think about was whether he could fold that bastard up and fit him in the tiny, wooden box.

When Jack saw William, he straightened up, arching his back, which audibly cracked. "Well, Will Jake," he said as he poked a Quirley into the corner of his mouth and struck a match. Exhaling a plume of blue-grey smoke, he said, "What can I do for you? Hope you ain't here for a box."

William shook his head. "Not me," he said. "I need to find Jebediah Jones."

Jack hissed; his tobacco- and Arbuckle-stained teeth looked as if they'd been varnished by the same stuff they used for the coffins. "Pull in your horns, Will," he said. "Ain't wanting no shindy in my yard."

"Won't be none if you tell me where he is," William said. He could see that the elder Pitt was rattled; he could also see that Jack knew exactly where Jebediah was at. "He with your brother, Jack?"

Jack put the planer down and stepped from behind the coffin. "You aren't thinking of kicking up a row with James, are you? 'Cos you'll be waking up the wrong passenger is you do."

"Ain't here for James," William said. "Both of you have always been alright by me. That rip Jebediah's been shooting his mouth off about Lou, and I need to have it out with him. That's all."

Jack considered this in silence for a second, occasionally drawing on his roll-your-own. William hadn't seen either Pitt brother for a few months, and he was surprised at how…*old* Jack looked, as if he had the weight of the world on his shoulders. Glancing at the baby coffin, William realised that wasn't far from the truth.

After almost two minutes, Jack hollered, "James! Bring that *fool* out here!"

William sighed, nodded in appreciation.

"Like I said, Will," the coffin maker said, "any trouble with James is trouble with me, you hear?"

"Appreciate it, Jack."

Just then, the younger brother, James, stumbled out of the workshop, clearly inebriated. Tailing him was Jebediah Jones, who appeared to shrink exponentially as he spotted William.

"Well, William Jake," James slurred, grinning like an odd stick. "What brings you around these parts?" His jovial manner did little to alleviate William's anger.

"Step aside, James," his older – and wiser – brother said. "These two need to talk."

Glancing from one to the other, James continued to grin. "Sure looks like they do," he said, noticing the aggrieved countenance of William and the petrified expression painted on Jebediah's face.

"What's this about?" Jebediah asked, though he knew exactly why William had sought him.

William jabbed a finger at the drunken idiot. "You've been yattering to people about Lou," he said. "I want you to tell me exactly, and I mean word-for-word, what you told Emmet this morning."

Jebediah held up a placatory hand. "I only told him what I seen, Will. Ain't no use in lying to you."

William wanted to knock him galley west in that moment, but there was something about the way the man looked – almost *sincere* – that kept him from doing it. "And what did you see? I need you to be really clear about this, because right now I'm fixin' to kick up a row, and you're more'n likely gonna be on the receivin' end."

Never, in the history of alcohol, had a man sobered up so quickly. "I saw a man go into your house after you left this mornin', Will." He wiped nervously at a string of drool that hung listlessly from his stubbly chin. "I swear, that's the truth. I only mentioned it to Emmet in the hopes he'd pass it on. We all know he can't hold his own water, and I didn't want to be the one to have to tell you."

William felt like he'd been kicked in the stomach; this, he thought, is what those poor tuberculosis sonsofbitches feel like just before they die. "Lou would never take another man," he said, although as soon as the words crossed his lips he knew he was lying. She had taken *him* while otherwise engaged.

Why would she not do the same again? William began to shake his head frantically.

"Looks like she gave you the mitten," James mumbled, somewhat unwisely.

"Shut the hell up," his older brother warned. "Ain't smart pissin' on a man's boots when he just cleaned 'em."

William tried to push away the thoughts of Lou embroiled in sordid and surreptitious encounters with another man. It was impossible. Then he started to recall times where she may have slipped up, occasions when he should have realised something was amiss. Whether these occurrences were genuine, or created by his own mind now that he knew the truth, he didn't know. What he *did* know was that somebody was about to get shot.

"I'm sorry, Will," Jebediah said, and the solemn look on his face suggested he meant it. "If you're going to do something about it, I should tell you that the guy I saw was bigger'n anyone in town. I mean, bigger'n anyone I've ever seen before. I din't get a close look, 'cos he had on this long, black fish…" He trailed off there.

William turned and left the yard. The sun scorched his back, sweat painted his brow, but he wasn't going to stop until he reached the house.

The house in which a cheater lodged.

*

He pushed open the door and silently stepped into the house. Part of him wanted to call out, to alert them so he didn't stumble onto something that would leave an impression forever on his brain; the other part wanted to catch her at it like the sick adulterous witch she was. He eased the door gently shut, blocking out the impossible heat, though it wasn't much cooler inside.

No doubt the heat from *them*, he thought, and quickly regretted it.

He headed through the house, tiptoeing like some bandit about to plunder. The floor creaked beneath him, but not loud enough to forewarn Lou and her mystery-man. Still he fought the urge to call out. At the door to the back room – the room where they slept, read to each other, made love – William paused to listen.

He could hear Lou whimpering, and another sound – a deep, guttural grunt that made him draw his gun without further deliberation.

He leaned back on his right leg and kicked the door as hard as he could, splintering it from its frame. Levelling his gun at the dark shape in the centre of the room, he realised he'd made a big mistake.

The thing was a tower, and not a man at all. The cowboy slicker had been removed and lay strewn across the bed. William could only focus on the wings – two huge appendages that jutted from either side of the creature's shoulderblades. As the door exploded inwards, the creature turned, irritated by the intrusion.

Beyond the thing, Lou stared out through hollow eyes. The cavity in her chest afforded him a view all the way through her. She whimpered one final time before slumping to the ground, the life snatched right out of her.

"Mothman," William whined. He'd heard the legends, he'd partaken in many a drunken discussion about the mystical creature, but he had never anticipated meeting the thing face-to-face.

The herculean beast turned on him; black strings oozed from its wide open maw. Its eyes were inches apart, completely devoid of humanity. Coarse fur covered its body, except for its wings which were like black parchment. William fired two shots into it before it reached him, and when its weight came down on top of him he knew he'd reached the end. At first there was nothing but pain, primal agony that he wished would end before it drove him wholly insane.

And then there was nothing at all. The Mothman tore from him and fed as William stared out across the bloodstained floor, towards the tattered and rent heart in the centre of the room. Lou's heart. The heart he had doubted, if only for a moment.

Parasitic Embrace

Amanda glared at the television screen, her breaths coming in short, sharp intakes. To begin with, she was unsure if she had heard correctly. Was it even *possible*? It had never happened before in the course of human history – or at least not as far as she was aware – so why would it happen now?

As the newscaster moved on to the next story – though it was clear that she, too, was shaken by the words that had just crossed her lips – Amanda had a thousand thoughts all at once. She knew she had to call somebody. *Anybody*. Her mother was out on the farm by herself; she probably hadn't even heard the warnings. It was a rarity for her mother to even switch on the television set during the day.

Maybe she had heard it on the radio.

It was *likelier*, but not enough to settle Amanda's nerves. She picked up the telephone and dialled. For a few moments, she didn't think anybody was going to answer. Her heart raced; inside, her stomach was doing somersaults, almost enough to bring up the breakfast which she had not long consumed. When her mother finally picked up the phone, she heaved a massive sigh of relief.

'Hello?'

'Mom, thank *God*,' she said. 'I just needed to call you.'

There was a nervous laugh, before the elderly voice on the opposite end of the line said, 'What is it, Dear?'

'Mom, haven't you seen the TV...or...or heard anything on the *radio*?'

'You know me, Amanda,' her mother replied, chuckling to herself. 'I can't bear to watch that rubbish. I've got my books, and that's all I need.'

Amanda allowed herself to lean against the wall. She hadn't realised but she was pulling the phone-cord so hard that it was only an inch from being yanked completely out of the receiver. 'Mom, there's been a volcano eruption in Spain, a *big* one, they think it's going to—'

The sound of her mother laughing on the other end of the line interrupted her. 'Amanda, you've called me to tell me about a volcano going off miles away? There's an ocean between us and Spain.'

Angrily, Amanda continued. 'It's not the fucking

lava I'm *ringing* you about,' she spat, trying not to get too worked up, though it was difficult. 'They said on the news that there's a massive ash-cloud, that it's going to reach the UK in the next six hours.'

Her mother was silent, obviously trying to digest the information her daughter was telling her. 'We had one last year, didn't we?' she asked, and then without waiting for a reply, she said, 'I remember it. They had to ground all the planes; it was a nightmare.'

Amanda sighed. 'This one's much worse than that,' she said, and it *was*. Mayhem at the airports was the least of their worries. According to the newsreader, the cloud was black, darker than anything they had ever recorded before. The volcano, Teide, had erupted with such force that the surrounding villages were destroyed almost immediately. There had been no warning, no rumblings from the belly of the beast prior to the eruption; not even seismic tremors, which would have at least offered the villagers below the chance of evacuating.

And it was only the beginning. The cloud would be over the UK in six hours, and according to the report Amanda had just watched, the best thing to do was stay inside and remain calm.

When Amanda finally finished the call to her mother, calm was the last thing she felt.

*

It was 2:27 when Paul turned up at the house drunk. She hadn't been expecting him, and nor did she want him anywhere near her while he smelt like a brewery, but he seemed to be genuinely concerned about the cloud, so Amanda made them both coffee and listened to what he had to say. It was only fair; they had been together for four years before finally separating six months ago.

He sat across from her, his coffee-mug trembling in his nervous hand. 'I just needed to talk to someone,' he said as he glared towards her with watery eyes. 'This whole thing, this *cloud* fucking thing, it's made me realise how insignificant everything is.'

She knew where he was going with this, and tried to pre-empt him. 'We broke up months ago,' she said, trying desperately hard not to add to his palpable woe. 'You know that things were never going to work between us.'

His head dropped forward; *yes*, he knew, but that didn't mean that he had accepted it yet. He sipped morosely from the cup and sighed. 'Are you just going to stay here?' he asked. 'When the cloud reaches us?'

She nodded. 'That's what they said on the news.' She gave her watch a cursory glance and hissed as she noted the time. There was less than two hours to go, if the scientists and god-knows whoever had worked it out right, and the last thing she wanted was to be trapped in the house with Paul for the next day or two. It was rude to just ask him to leave, but there was no harm in hinting.

They drank their coffee in relative silence; Paul didn't mention their relationship, though he brought up the cloud a couple more times, which only further convinced Amanda that he was genuinely scared. It wasn't like him, but his emotions had changed, and she couldn't be sure of how much alcohol he had consumed.

He finally left at 3:15, less than an hour to go before a terrifying shadow enveloped the sky above.

It was times like this that Amanda wished she still drank.

*

She was standing at the kitchen window when the sky turned yellow. In the background, the sound of a rolling report continued to blare out of the TV. The neighbours – fools that they were – had wandered out into the garden for a better view. Amanda watched as Douglas West pointed towards the sky. His wife, Maggie, nodded as she listened to what must have been her husband's take on the cloud. Amanda wanted to yell, to tell them to go back indoors where they would be safe, but it was none of her business. There were idiots everywhere, even if they *themselves* weren't aware of it. She poured herself another cup of coffee – her ninth for the day – and stood watching at the window as the orange miasma began to tint the atmosphere.

It said on the news that the yellow comes before the grey and black, which wasn't comforting in the slightest. Amanda wanted to climb the stairs, fall into bed and pull the sheets up over her head until it was all over and done.

She lit a cigarette and exhaled a plume of blue smoke into the kitchen. The irony of her actions were not lost on her, and she nervously laughed as she realised that it was probably safer out in the garden with the Wests. She walked across to where the phone hung on the wall and picked up the receiver. Only after punching in the first six numbers did she realise how silly she was being; her mother would have told her exactly the same if she had continued to dial. She replaced the phone in its cradle and turned back to the window.

It was getting darker. The kitchen was gloomy, ominous, and shadows that had been visible only a moment before were now nowhere to be found.

Amanda took two aspirin and moved into the living-room, where she could no longer see the nightmare unfolding through the kitchen window. She switched on the TV and was not surprised to find the news still covering the volcano and subsequent ash-cloud.

A reporter was standing on the roof of the BBC centre. Wearing a dust-mask – the kind which could usually be found on someone inspecting asbestos – it was difficult to understand what he was trying to say, but he was certainly frightened by the strange phenomenon and kept fluffing the report. The camera panned around, skyward, and it was almost impossible to pinpoint just what the cameraman was looking at, such was the darkness. The sky was the colour of strong coffee; around the clouds there were highlights of orange, but they did little to create any sort of visible light. The sun was up there somewhere, through all of that mire and ash. According to the reporter, who was shifting from one foot to the other as the temperature suddenly dropped, 'We have no idea how long this is going to last, or how much worse it is likely to get.' The camera moved back around to his masked face. 'If you don't have to go out, then please remain indoors. The cloud is toxic, and *dangerous*. If you, or anybody that you know, are asthmatic, make sure that they are kept in a room where there are no openings and no way for the noxious dust to get in. Daniel Brown for BBC News.'

The reporter was replaced by a concerned-looking anchor, who shuffled papers and did everything she could not to look into the camera. Amanda watched as the woman rambled nervously on, trying to explain the cloud in scientific terms that were beyond her.

A chill ran through Amanda as the room seemed to drop several degrees. She stood and made her way across to the living-room window. The curtains were drawn, and had been since the cloud appeared; there was no point staring out at it, Amanda thought. It was terrifying enough to know that it was *there*, without having a constant, visual reminder.

Though she knew she had to look, and tugged the curtain slowly to the side.

The street was darker than night; the lights framing the road were all on, tricked by the sudden phenomenon. Amanda looked towards the deathly cloud, which was moving with unnatural liquidity across the sky. She had seen things during her life that had scared her, terrified her, even, but the way in which that endless obsidian sea trickled by overhead intimidated her. She could hardly breathe as she gazed up into the sheer vastness. Then, she could smell sulphur, and she rushed across to the front-door and slapped a trembling hand over the keyhole. Beneath her, a slow, murky mist began to appear at the bottom of the door; she ran to the kitchen and grabbed a towel. She rushed back and wedged it in place.

How could she have been so stupid? The news had warned about the sulphur smell, and she had completely forgotten what to do; she had been too busy standing at the window in awe of the spreading monstrosity outside.

The smell dissipated, and Amanda slowly made her way back to the sofa. The truth of it was: she was exhausted. She could have slept for days, if only that fucking thing wasn't out there. She knew there would be no sleep at all that night. How could *anybody* sleep?

The newsreader was now sticking a finger in her ear, listening to some faceless producer. Her expression changed once again, from mild anxiety to downright panic. When she finally managed to speak, she did so into the wrong camera such was her disorientation.

'Erm...I've just been informed that we have some breaking news,' she said, finally realising that camera two wasn't even switched on. She hurriedly repositioned herself for the correct camera before continuing. 'There have been reports that something, we don't know *what*, is in the cloud.' She looked off-camera, for support, before realising that the people in the studio knew even less than she did. The producer in her ear said something else, which she repeated aloud. 'The cloud seems to be making people crazy,' she said. 'We have reports of mass confusion in the middle of the city, where people...' she shook her head as the news was repeated to her via the tiny earphone. 'People are *killing* each other. The police are at the scene, but we can't show you any pictures right now. You are all advised to remain indoors, keep everything locked, and await further instructions.'

This was getting worse by the minute. Amanda didn't know what was worse; the fact that a toxic cloud the size of Ireland was hovering over them, or that people were so confused by the whole thing that they were killing each other.

Amanda was perched on the edge of the sofa, trying to slow her own increasing heart-rate down, when the female anchor threw back to the reporter on the roof.

'Daniel, what can you see up there?'

Daniel was standing on the edge of the roof, staring out at the city. He either hadn't heard the woman's question, or there was something there that had him intrigued. The cameraman whispered his name, which got his attention. Daniel span, made his way back to the centre of the roof.

'I don't know what's going on down there,' he said, trying to remain calm. 'People are fighting; there have been several beheadings. It's hard to say at this moment whether the ash-cloud is in any way to blame for these acts of random violence, though it would seem to be the case.' He paused, wiped grey dust from his forehead, and sighed. 'There seems to be...something...I feel strange.' He doubled over, panting, desperately trying to regain some composure. This was going out live to thousands of concerned citizens, and here he was having a funny turn on air. His head was pounding, though, and all he could see through the haze was tiny, red dots. He gasped, grabbed at the air with taut hands. It felt like he was dying.

The cameraman appeared in shot, making his way across the roof to where Daniel Brown struggled for air. He reached him, placed a hand on his back, and said something inaudible. The camera was still rolling, although the gathering miasma up on the roof made it difficult to see clearly.

Suddenly, Daniel grabbed the cameraman's arm and sank his teeth into it. The cameraman screamed as his flesh came away from the bone. With a mouthful of sinewy tendon, Daniel grabbed the man around the throat and dragged him to the ground, pounding his skull with such force that the cameraman's head caved in with just the second blow.

Amanda was on her feet, her hand covering her mouth to prevent the inevitable scream. She couldn't take her eyes off the screen, though. What had she just seen? What had half of the *city* just fucking seen?

Daniel Brown punched and elbowed the bloody mess that had once been a head for almost a minute. Eventually, he rolled across and lay on his back, still gasping for air. His belly rose and fell, rose and fell, and then it suddenly erupted. The reporter gagged and choked as his mouth filled with blood. He looked down with wide eyes as something began to pour out of him. It wasn't blood, or any form of fluid; an army of strange creatures were clambering out, scuttling across the roof. They were spiderlike, but the camera was positioned so far away that it was impossible to tell *what* they were. All of that was still going on when the camera died, and the TV screen was once again filled with the terrified face of the female anchor. She must have seen what had just happened up on the roof, for she was up out of her seat, tearing the earpiece out, and within a second the screen was empty apart from a spinning chair and a rolling banner that hadn't updated for quite some time.

Amanda ran into the kitchen; she didn't know

what else to do, but getting away from the television screen was important. She rushed to the sink, drew herself a glass of water and swallowed it down in three hungry gulps. She hadn't realised, but tears were streaming down her face, confused and panicked sobs racked through her entire body. She slammed the empty glass down on the counter and closed her eyes. When she opened them again a few seconds later, she screamed.

A face at the kitchen-window, pressed so close that breath-steam concealed the bottom half, almost sent her flying back into the table and chairs.

It was Douglas West; the idiot from next door. His eyes were rolled up into his face so that only the whites were visible; Amanda could see through the glass that they were unnaturally bloodshot, as if every blood-vessel in his face had exploded. His neck-cords were unnaturally taut, and with his hands he scraped incessantly up and down the window, squeaking and scratching until Amanda thought it might drive her insane.

'What do you *want*?' she screamed, hoping that he would hear her. 'Mr. West, go back inside! It's not *safe* out there.'

Amanda noticed that Douglas's hands were covered in blood, and that was when she realised that it was too late for him. Had he slaughtered his own wife? *Why*? She thought about the reporter, the poor bastard up on that roof at the BBC centre who had savaged his cameraman. Did Douglas West have those things inside of him? Those...whatever-the-fuck they were?

Douglas scratched and clawed at the glass a few more times and then, as if he resigned himself to the fact that he couldn't get in, slid off the window and disappeared into the darkness.

Amanda couldn't breathe; something horrible was happening, and the cloud had something to do with it. She pushed herself forward, ignoring her instincts – which were telling her to run upstairs and hide – she glanced out of the window just in time to witness Douglas West's demise.

He was doubled over in the middle of the garden – *her* garden – and he was violently trembling, the way a dog might just before a particularly nasty shit. Amanda stifled her own screams as she watched. Douglas's mouth opened wide, wider than it was physically possible. His jaw must have dislocated, and was now hanging down a few inches below the rest of his face, swinging from side-to-side as the pain racked through him. And then, a torrent of those things spewed from his mouth. In that moment, his eyes rolled back down into place, and he seemed to realise that something was not right. Hundreds – perhaps *thousands* – of them began to hit the grass and scamper away in every direction. Amanda was paralysed with fear; her legs gave beneath her and she hit the kitchen-floor with a meaty thump.

She cried; the water that she greedily finished a moment before threatened to make a reappearance. Where had this nightmare come from? How could this...

She had to call her mother. She clambered to her feet, angry with herself for being so weak. Although it was almost impossible to get her legs to work in tandem, she staggered across to where the telephone hung on the wall and snatched up the handset. For a moment, the number evaded her; it was ridiculous, for she had called that same fucking number every day for the last three years. She took a deep breath, allowed the temporary amnesia to pass, and sighed as she keyed in the number. Pushing the handset to her ear, she prayed for the voice of her mother to appear.

Two rings...

Three...

'Hello?'

Amanda could have burst into another bout of hysterics, but it was not the time. *'Mom, thank God. Are you okay? Is the door locked?'*

The silence that came was enough to send Amanda over the edge, and she leaned forward as the stomach-full of water gushed into her mouth, which she opened to let the clear vomit hit the tiles. In her ear, her mother was saying something about the garage, something about being stuck in the garage with another man.

Amanda wiped the spittle from her lips and chin before attempting to speak. 'Mom, who is the man? Where did he *come* from?'

'He was stuck, out on the road,' her mother replied. 'He looked like he needed help. He doesn't look well, Amanda. Not well, at all.'

Amanda screamed down the phone. *'Mom, you have to get away from him. Get into the house and lock the fucking door!'*

A muted voice said something, and then the sound of her mother responding; it sounded, to Amanda, like "Stay *back*" or "Get *back*", though it was muffled and incoherent.

'Mom, get to the house. Leave the sick man where he is and get—'

The phone went dead, leaving Amanda screaming to herself. Her head pounded, the beginnings of a violent migraine. She dropped the phone and watched as it swung left and right, clattering against the wall. In the background, the television was reiterating the importance of remaining indoors, that the cloud had something to do with everything that was happening.

No shit! Amanda thought.

She stumbled into the living-room and fell to her knees in front of the TV; the empty studio had been replaced with a darkened room. It looked like the entire production team had gathered, though obviously it was too much of a good story to stop filming. The camera was capturing everything, and although it was gloomy in the room, several figures could be seen moving around, hastily blockading doors. At the far end of the room, the female anchor was being soothed by an elderly man, probably the executive producer. A face suddenly filled the screen; it was so close to the camera that Amanda could make out a thick arrangement of nasal-hairs, despite the darkness. The face started to whisper.

'We have confirmation that the cloud is carrying something...some sort of...of *microparasite.* I don't even know what the fuck that *is*, but...but that's what appears to be happening.' The face glanced across his shoulder at the shuffling figures before continuing. 'In truth, I have no idea *what's* happening, but we're going to go off air for a while. Just please, everybody stay the fuck away from the cloud; stay *inside*...and stay safe.'

The camera switched off, leaving a test-screen of parallel coloured bars.

Microparasite? That was what the man said. The word made Amanda want to scream; those things breaking out of people were somehow coming from the cloud, using their hosts for a few minutes before emerging. Even Amanda knew that that was pretty rapid evolution, even for a fucking parasite.

She stood, her legs still bandy and unreliable. A terrible thought suddenly danced into her mind. She had smelt the sulphur, she'd been exposed to the cloud, or at least its pungent redolence.

Was she infected? Were those fucking parasites growing inside of her? The mere thought brought bile up into her throat. She coughed and spluttered, trying to push the ghastly inference out of her mind. She tried to reassure herself that, from what she had seen, it didn't take long for the parasite to evolve, and she was not feeling any signs of affliction, so she must—

The door knocked; Amanda almost fell back into the television-set. *Bang bang bang...*Violent, somebody trying desperately to get in. Her heart was in her mouth. She bit her tongue in an attempt not to scream, and she tasted iron as her mouth began to fill with blood.

'Amanda!' a voice bellowed. She knew straight away who it was, though that failed to alleviate her concerns. 'Amanda, *please*! I know you're in there; I need some help!' He finished the sentence off with three more bashes on the door.

She wanted to speak, to tell Paul to leave her alone, but she couldn't. Instead, her mouth opened and closed like a goldfish; silent gasps that only she could hear.

'Amanda! Please!' And now he was sobbing, slamming the door with open hands. 'It's crazy out here. I don't know what the fuck is going on, but I—'

Amanda listened, but no further words came. Everything was deathly silent; maybe her prayers had been answered and Paul had simply given up.

She managed to tiptoe around the sofa, not taking her eyes off the front-door. Her heart pounded so fast that her arms and legs trembled with each beat. The threatening migraine was no longer there; it had been replaced with something much worse, a pain that no amount of Aspirin could ease. Again she panicked, putting two and two together to get five. Was the agony inside her head caused by the fact that she had come into contact with the cloud? Was she now a host to thousands of insectile creatures?

She reached the stairs and put a foot on the bottom step. Her sudden fatigue might not allow her to climb to the top, though she would fucking *try*.

She managed to get to the third step when the door crashed in behind her. She turned just in time to see Paul rushing towards her, his eyes white and bloodshot, his mouth contorted into a pained grimace. She tried to scream, but it was too late. Paul thumped into her, crushing her back against the stairs. Her head smashed against a baluster, splitting her temple in two. As white stars began to dance between her eyes and eyelids, she could feel Paul grabbing at her, trying to tear her apart.

'I said let me fucking *IN*!' he screamed, though not in any voice that she recognised. His hands slipped around her throat; she opened her eyes to find his face only an inch away from hers.

And then his mouth opened.

She could see legs, hundreds of tiny, spindly legs, creeping their way out of his throat, manoeuvring their way around his teeth, and then they were spilling out of his mouth and into hers.

She closed her eyes, gasping and choking as the things slipped down her own throat. Paul was too strong for her; preternaturally strong. She couldn't push him off, couldn't even move his hand away from her neck.

All she could do was *accept*.

When her eyes opened a few seconds later, they were achromatic, surrounded only by the crimson of broken blood-vessels.

Paul kissed her once on the lips and rolled off so

that they lay, side by side, on the stairs.

Which is where they remained as the ash-cloud danced in whorls through the shattered door, the smell of sulphur more discernible than ever. Amanda reached down and held Paul's hand.

And then they waited.

Benji

The room was a mess, and had been for almost three solid months. There was just enough space on the floor to change nappies, or apply cream, but that was it. How it had come to be like this wasn't a mystery; there just weren't enough hours in the day to clean, and subsequently the house had fallen into complete disarray.

Apart from the lack of space, the nursery was typically furnished. There were various wall adornments, with counting and reading materials scattered haphazardly around. The wallpaper was no longer visible, such was the concentration of pointless exercises and measuring charts. Although the height graph hadn't been updated for almost a year, it remained pinned to the wall, a reminder of the first few months' growth-spurts.

Sitting in the corner of the room, with various clothes hanging over its back, was a small rocking chair, which had been intended for Jacob to sit on when he was big enough but was now nothing more than a glorified clothes-horse. In the seat was a box, a general collection of sewing materials and implements, but sitting on top of the box was a toy that Jacob had never held; he wouldn't even know it existed. The small, brown bear, which for some reason or other Donna had named Benji, was obsolete, a pointless gift from one of Jacob's uncles or aunts that would have been moved only once or twice, when Donna was in need of thread or a fine needle. And yet, when the box was returned, Benji was placed back on top of it, as if it had earned the right to belong.

David glanced around the room with the same look of contempt as always; he couldn't, for the life of him, see how things had become so untidy. Sure, Donna had things to do while he was at the factory. Jacob and Isobel were a full-time job, and David knew that he had somehow managed to draw the long straw when it came to responsibilities. His wife, on the other hand, was struggling, that much was clear.

It was time to do something drastic, anything to ease the pressure without making Donna feel as if she was failing.

David sighed, gave the nursery one more cursory glance, and headed downstairs to dinner.

*

'And you're going to help me?' Donna asked as she scraped the mashed-potato from Jacob's chin and pushed it into his agape mouth. 'Tonight?'

David smiled and poured another glass of wine. 'When do we ever have time to do it?' he said. 'It's a mess up there, and the only way we're ever going to get it cleaned up is by chucking anything that we don't need or want.'

Donna was slightly shocked by her husband's offer; it was a rarity for him to vacuum, and here he was offering to help clean up the nursery, without needing a prompt. It was very strange, indeed, but she knew an opportunity when she saw one.

'Okay,' she said. 'And you're okay with it? You're not missing anything?'

He shook his head and began to laugh. 'I wouldn't have offered if there was a game on, believe me.'

Donna began to cut Isobel's food up before taking a sip of her wine. 'Then I really appreciate the help,' she said, and she *did.* It was hard work, and the last few years had taken their toll on both the house and the marriage. She had almost forgotten the fact that she was a wife; being a mother had taken precedence, and David had been happy to help wherever he could, but there was only so much he could do whilst maintaining his day-job.

'On one condition,' David said, forcing a forkful of cauliflower into his mouth. When he finished chewing, he said, 'We're going to be ruthless. I don't want to hear any sentimental stories or stupid anecdotes about that stuff. If it was a gift from your family, fine, it goes up the loft, but anything else gets bagged and either trashed or taken to the charity-shop.' He knew that being assertive was the only way to get the room cleared; Donna could become emotionally attached to a pubic-hair if David wasn't there to keep her in check.

'Ruthless,' she reiterated, smiling. 'We take no prisoners; once it's clean, I can keep it that way.'

They chinked glasses and finished dinner.

*

Jacob was asleep for eight – which was a miracle – and Donna had managed to put him down in their bedroom, where he wouldn't be disturbed by the clean-up mission going on in his own room. Isobel was watching cartoons in bed, but she too would succumb to sleep within the hour. They had as long as it took to clear the nursery, and Donna – for the first time in what felt like an eternity – was genuinely optimistic.

'Remember,' David said as he opened a black bag and began to scour the room for irrelevant objects, 'ruthless. I want these bags filled before we go to bed, do you hear me soldier?'

Donna laughed as she started to work through the piles of outgrown clothes and broken toys. 'Have you heard yourself?' she said. '*Slavedriver.* If this is what you're like at work, no *wonder* nobody likes you.'

David feigned a choke. 'Who *said* nobody likes me. I'll have you know I'm a well respected member of the workforce.'

Donna shoved a handful of empty boxes into her bag. 'That's not what *I* heard,' she chuckled. 'A little bird told me that people spit in your tea when you;re not looking.'

David dropped a dirty nappy – it was best not to ask too many questions, though he did wonder why there were soiled nappies lying about the place – into his black bag before turning to his wife. 'I'm glad,' he said. 'I like my tea like that.'

As they worked through the scattered mess, which looked like something you might see on the news after a particularly nasty flood or tornado, both of them became less talkative and more focused on the job at hand. Donna was about to start on the toybox at the far side of the room when David spoke.

'What about this one?' he said.

She turned to find him holding Benji in one hand and an almost-full black bag in the other. To be quite honest, the poor bear was already halfway towards the bag, as if David had already made the decision.

'You don't like Benji?' she asked, stretching her back which had started to ache from being doubled over.

'You *do*?'

Donna tried to recall where the bear had come from, though it was difficult. Jacob had been inundated with so many plush toys in his first year, it was almost impossible to remember who had given him what.

'He might like Benji when he gets a bit older,' Donna said.

David glanced down at the bear, trying to find a redeeming feature. 'Really?' he said, staring into the black glass eyes. 'Then, when he's older, I'll get him one just like it.' And with that, he shoved Benji into the bag and began to tie a knot in it.

Donna simply returned to the toybox, knowing that her husband was right.

It was just a bear; at least the sewing-box would be easier to get to.

*

'So how was your day?' David asked as he fell into the sofa beside Donna. 'Kids been good?' He glanced over to the rocker, where Jacob was fighting the sleep and rubbing his eyes.

'Had worse days,' Donna sighed. 'He looks exhausted,' she said, pointing to Jacob who was now yawning, 'and I'm the one running around all day.' She smiled and grabbed David's hand. 'I'm gonna take him up before he gets his second wind.'

David started to stand. 'No,' he said. 'You've been on all day long. I'll put him down, and then we can watch a film or something.'

Donna, through habit, began to protest, and then decided against it. 'Thanks.'

David unstrapped Jacob and lifted him from the rocker. 'Come on, you chunky-monkey. Let's get you into bed.'

Donna watched as her husband carried Jacob out into the hallway and up the stairs. She couldn't help thinking that David was overcompensating for something; he had never been so good, so thoughtful. Perhaps he realised – finally – that Donna was on the verge of a physical breakdown, or maybe he just wanted to spend more time with Jacob and Isobel, and this was his way of going about it.

Either way, Donna was much happier. She relaxed into the sofa and began channel-hopping for a half-decent movie.

*

Jacob was suitably blanketed and seemed comfortable in his cot. David playfully tweaked his nose and made the sound of a honking horn, which always managed to get a laugh from Jacob. 'Goodnight,' he whispered, and wound up the musical mobile which hung above the cot. As the farmyard animals began to mechanically rotate along with the music, David turned and headed for the door.

But something stopped him, and he found himself doing a double-take, just in case he was mistaken.

No, there it was, sitting atop the sewing-box the way in which it always had. Confusion washed over David as he tried to figure out what the bear – *Benji*, Donna liked to call it – was doing back in the house. He had taken it out in a bag, along with two other bags that very morning. And wasn't it bin day? The bags had been collected, taken to the refuse-centre.

David smiled. There was only one explanation; Donna had reclaimed it from the trash. He knew she had trouble letting go of things, but never to the extent of riffling through the bins. He switched the light off and gently pulled the door behind him as he left the nursery and the mellow, mechanical music of the rotating mobile.

'If you liked it so much, you should have said so last night.'

Donna waited for her husband to make himself comfortable on the sofa before questioning his meaning. 'Liked what?'

David playfully snatched the remote-control from Donna and began to flick through the channels in the way only a man can: Quickly and indifferently. 'The bear,' he said. 'Benji, or whatever you like to call it.'

Donna glared at him, still not understanding what he was getting at. 'David, have you been drinking, because I have no idea what you're rambling on about.'

David ceased flicking channels momentarily and sighed frustratedly. 'The bear,' he said. 'If you didn't want to throw it away, you could have just said. I wouldn't have been—'

'The bear we threw away last night?' she interrupted. 'What about it?'

David pinched his nose between his thumb and forefinger; the conversation had become a muddle, and his wife wasn't making it any easier.

'So you decided not to throw it away,' he said. 'All I'm saying is, it wouldn't have been a—'

'We did throw it away,' she interrupted once again. 'I watched you put the bins out this morning.'

Now David really was confused. 'Wait, wait, wait,' he said as he pushed himself forward on the sofa. 'You mean, you didn't take it out of the bag.'

Donna shook her head. 'What do I look like?' she said. 'A *fox*?'

David stood, panicking. 'Then why is it back in the nursery?'

At first, Donna thought he was cracking wise, the way he sometimes did. Then she noticed the concerned expression on his face and ruled it out completely. He just wasn't that good an actor.

Before she could speak, David was dragging her by the hand, up the stairs and into the nursery.

The tinny lullaby was just about to finish, and as they both stood in the middle of the room, staring at Benji as if it was a boa-constrictor or a crack-dealer, Jacob started to cry.

*

It wasn't a funny joke, Donna thought, but too much time had passed and there was no way that David was going to admit it now. After swearing on his life, and even Jacob's – which she reproached him about – that he had not retrieved the bear from the bag, she decided not to push the issue further. She had bagged the bear up once again and hand-delivered it to the Hospice at the edge of town.

'What a strange-looking bear,' the elderly lady behind the counter opined as she handled Benji. 'Never seen one quite like this before.'

Donna didn't know what to say; it looked just like any other bear, and she had seen thousands, exactly the same.

'Well,' the lady said, licking her top lip which was home to a silvering moustache. 'I think it'll make somebody very happy. If your little one doesn't want it anymore,' she glanced across the counter to the pushchair where Jacob was sleeping. 'Thank you for your donation,' she smiled. Jacob continued to sleep.

And that was that.

As they left the shop, Isobel asked Donna why the old lady had a moustache.

'Sometimes,' Donna replied. 'Old ladies have moustaches.'

It was the easiest answer she could think of.

*

David's parents offered to have the children for the night, which was always a bonus as far as Donna was concerned. As a couple, it was a rarity for them to go out – and not in a paint the town red kind of way, which they were both way too old for, now – and such opportunities were to be pounced upon.

David booked them in at a Tapas restaurant in the city, which Donna loved primarily because it was where they had frequented on their first, fourth and seventh date. She just couldn't get enough of the meatballs.

After dinner, they headed home; suitably stuffed and reasonably tired. Sleep wouldn't be an issue, not with the kids away and a Saturday morning lie-in to look forward to.

'I'm just going for a piss,' David said as soon as the front door was open.

Donna laughed and watched him bounce up the stairs like an excited child. 'Who said romance was dead?' She entered the lounge and tossed the car-keys onto the shelf. Upstairs, the sound of urine hitting the bowl with some force made her smile again.

As she perched on the edge of the sofa, the effects of two bottles of Merlot suddenly making an appearance, she felt quietly satisfied.

And then David shouted from the top of the stairs as Benji came bouncing down.

Donna screamed

*

'I don't *understand*,' Donna cried. 'I took it to the

fucking hospice this morning. I *swear*, David, I'm not playing some stupid game.'

David paced the length of the lounge three times, with Benji clenched in his white-knuckled fist. 'So, *what*?' he said. 'Just walk back here on his *own*, did he? Come on, Donna. Admit it. It's a stupid joke that wasn't funny the first fucking time around.'

Donna, wiping the stream of tears from her face, gasped. How was this *possible*? Was this part of David's joke? If it *was*, then he was not the man she thought he was. Donna was reduced to tears, after such a wonderful night. If this *was* David playing a silly game – and it had to be, didn't it – then she needed to seriously rethink their relationship.

'I don't get it,' she sobbed, trying to stand from the sofa but the effects of the alcohol were somewhat multiplied by the sudden events. 'The lady with the moustache had him,' she said. 'I'm not lying to you, David. Please, I just need to figure it out.'

David angrily slammed a fist down on the shelf; the car-keys bounced a few inches into the air before landing in the middle of the room. Donna could see that nothing good was going to come of the situation, and the best thing to do was get out, go...anywhere. She turned for the door but was tugged back by David. His grip terrified her, but she knew that he wouldn't hurt her on purpose. He never had; it wasn't part of his personality.

'I'll tell you what we're gonna do,' he said, menacingly. 'Let's take Benji out the fucking back, shall we?'

Donna pulled her arm free of David's grip and rubbed it where it was already beginning to get sore. There would be a bruise in the morning, but she had the propensity to bruise easily, anyway, so that was no way to gauge her husband's intent.

She glanced down at the bear, still fathoming how it had managed to reappear in the nursery for the second time in as many days. She couldn't come up with a reasonable explanation.

'And do what?' she asked, slightly slurring the words. 'Bury it?'

'That won't be enough,' David said, shaking his head maniacally. 'Follow me.'

It was freezing outside, and a slight drizzle had coated everything. The gentle pitter-patter of the rain on the barbecue cover was soothing, and as David put the little brown bear into a dry bucket from the shed he realised how stupid this all was. As he carried the bucket out onto the garden, Donna watched from the doorway. There was no point in them both getting wet.

'Let's see if he comes back from this,' David said, before pouring Kerosene into the bucket. 'Little shit.

Little bastard! Fucking little bastard!' The first match he struck went out; the rain was starting to worsen. The second match, however, worked just fine, and David grinned one last time before dropping it into the bucket.

There was a *whumph* as the bucket – and Benji – ignited. David took a step back from the bucket, wiping rain from his eyes so the he could watch. The flames licked around the bear at first, as if they were frightened, and then the whole thing went up. Bits of blackened stuffing began to crawl into the air, and there was an audible crack as both of Benji's eyes succumbed to the conflagration.

David began to laugh, watching as the smoke billowed out from the bucket. 'Let's see the furry little fucker come back from this one,' he sniggered.

Donna turned and went back into the house. When David finally entered the bedroom that night, neither of them spoke.

*

'Is it my turn to put Jacob down?' David asked, sipping the remnants from his beer-can. They had constructed, between them, a rota, and as far as Donna could recall it was a Tuesday, which meant that it was David's turn. She glanced down at the empty beer-can in his hand, though, and decided it was probably safer if she carried the baby up the stairs.

'I'll do it,' she said, rubbing David's cheek with the back of her hand. 'Just find us something good to watch for when I come back down.'

David picked up the remote-control and began to surf the channels, not expecting to find anything worth watching, but you never did know.

He was just about to order a violent pay-per-view movie when Donna's scream filled the house. He crushed the empty can in his hand and raced up the stairs.

He ran through into the nursery; Jacob was crying, and Donna was pushed as far up against the wall as she could manage. Her eyes were bulging, and she was struggling to breathe, but it was pretty clear what she was looking at with wide, terrified eyes. David couldn't believe what he was seeing.

There, sat on top of the sewing-box, was Benji. No longer burned; not a mark on it, in fact, and yet they both knew it was the same one, the one that had always been there.

The one that would be there forever.

Food of Love

It was just after dark when she called. Bryan didn't know how long he'd been asleep, but the book he had been reading was still sitting open on his lap, and the half-filled whiskey-glass was still in his left hand. Minutes, he guessed. And now, Claire was calling in that whiny, needy manner of hers.

She was hungry.

Bryan pushed himself up from the chair, necked the remaining whiskey, and slammed the glass down on the mantelpiece.

'*Bryyyyyaaaaan*!'

How long had it been since she last ate? It didn't seem long since Bryan had taken her a tray of fries, three burgers and a litre of milkshake. How could she possibly still be hungry. Maybe she needed a piss. Perhaps she needed him to flip her again; those sores on her back were getting worse. Pustulous, *ripe*, Bryan didn't want to be anywhere near her when they finally went.

'Bryaaaaaaaaaaaaannn, pleeeaaaassse!'

'Coming, baby!' Bryan said, hoping that she heard him over the sound of the bedsprings giving way beneath her. He flipped the light-switch and made his way across the hall to where she slept.

To where she ate.

She was in the same position as when he'd left her; half-sitting, half-slouching. The dark wooden tray was somewhere down by her feet, barren apart from screwed-up wrappers and inedible sachets. Claire's face was painted with sauce. Ketchup was smeared along her left cheek, while dots of mustard haphazardly peppered her chin. She looked as if a team of blind make-up artists had gone to town on her, and yet she looked *beautiful.*

'What can I get you, baby?' Bryan asked as he tidied the clutter at the foot of the bed, piling wrappers on top of wrappers before snatching the tray up. The only sound in the room, apart from the rustle of discarded fast-food debris, was the monotonous beeping of the heart-monitor. How he loathed that sound, and yet it was vital.

'I'm huuuungry still,' she said, her voice akin to that of a petulant child. 'My belly's rumbling.'

Bryan sighed, rolled his eyes. 'You want me to do another stop?' he asked, although he already knew the answer, so he added, 'I'll get you a few more burgers, but that's it for the night, baby. I need to sleep. You wouldn't want me to sleep all through breakfast, would you?'

Her face took on something of a shocked expression, as if what he had said was unthinkable or one of the worst things imaginable. '*Noooo*,' she said, her mouth flapping, jowls slapping against the fat of her neck. 'Breakfast's the most important meal of the day.'

'Exactly,' Bryan agreed. 'So I'll do one more trip tonight, then I'm going to sleep.'

The monitor double-beeped momentarily. Bryan turned his attention to it, gazing across the room to where it stood; the machine of utmost importance, the contraption that told him his beautiful wife was okay. They'd had a few close-calls, that machine and Bryan, but Claire had always pulled through.

She was a fighter; a hungry, resilient goddess. Bryan often wondered if she was immortal. Forty-six stone, now, and showing no signs of slowing down, it was difficult to remember what she had been like before. Their wedding photos had been filed away in the attic; Claire had suggested burning them, since the woman in the picture was nothing like the one Bryan adored so much, now. She despised herself in those pictures, all cute and verdant. She'd looked like some atrophying old lady, with her dress all abloom and her hair all plaited, barely able to support herself as the photographer tried again and again to catch her on her good side.

Back then, there *wasn't* one.

It was shortly after the wedding that she realised she wanted to be fat, and Bryan had agreed.

'I'll get you up to where you want to be,' he'd told her. *'I'll love you, no matter what.'*

And he had, and he *did*, now more than ever.

He stood at the door, blew her a kiss, and headed off to fetch her the last meal of the day.

Claire closed her eyes and smiled. She was the luckiest woman alive.

The machine in the corner beeped maniacally, as if in complete agreement with her.

*

The skinny guy appeared at the window with the brown paper bag of food. When he saw Bryan, he smiled. 'Can't get enough, huh?' he said, his lips seeming to curl up into a disgusted sneer.

Bryan snatched the bag from the kid's grasp before counting out the money. 'You look like you could do with a good meal yourself,' he said, though he couldn't, for the life of him, figure why. He didn't need to justify himself to this little shit; he didn't need to *explain* why he was back, ordering more food. It was none of this prick's business. Minimum-wage was nowhere near enough remuneration to get up close and personal with the customers. This sonofabitch was simply being disrespectful. When Bryan handed the kid the money, the kid took it without as much as eye-contact.

Yeah, you little fuckwit! Keep your mouth shut in future . . .

On the drive home, Bryan got to thinking. Claire had looked simply divine when he'd tended to her. The sauce up her face did nothing to diminish her beauty. If anything, Bryan found himself getting hard as he pictured himself licking it off, slurping it out from the folds of her neck. He ran two red lights as images of Claire's immense form plagued his thoughts. There was just . . . so *much* of her. Not like when they'd first met and her bones had been visible, jutting out from her parchment skin at odd angles. He'd loved her then, but now, now he fucking *cherished* her.

He was glad when she'd reached her first milestone; it seemed so long ago, now. They'd stood together in front of the Bariatric scales, Claire looking petrified, Bryan trying to hold back his anticipation so that she didn't feel the pressure she was obviously under. And then, she had taken a tentative step forward, and the needle on the scales had rocketed forward, the numbers passing it by quicker than the eye could see. When it came to a halt on twenty-eight stone, Bryan had almost clapped for joy. Claire had cried so hard that her make-up painted little inky lines down her chubby cheeks.

So long ago.

It was six months later when the scales were obsolete and Bryan made the purchase of a set of crane-scales. The first time Claire hung from the bedroom ceiling in a harness, Bryan realised he'd never imagined just how beautiful she would become. Only to *him*, though. Other people were disgusted by her, repulsed. Her family were no longer in contact, as they had been in previous years. They disagreed with what she was becoming and wanted no further part in the sickness.

But to Bryan, she was an emerging butterfly, shaking off the restraints of the cocoon.

The digital readout that first time, suspended from the ceiling, had read 476 pounds and, as with anything, they set the target of 500, to be reached in time for Christmas that year.

They surpassed it, and by Christmas Eve she looked magnificent, a 550lb beauty. Bryan could no longer make love to her, but it was a small price to pay. That wasn't to say they didn't still have their fun; it just involved a lot less penetration.

And now, at forty-six stone and counting – and with her family still out of the picture – they were reaching the goal that Claire had so optimistically set in 2009.

Fifty stone.

"If I can make it to fifty," she'd told him with a mouthful of ice-cream, *"then I can die happy."*

She *was* going to die, and soon; they both *knew* it, but it was something they had come to terms with. Fat people die young. Common knowledge, and neither of them were stupid. Her breathlessness now was almost uncontrollable. In fact, the only time she could breathe properly was when she was eating. There was irony in that, Bryan thought. A sick paradox that they both found amusing. It wouldn't be so funny when she died, of course, but for now it kept them laughing.

He arrived home with the burgers a little after ten. Claire had managed to switch the TV on using her fat foot; he'd forgotten to replace the control where she could reach it, and so she must have had a hell of a time trying to kick the darned thing into life.

'Where have you been?' she whined. 'I was worried.'

Bryan smiled. 'About me, or about your food

going cold?'

She laughed, nasally. 'About *you*, of course. You know I don't have a problem with eating cold food.'

After unpacking the paper-bags, Bryan sat on the edge of the bed and watched her eat. She didn't mind; she was too engrossed in some celebrity game-show and her food to even notice him. When she was done – and her face was once again caked with sauce and cheese, *mmmmm* – Bryan gathered up the wrappers before kissing her on the forehead.

'I'll bring your breakfast in at seven,' he told her, hoping that she could go through the night now that she had eaten late. 'If you need me, I'll be in the next room.'

'Why don't you stay here tonight?' she asked in her most annoying child-voice. 'It's been a while since we last fell asleep together.'

As much as Bryan wanted to, he needed to sleep, and lying next to Claire while that machine tormented him from the corner of the room with its incessant beeping would not only keep him awake, it would drive him insane.

'I'm in the very next room,' he said, stroking the folds of her belly, slipping his entire hand between her flesh. 'Now, come on, it's getting late, baby. I love you so much.' He stood, pulled the sheet up to her breasts, which were warm and shone with a thin film of sweat.

'I love you, Bryan,' she said, feigning a smile. Deep down, he knew that she was already thinking about breakfast; the bacon, sausage, eggs, fried bread, mushrooms, beans, toast, black-pudding, fried tomato, hash-brown, more toast. He would keep it coming until she could eat no more, because she was right: breakfast *was* the most important meal of the day.

He switched the light off on the way out; only the hazy blue light from the TV screen illuminated the room. As he closed the door, he heard Claire fart and burp simultaneously. It made him smile.

He loved her so much, but for now he had a date with the armchair and a few more glasses of whiskey.

*

Bryan woke to the sound of mail being rammed violently through the letterbox. He sat forward in his chair, pinching his nose between thumb and forefinger as the pain of last night's alcohol hit him.

The bottle sat empty on the floor; the glass next to it was still half-full. He thought about finishing it off, but didn't. He felt like death warmed up, and he had a huge breakfast to prepare for Claire – not the best thing in the world to be doing when you felt like absolute shit. He would be fighting to keep the bile down the entire time, he just *knew* it.

He stood, stretched, and realised how late it was. The clock on the mantelpiece informed him that it was almost nine.

That couldn't be right.

Perhaps Claire had called out to him a few hours back, realised he wasn't ready to get up yet, and fallen silent again. *But she must be starving*, he thought as he brushed the greasy hair away from his face with his fingers and made his way into the hall.

It was dark, with only a slice of light peeking out from beneath the door behind which his beloved slept. It was also silent, which terrified him more than anything. The machine should have been beeping, audible, but there was no alarm to suggest that Claire was in trouble, only the deafening silence that told him it was *much* worse than that.

He lunged for the door, pushed it open with his shoulder, and fell into his own personal hell.

The bed was empty, though her outline remained; a perfect indentation in the bedsheets that made it appear as if a ghost still lay there. The morning light streamed in through the open curtains, highlighting the horrors of the room. In the corner, the machine's screen was blank, as if a power-cut had knocked the insidious thing off. Bryan knew, however, that the machine would have rebooted, powered back up to blink annoying red digits until someone came along and reset it.

There were no red digits; only the dull brown of the screen where they should be.

'Claire!' Bryan yelped, his voice cracking as if he was afflicted with some insufferable throat defect. He staggered forth into the room, deeper into the mire and misery knowing full well what he was about to discover.

There she was. She filled the floor on the left side of the room, her entire body spread across it like a fleshy puddle. She must have landed on the machine's cord because it lay on the carpet, unplugged, a few feet away from the socket.

He tried to call out again, to rouse her, tell her everything was going to be just fine; her baby was here, and it was almost time for breakfast. He *tried* to speak, but nothing would come. He stood with his hands on top of his head, his mouth flapping open and shut, only air escaping, and there didn't seem to be enough of it in the room.

Bryan dropped to his knees. As he did, a cloud of flies flew from her bare flesh up into the air. Her skin was speckled purple, bruised, *decaying*? He didn't know, but the *flies* did, and wouldn't be venturing too far away from the body for the foreseeable future.

Two flies played around her nose, buzzing in and out of her nostrils, and although her hair was matted and draped across her face, covering her eyes – thank *God* – Bryan watched the flies crawl in and out of her nose as sobs caused his entire body to shudder. He closed his eyes, kept them shut, hoped that when they opened again he would be in his chair, just waking, and Claire's voice would be emanating from her room, begging and pleading for the big breakfast he'd promised her.

He opened his eyes, and there she still was, mottled skin and foraging flies. Her chin was caked with dried sauce from the burgers he'd brought her only a dozen hours ago. Suddenly, he found himself sitting at the foot of the bed, watching her eat, one after the other, sometimes not bothering to chew. She'd sat watching that stupid TV programme, and he'd watched her watching it.

And now she was dead, gone, *fallen* . . .

Bryan couldn't move for the longest time. He didn't want to. His job was to keep the flies away, which he did with aplomb. As the swarm descended, landing atop his wife's bare folds – *oh, how magnificent they looked, even in death* – he waved his hands maniacally. The flies, sensing the imminent danger, flew up into the room, a cloud of scavengers wanting to devour Claire where she lay. It was a waiting-game;

a battle of wits. Who would move first? The flies were certainly persistent.

After three hours Bryan could cry no more. He was dry, hollow. His head pounded, his jaw ached, his teeth hurt from where he'd ground them. His ass was sore from the bedroom-floor, his toes were numb, his beautifully corpulent wife was number.

He knew he had to do something. He couldn't remain on the floor, shooing the flies away. He couldn't keep looking at her, lying there, fading away. He couldn't watch as all their hard work was undone, all those years of gaining and building; she would slowly rot, her meat – *their* meat – falling away from her like flesh from a chicken-bone. There would eventually be nothing left of her, and that simply wouldn't do.

Stumbling to his feet, Bryan clenched his eyes shut. The pain momentarily dissipated, long enough for him to think clearly. He knew what to do, what he *must* do. It wouldn't be easy, but love never was.

He made his way into the lounge, finished off the whiskey that had previously sickened him, and returned to the bedroom, freshly invigorated and determined.

He positioned the crane above Claire's body, connected the hooks to the straps on her waist, arms and legs. He was thankful they had decided to leave the straps permanently on her; there would have been no way of positioning her to wrap the belt around her waist if they hadn't, and Bryan's plan would have gone straight out the window.

The flies were keeping their distance now; watching, unsure what this crazy sonofabitch was about to do, and intrigued to see how it all panned out.

With the hooks affixed, Bryan took a step back and pushed the top button on the crane's remote. Up she went, an angel taking a final flight before having her wings hacked off for good. As she rose, her rigid arms pointed away at the ceiling, as if she had spotted something and wanted to make Bryan aware of it. A crack in the plaster, perhaps, or a perversely large spider.

'No need to worry about that now,' Bryan managed. 'No need to worry about *anything*, any more, baby.'

Up she went. The crane seemed to struggle for a second, and Bryan glanced across to the flashing red light to his right.

Six-hundred and fifty-eight pound.

Bryan smiled. She'd never been so heavy before. It wasn't quite the fifty stone they were aiming for, but it was as close as they were going to get. *It's all downhill from here, baby. You've reached your peak.*

Bryan settled onto the bed. He almost fell into the crevice her body had created. He gently lay back, and guided the crane across so that his wife, his beautifully obese Claire, was hovering above him, swinging slowly back and forth as the flies began to land on her once again. He lay like that for a while, smiling as memories of their life played on his mind's projector-screen. Here they were on the beach; Claire in an ill-fitting swimsuit that contained nothing of her immense flesh, Bryan in a pair of tight, yellow speedos. Here they were eating birthday-cake; Claire's slice was almost three quarters of it. Here they stood at the bottom of the Eiffel Tower, laughing about how it might buckle if she went up it. The images appeared to him only once before disappearing in a dark miasma.

'I love you, Claire,' he said.

He pushed the button on the remote and watched as his wife got closer, and closer, and closer . . .

SPARROWS

'Oh, *Kayleigh*!' Lucy said, leaping to her feet and pulling the girl away from the soda-drenched picnic blanket. 'I've told you to be more careful.'

The girl looked apt to cry; her legs shimmered in the sunlight as a result of the clinging soda. Lucy began to wipe at her, somewhat irritably, and continued to reprimand her daughter.

'Go easy on her,' David said, pushing a cherry-tomato into his mouth. 'She's just clumsy.'

The look that Lucy shot him said it all. 'It's *all* the time, David,' she told him. Kayleigh stared up into her mother's annoyed face as she continued to scrub the stickiness from her legs. 'Look at the mess. There's *coke* in the salad, for Christ's sake.'

David, sensing his wife's chagrin, decided to remain silent. He pushed another tomato between his lips and turned his attention to the children on the opposite side of the field. They were playing on a rope-swing, taking it in turns to push. David was waiting for the rope to break – and it *would* – so that he could leap into action, rush to their aid. He hoped, in a strange way, it would break sooner rather than later; they would be leaving soon. The picnic was drawing to a close, and Lucy would certainly push things towards a premature end now that Kayleigh had spoilt the blanket.

'Pass me that,' Lucy snapped, jabbing a finger towards a rolled-up, green towel next to the woven hamper.

David tossed her the towel and smiled. 'You're really *pissed*,' he said, deciding that her strange mood-change needed to be addressed. He had noticed her temper worsening recently, and he was – in all honesty – growing tired of it. 'It's just a picnic. You need to calm down. For *fuck's* sake, breathe and take a chill-pill.'

That did it. Lucy, who had been rubbing salad-cream from Kayleigh's face, suddenly stopped. If looks could kill, David would have been dead twice over. There was no love for him in those eyes; only the sun and its incessant glare reflected there.

But she didn't speak; she didn't *have* to. Kayleigh was listening, waiting, seeing how this little scenario panned out. Their daughter had been present at a lot of their arguments – and there were a *lot* – and was accustomed to the warning signs. This, Kayleigh's expression said, was going to be a good one.

But it didn't have time to develop. If it had, it would have been momentous; marriage-ending, but something distracted David, and then Lucy was glancing in the same direction as her husband. And Kayleigh, who was expecting fireworks, followed their eyes with her own, and screamed as the children across the field were swarmed, enveloped, by something dark and ominous.

Lucy plucked her daughter up into her arms and placed a hand over her eyes. Kayleigh continued to scream, for the image was tattooed on her retina. Those boys swinging at the air, batting the birds away, trying to run away from the rope-swing and into the surrounding woods.

'Get to the car!' David yelled as he scrambled to his feet.

Lucy was up, though her legs were dead from kneeling for so long. She almost lost her balance, and would have gone over backwards had she not been carrying Kayleigh. 'we have to *help* them!' she screamed. 'Why are the birds attacking them? Did they do something to provoke them?'

David didn't know. If the children had somehow incited the sparrows then he certainly hadn't witnessed it. 'I don't know,' he said. He watched as one of the boys broke for the trees, only to be dragged to the ground by hundreds – *thousands*? - of tiny, brown birds. The boy started to scream, but was cut off as the host washed over him.

'Lucy! The *car*!' David said, hoping that his wife would – for once in her life – pay him some heed.

The car was parked up on the verge a hundred feet from where they stood. David could see it, could see the luminous green dice hanging down from the rear-view mirror, and yet it seemed so far away, impossible to reach.

They began to run; a family in fear. The sound of the birds behind them pushed them forward. The murderous song of a thousand sparrows. Were they feasting on those poor boys, or simply attacking in retaliation? In that moment, it didn't matter. What mattered was reaching the car.

David glanced across his shoulder, noticed that his wife had fallen back a little. 'Come on!' he bellowed, and that was when he saw the birds shift position. One second they were across the way, too preoccupied to take any notice of the escaping family, and the next they were up in the air, flying in a formation that was both beautiful and unnerving. Twenty feet, thirty feet, fifty feet up, and then they were coming, all of them, the pecked bones of three adolescent boys lay strewn in their wake

'Shit, Lucy, *come on*!' David yelled once more. He was breathless with exertion and fear, and his words came in short, staccato bursts that were almost incomprehensible.

The birds were shooting through the air, their chittering enough to make gooseflesh rise despite the burning mid-afternoon sun. David looked to his left as a shadow appeared in his periphery. Sure enough, a swarm roughly the size of the car they were approaching – not fast enough – was flanking them. He gasped. Behind him, Lucy screeched at the sight of the nearing birds. David wanted to tell her to shut the fuck up, that screaming was doing nothing to help, but he didn't have the breath or the energy to waste.

Somewhere on the field – though David wasn't sure where as his eyes were trained on the glistening bonnet sitting over on the verge – a woman screamed. It wasn't Lucy, nor Kayleigh, so he assumed there was a spectator, or perhaps another victim of the sparrows' terrible rampage. He didn't want to look, and the sweat stinging at his eyes made it almost impossible to see now, anyway. A moment later and the screaming stopped; the poor caterwauling woman was being stripped to the bone by a hundred pecking beaks, her mouth stuffed with feathers as the sparrows attacked. It was *that* which silenced her; that and the fact her thorax had been hollowed out, the tiny flapping creatures already inside of her, eating their way out. Of course, David didn't see any of that happening, and thankfully neither did his wife and daughter.

They were racing for the car, silently praying, hoping that they made it in time.

'Daddy!' Kayleigh screamed. 'Daddy, I'm scared!'

Without turning, David said, 'Everything's going to be alright!' He wasn't sure whether it was a lie; hell, he wasn't even sure that she heard him. The noise coming from all around – incessant chirruping that was nothing less than hellish – stifled his voice. He was gasping for air, but there didn't appear to be any. His heart was beating so rapidly that he was preparing for the worst coronary imaginable, but he kept running, kept looking at the verge, at the car, at the birds flanking them on both sides.

They were taunting them. They *had* to be. It would take less than a second for them to alter course, to swoop across and savage them where they ran.

Which is just what they did. David followed the dark formation on his left as they suddenly rushed across. He spun, watched as Lucy was snatched from the ground. Kayleigh, who had been pressed tightly to her mother's chest, spilled free and rolled over and over like a stuffed toy. David made a guttural sound in his throat; the sight of his daughter's mangled body rolling like that, as if she was a marionette and some sonofabitch had just cut the strings, worried him more than the sight of his wife being carried away over the field.

David plucked Kayleigh up from the ground. She was unconscious; something that he was somewhat grateful for. He turned, continued for the car. The birds to his right were relentlessly approaching. The ones that had been on his left were not missed, but David couldn't help but imagine the horrific tortures they were enacting upon his poor wife.

She was *gone*.

Kayleigh wasn't. Not *yet*, anyway. The car was just a few steps away, up on the verge. David began to clamber up the incline, his heart still threatening to explode inside him. He reached into his pocket with his free hand, the one that wasn't clinging onto the motionless dead-weight that was his daughter, and pulled out the car keys. He pushed the button on the remote.

The car's lights flashed twice to signal that the doors were open. David lunged for the back door, which was the nearest, and pulled it open just in time. The sound of a hundred birds hitting the door, like machine-gun fire – *thunk, thunk, thunk, thunk* – served to remind him how close he was, how close they both were, to being torn to shreds.

Kayleigh squirmed in his arms as he began to force her into the back of the car. She crawled forward, allowing him room to clamber in after her. He reached back and pulled the door shut, but not before several of the miniature demons flew in.

'Daddy!' gasped Kayleigh. Three sparrows were already slamming into her face, trying to peck their way inside. She was flailing maniacally, managing to push them away only for them to choose a different trajectory.

David plucked one of the birds from the air; it squealed shrilly. He could barely keep hold of it such was its crazed fluttering. Its beak was pecking at his knuckles, drawing blood, but he felt nothing, and when he slammed the bird into the closed window with everything he had left the bird ceased its spasms and dropped onto the back seat, dead.

Kayleigh was still fighting the two remaining birds off; the car was rocking so violently that David was disorientated. One of the birds landed, dazed, in his lap and was in the process of gathering itself back up when David brought his fist down onto it. Immediately, it ceased moving and stared up at its killer with glazing eyes. The third, and final, creature was lucky. Kayleigh was unable to do what she had just witnessed her father do, and had decided to to opt for the more humane method. She reached across and lowered the window ever-so-slightly. She had the bird in her grasp, holding it tight enough to cause its eyes to bulge from their sockets.

'What are you *doing*?' screamed her father. 'Close the fucking window!'

She pushed the bird up to the partially open window and released it. It dropped out of sight, and Kayleigh frantically wound the window shut. Why had she decided not to kill it? The bastard could very well have been one of the ones that had dragged her mother off across the field.

David pulled her into a hug, held her tightly for a few moments before forcing his way into the front of the car. He jammed the key into the ignition.

The car was rocking once again, but this time it wasn't from its occupants' flailing. It was the birds, slamming into the doors, bouncing off the windows, thumping into the axles – and probably killing themselves in the process.

David turned the key.

The car roared into life and then, with a dramatic splutter, died.

'No, no, no, no!' David was trying to hold it together in front of Kayleigh, for that was what father's do. They act brave in moments like these; they remain calm and tell everyone that it'll be okay, that nothing bad will happen.

But bad things would happen. *Had* happened...

The *exhaust*, David thought. They must have blocked the exhaust. That would prevent the car from starting. Those evil little bastards had forced their way into the pipe, wedged themselves in like feathered fucking parasites.

Kayleigh climbed into the front passenger-seat; her expression said it all. She had doe-eyes, terrified, seeking answers that her father couldn't provide. 'Why aren't we *moving*?' she managed through devastated breaths.

David relaxed, allowed his head to rest against the steering-wheel. 'We will,' he told her. 'We're just going to stay *here* for awhile.' He reached down and turned the dial on the radio. A few channels were still playing music, as if nothing remotely disturbing was happening outside. Perhaps this was an isolated incident; maybe this particular flock had just been having a bad fucking day...

'*...have been reports of attacks coming in from all over the country,*' a voice said. David moved his hand away from the dial; this was exactly what he was looking for. '*All we can tell you at this point in time is to stay indoors. If you can, block your windows and any air-vents. Use anything you can to barricade yourselves into your homes. I can't believe I'm fucking telling you this...this is crazy, but it's* *happening. If you've just tuned in then you probably have no idea what I'm mumbling the fuck on about, but there's...there's something happening outside...it's...it's the birds...they've all gone fucking nuts. We have reports coming in from all over the country. The birds are...killing people. I repeat, if you're out there....get indoors and stay there until further notice...and God help us all...'*

David stared into his daughter's terrified eyes and smiled. He didn't know *why*; it just seemed like the most comforting thing he could have done in that moment. She didn't smile back. She simply stared out across his shoulder, at the thick, black clouds of birds as they swarmed over everything and everyone. The car continued to rock back and forth, the machine-gun fire of sparrows bouncing off the doors enough to drive them steadily insane. And so they waited.

And the man on the radio continued to warn the country.

Can You Read That Asteroid from Here?

"This way, please," the woman with the frog-eyes said from behind her clipboard. "Is this your first attempt?"

I shook my head. "Third," I said. "But I only failed the first two due to unforeseen rock formations." That wasn't quite true; I'd failed the second test after rear-ending a Russian satellite. Still, Frog Eyes didn't need to know that.

She led me along a thin corridor with more flashing lights than a Bavarian disco. It was, I thought, a good job I didn't suffer with epilepsy. I wondered how many afflicted pilots had suffered at the hands of those ridiculous lights. At the end of the corridor, a set of double-doors went *whoosh* and I followed she of the reptilian corneas into what appeared to be a waiting-room.

"Take a seat," she told me, which was funny as there didn't seem to be any free. "Your instructor will call you when he's ready."

I thanked her and found a nice quiet corner to panic in. There was a strange smell in the room, as if someone – and it certainly wasn't me – had a special way of dealing with stress, one that would require a clean set of underwear upon test completion.

"You're a pretty one, aren't you?" a robotic voice said. I turned to find a droid giving me a depraved once-over. It wasn't one of the newer models; this one had wires protruding from its face, and I found myself thinking: *They don't make 'em like they used to…*

"Thanks, I *think*." I wasn't in the mood for conversing, and certainly not with a perverted droid.

The machine beeped, and for a moment I thought I'd stepped on its toes. "Nervous?" it asked.

"I wasn't until you came over," I said, trying not to upset the poor bastard. I smiled, as if that would help.

"Ah, I remember the first time I failed," it went on. "Bloody planet came out of nowhere, it did. You ever crashed into a thousand-mile-wide unpopulated hunk of rock before?"

"Can't say I have—" I looked at the name printed on the droid's front panel. "—Z140"

The droid laughed, as if I'd just told him a brilliant joke. "Just call me Zed," it said. "The 140 isn't necessary for pretty girls like you."

I had to nip things in the bud right then, and so said, "You do know that sexually harassing human females is punishable by recycling. Keep it up, Zed, and you might find yourself reincarnated as a vending machine."

The droid was about to retort when a mechanical and bodiless voice said, "Cassie Opa to the launch deck please."

As I walked across the waiting-room, I could feel Zed's dirty cameras observing my ass, and so put on a little dance for him. The smell of melting wires and fusing steel proved that I still had what it took. I didn't even feel guilty when a team of droid paramedics – *Bot-Fixers* – rushed past me to where Zed was clicking and whirring and slowly melting in on himself.

When I reached the launch deck, I was ready for the test. I knew it was my final attempt; that nobody in their right mind would offer a pilot's job to a candidate who had failed more than three times. Sure, there were employers out there willing to take a chance on a pretty pilot, but most employers had a fondness for their freight – which was, more often than not, incredibly valuable – and thus expected it to be delivered intact. No amount of beauty would supersede millions of pounds of busted cargo.

"Miss Opa," the instructor said as he bounded across the platform as if gravity was something that seldom affected him. He was wearing a suit that said, *Sure, I like to dress smart, but only in clothes three sizes too big for me…* "My name is Thaddeus M and I will be testing you today."

You're testing me already, I wanted to say, but didn't. "Very much looking forward to it," I lied. "Will we be taking the usual route, past the three golden stars, around the pink moon, and back along the asteroid belt?"

Thaddeus shook his head. "Unfortunately not, Miss Opa. You see, we like to chop and change around here. Since you've already taken that route twice before, it's only right that we alter the test. We can't have you memorising every little piece of floating debris now, can we?"

Bastard! "Of course not," I said, giggling like a foreign exchange student at Disneyworld.

"Right, let's get a wriggle on, shall we," he said, pushing a button on the small, ticking device in his right hand. The floor opened up (which had been a lot more impressive the first two times around) and up came the ship. No matter how many times you see one, a spaceship with a large red L painted on its side always looks ridiculous.

We climbed into the ship – mirrors, seatbelt, check make-up, light cigarette…

"There's no smoking during the test, Miss Opa," Thaddeus said, coughing and spluttering out of the window. "Having failed twice already, I would have thought you would have read the terms more closely."

I extinguished the cigarette and smiled coyly. "Sowwy."

Thaddeus wrote something down on his little test-sheet before tapping the steering-wheel. "The test begins *now*," he said. He pushed a green button on that special little handheld device of his and the doors in front of the ship slowly crept open. "Take a right as soon as we exit the launch deck. Head for the second sun on the left, and whatever you do, do not enter Quorzian airspace; as you know they can get a bit cranky, and we're liable to get blown up should you accidentally stumble into their no-fly-zone."

Out into space we flew, which was just as black and boring as it sounded. I tried to perk things up by telling anecdotes about my great-grandfather and his mail-order bride from the Fhtagn territory, but Thaddeus was having none of it. It was just my luck to get the professional buzzkill. I'm pretty sure the M he'd given as his surname stood for *Monotony*…

"When I tap hard on the wheel," he said, leaning in to me. I was tempted to kiss his bald head, but that's just a problem I have. "I want you to perform an emergency-stop."

It was almost an hour later when he tapped the wheel, by which time I had completely forgotten what I was meant to do. I tapped along with him, as if we were composing a ditty for some Swedish death-metal band. Only when he grimaced did I remember what was expected of me.

I slammed on the brakes.

At least, I *thought* I did. Brakes – as far as I was aware – were there to slow the ship down, and yet there we were, careening through space, now at warp speed. It was then that I remembered – lefty brakey, righty speedy.

"What the hell have you *done*!" Thaddeus gasped at me, incredulous. "We're approaching Quorzian airspace…we *were* approaching it, but now we're slap-bang in the middle of it! Make a U-turn! Make a U-turn quick!"

I was panicking by that point, wondering what we would look like as thousands of irreparable pieces, forever floating through space. I probably wouldn't even get a refund for the uncompleted test.

When the first laser hit our tail-end, I realised I was almost certainly going to fail this time, too. There was something about the smell of burning space-ship – and the way Thaddeus was gripping the dashboard with white knuckles and, for some reason, his teeth – that didn't inspire confidence.

I pulled the wheel as hard as I could to the right, knowing we would be dead in the next thirty seconds if one of us didn't pull ourselves together. After skimming the terrain for a few seconds – red dust now peppered the windscreen, as if somebody had just sneezed with a mouthful of turmeric – I managed to get the ship under some sort of control, and after dodging several death-rays – operated by several highly pissed off Quorvians – I took the ship up into the darkness, past the second sun, and beyond the no-fly-zone belonging to the planet quickly shrinking behind us.

"Don't suppose I'll get points for saving our lives?" I said, but Thaddeus didn't hear, and if he did he chose not to respond.

Landing the ship back at the launch deck – perfectly, might I add – we disembarked and, after pushing his shoulder back into its socket, Thaddeus said, "I'm pretty sure you know what I'm going to say."

I shrugged. "Thank you for avoiding those death-rays? Would you like to go to dinner sometime? Is that your natural hair colour?"

Thaddeus M grimaced and rubbed at his bleeding jaw. "You're certainly a character, Miss Opa," he said. "But unfortunately, you're not ready for a license."

I sighed. "Those Quorvians really are irritable, aren't they?" It was no use; my instructor had already made his way across the launch deck, where he'd disappeared through a set of hissing double-doors.

And so, that was how I failed for the third and final time. Shortly afterwards I became a space bus-driver, which was the one pilot's job that any reckless, drunken, license-less person could do, though it does help if you're pretty.

Hair

She boarded the bus at Trafalgar Square, flashing her pass at the driver, who grunted before pulling, somewhat unceremoniously, from the station. As she stumbled down the aisle, looking for a seat and trying not to topple on her ass in the process, Luke shifted nervously, hoping that she saw the space next to him, knowing it wasn't in her best interest, and yet pulling her forward with invisible hands.

As she reached the empty seat, Luke smiled, hoping he didn't frighten her off. When she returned the smile and took the seat, he realised he'd had nothing to worry about.

He wasn't ugly; though he wasn't handsome, not in the conventional sense. A scar, deep and white, stretched the length of his cheek; in the afternoon sun it must have looked like The Grand Canyon.

The girl – for that's what she *was*, really, despite the make-up and power-suit – accidentally brushed Luke's knee, and immediately apologised, so much that you might have believed she'd produced a knife and slammed it into his thigh.

"No problem," Luke grunted, trying not to make eye-contact with the girl. He couldn't get into this now.

The girl removed a compact from her purse and began dusting her nose; it was then that Luke caught a sniff.

Apples; beautiful, sweet apples. He had to steal a look. In that moment he was a donkey, and this girl – who had chosen to sit beside him rather than stand in the aisle – was a dangling carrot.

Pretending to look past her, as if there was something worth witnessing beyond the windows opposite, he managed to surreptitiously glimpse her profile. She continued to daub her nose with powder, unaware of his gaze, which afforded him just enough time to ascertain that she was good enough.

It was the hair. Auburn, darker at the roots, she was something of a vintage for a connoisseur like Luke. The scent of apples teasing his nostrils emanated from there, on top of her wondrous head. He pictured her, standing in the shower, shampoo oozing down between her breasts as she worked the liquid into a lather. Her pubic hair didn't quite match the chestnut of that upon her head, or perhaps it did and the shower's jet had simply darkened it.

Stop it, he told himself, allowing his arm to drop from the slim window-ledge to cover his irrepressible erection. He suddenly felt very uncomfortable; the girl clipped her compact shut and stuffed it back into her purse, completely unaware that the strange man sitting beside her had pictured her naked and was now suffering the consequences.

The bus pulled to the side of the road; the air-brakes hissed as the driver pulled the lever for the door. Two men wearing hi-visibility jackets and sooty faces boarded; an elderly woman with a hunchback alighted. Luke felt his erection wane further.

The auburn girl – was she an Emma? A Lucy? – began composing a text message on her phone, and Luke was fascinated at how expertly she worked the tiny buttons with such prolific nails. He furtively watched, his head facing forward but his eyes on the prize.

The text was to a girlfriend; he could tell by its content. *How did it go last night, m8? You were pretty drunk when I left. Hope he treated you well. ;) x*

The winking face concluding the message reminded Luke what he was dealing with here: a girl, not long out of glitter and tiaras. The power-suit, crisp and new, suggested she was on her way to an interview, which would also explain why she was paying such close attention to her make-up.

After a few minutes, the girl's phone beeped. *He treated me VERY well, Kelly. :D You didn't seem that drunk. I thought you just needed to get off early because of your interview. Good luck, btw. If you get it, drinks are on you. Xxx*

Bingo! He'd been right about the suit; that Kelly – though she didn't *look* like a Kelly – was hoping to get a new job. Luke was also pleased to hear that this friend of hers had received a good dicking last night. *Good for her.*

Kelly reached up and pressed the red button. A bell tinkled, and a sign at the front of the bus lit up, announcing that it would be stopping at the next station. Luke sighed; this wasn't where he'd needed to get off. He had no idea where he was, which was something he always tried to pay close attention to, for obvious reasons.

Kelly stood, straightened her jacket, and made her way to the front of the bus. The men in hi-vis jackets muttered clandestinely to one another as she passed, casting perverted glances over her as if she was nothing but meat in a suit.

Luke despised them for it.

As the bus slowed, he stood and made his way along the aisle. Looking through the windows to his right, he saw a row of shops. One of them, a tattoo parlour, announced itself as *Jack O' Diamonds Ink*. The store next door, which seemed to specialise in the reparation of household goods and retail of general hardware, offered him much more in the way of clues. *Ripple Road Repairs.*

Ripple Road. He knew exactly where he was, now. If things went awry, he could easily find his way back to Trafalgar Square.

Not that he'd let anything go awry; he was nothing if not professional.

The bus slowed, air-brakes screeched, and Kelly stepped down onto the street much to the detriment of the glowing degenerates still seated, still mumbling to one another about what they'd do to Kelly, given half a chance.

It was a chance they would never get.

Luke thanked the driver – who grunted; clearly a man who disliked his job – before disembarking and lighting a cigarette.

Kelly was already striding away, intent on making a good impression with her prospective employers by arriving early. Luke allowed her a few hundred yards before heading after her.

This was the part of the game he liked best; a little sport before the inevitable denouement. This section of the kill he liked to call The Shadowing.

As he walked after her, he could smell the apples; a spot of blood in an ocean, and he was the shark, hungry, relentless. He tried not to picture her showering again, but it was impossible. The erection pushing against the zipper of his jeans discomforted him. Glancing down, though, he was pleased to see that his stiffness was concealed. He stopped, peered in through the window of a charity-shop as he readjusted his cock to where it wouldn't end up sore.

Must. Stop. Picturing.

When his pursuit of Kelly resumed, he realised he'd spent way too long fiddling with himself; Kelly, his auburn-haired goddess, was nowhere to be seen.

At first, panic hit him. He scanned the street ahead, frantically, picking up the pace, practically running. All the time he cursed himself for being such a fucking idiot. *You cunt! You silly fucking cunt!*

He rushed past a row of shops, glancing in through the window of each in case Kelly had stepped inside. A dog tied to a lamppost almost upended him, and as he untangled himself from the lead he spat and swore at the ridiculous creature dancing around his feet.

Then he saw her, and he calmed enough to sensibly step out of the dog-lead's impossible grasp and leave the miniature poodle – it was fluffy and white; one of those candyfloss looking motherfuckers that you usually find peering out of some cunt's handbag – to enjoy the rest of its meaningless existence.

There, through the window of *Nancy's Nails*, Kelly shook hands with an orange lady – shit, why do people *do* that to themselves? – wearing a white smock. His relief was palpable; his heartbeat settled, and a smile returned to his lips. He took one last look at Kelly, hoping she nailed the interview and got the job, regardless of what he was about to do to her.

She deserved one final bit of happiness.

Luke noticed a coffee-shop across the street, where he would spend the next hour, watching…waiting…imagining.

*

When she emerged from the nail parlour, Luke's belly felt distended with latte. As he stood and slipped out through the side-entrance, he could feel it sloshing around inside him; his own fault for opting for *Grande*.

Kelly was smiling as she walked, which probably meant she'd got the job. What qualifications did you need to paint some fucker's nails, anyway?

He trailed her to a junction at the end of the street, where she composed a text message and withdrew cash from an ATM. Luke guessed she was about to go off celebrating, perhaps meeting up with her cock-hungry friend for afternoon shots. He couldn't allow that to happen; it would ruin everything.

Kelly was practically skipping. Luke imagined chalk-marks on the pavement, pictured her in a frilly dress; it helped pass the time, though he knew he was quickly running out.

When she turned into an alleyway – a shortcut, he assumed, to her bar of choice – he realised it was his only opportunity to get this done. He went after her, no longer caring if she turned and glimpsed him, no longer maintaining the stealth that had seen him successfully shadow her for the last two hours.

The alleyway was thin and, thankfully, deserted. *Just me and you now, honey*, he thought, his face contorting with anticipation. The gap between them had closed exponentially; the scent of apples from that magnificent chestnut hair taunted him, willed him to snatch out and grab a handful, which he did just as she turned.

Her eyes widened. A scream was about to fall from her mouth when Luke slapped a hand across it. As he pushed her against the wall, lying to her in excited whispers that he wasn't going to hurt her, he retrieved the knife from its sheath on his belt, a scabbard that had been cleverly concealed by the perfect length of his box-jacket.

Her muffled protests meant nothing to him as he ran the blade along the perfect pink flesh of her throat, drawing a thin red line that soon began to spray arterial fluid. She choked and spluttered, trying to make sense of how her perfect day had taken such a ghastly turn for the worse.

Luke smiled, avoiding the jets of warm fluid squirting from her carotid. The beautiful whiff of apples and her muted gargles was all too much, and he shuddered as he came; the warm dampness of his jeans a worthy tribute to an afternoon well-spent.

*

He turned the key in the lock and pushed his way into the room. It was small and pokey; the kind of place he would always find himself. Locking the door behind him, he flicked on the lamp standing in the corner of the room and turned on the television. Not the news, though; there was nothing but terrible things happening in the world. It depressed the life out of him.

He pulled a small bag from his pocket and emptied its contents onto the table, being extra careful not to drop any.

Auburn hair. It was just a swatch, yet the sent was almost overpowering. He lifted it to his nostrils and sniffed, revelling in its perfection. For a few seconds, he thought he would orgasm again. It was something of a disappointment when he didn't.

He made his way to the kitchen, where he retrieved a tube of glue from the drawer. On the television, some old biddy was trying to barter with a posh fucker over the price of her dead grandmother's Queen Anne table.

He applied glue to the roots of the hair, being careful not to get any on the beautiful redness a little further along the strands. With that done, he turned to face his mannequin, which glanced at him with gratitude for what it was about to receive.

It already had a full head of hair. Perched upon its head there were browns, blondes, reds, ravens; a multi-coloured wig that Luke hoped to one day wear.

He attached Kelly's hair to the toupee and stepped back to admire his handiwork.

"Beautiful," he said, wiping a tear from his cheek before dabbing his eyes with the back of his hand.

After an hour of bullshit TV, Luke found himself at the door to his room, his bus-pass in one hand and an empty plastic bag in the other.

With one last glance at the mannequin taking up precedence in his home, and the glued sections of hair upon its pate, he headed out into the night.

Phoenix Rising

Jacob knew what the gift was, simply by its shape and size, and yet he couldn't fathom how his parents had managed to afford such a luxurious item. Besides, they were nothing but frugal when it came to needless expenditure, and this certainly fell into that category.

You see, Jacob still had a Robomate™; Percival was nothing like the model wrapped so neatly in front of him right now, but he *worked*, and he had been nothing but helpful the entire time Jacob had been linked with him.

'Well?' the boy's mother said, startling him a little from his confused reverie. 'Aren't you going to *open* it?' She was smiling; her perfect, white teeth seeming to stretch from ear to ear between her excitedly quivering lips. Jacob's father stood slightly behind her, his arm draped lackadaisically across her shoulder.

Jacob turned back to the gift. It was exactly the same size as him, only wider – much wider. He stepped forward and began to rip frantically at the brown paper. It rained down like confetti as his excitement got the better of him, and yet he felt guilty as he tore through to the prize contained within.

What was to become of Percival? Surely they didn't expect him to pack Percival away, or send him to Old Man Withers down at the breakers yard. That would be *terrible*! He would never allow that to happen. Yet *something* was going to change; Percival would be distraught at the sight of a newer model, a better model, one that could do so many things that he wasn't programmed to. There was no way that his mother and father would allow him to keep two Robomates™. Jacob could hear his mother already, complaining about the clutter, about how one of them had to go, and that the older model – poor old Percival – was obsolete.

And yet, with all of those horrible thoughts running around in his head like wayward mice, he continued to pull at the brown paper, a massive grin upon his face, until the prize was finally revealed. He stepped back and looked upon the creation with awe.

The machine had been built in his own image; it was uncanny to the point of being disturbing. The only differences were the hundreds upon hundreds of moving parts. Where Jacob had a nose, the Robomate™ had a button; where there were eyes on

Jacob's face, this mechanical being had glowing red orbs. It was *magnificent*, and he knew that his parents were waiting for him to speak, to express his undying gratitude for such a momentous gift on his twelfth birthday. After a few moments of opening and shutting his mouth – a result of the intense wonderment he felt at the sight of his new companion – he gave them what they wanted.

'I love it, Mommy!' he gasped. He reached across and touched the automaton with trembling fingers; a high-pitched whirr emanated from deep within its core as a response. 'What's its *name*?'

'Well, you can't very well call it GX5000 all the time, *can* you?' said his father, stepping forward and placing a hand on the new robot's chest-plate. 'What do *you* think?'

Jacob glanced into the glowing red bulbs and smiled. He hadn't named anything before. The last dogs on earth had died long before he was born, and cats were no longer kept as pets, not since they all became feral back in the 2020's. Percival had already been assigned a name by the time Jacob's parents acquired him, and it was too much trouble to have the poor thing reprogrammed, so it had simply stuck.

But now, Jacob was being offered the opportunity of a lifetime. He was to assign this new robot – this top of the range, energy-efficient, and frankly bewildering automaton – a name of his own choice. A thousand words and images whipped through Jacob's head as he concocted something unusual, something different. It was no good calling such a beautiful Robomate™ Frank, or Terry. Those were pedestrian names, likely to incite witticism from the other children in the street.

No, it had to be something special, something that instilled fear. His father was looking down at him, eagerly awaiting Jacob's decision. A few seconds later, and Jacob grinned.

'*What*?' his mother asked. 'Do you have a name?'

Jacob nodded. 'His name is Phoenix.'

They all stood there, admiring Phoenix, for quite some time. When Jacob had calmed a little, his father removed the bracelet from his wrist and synchronised it to Phoenix's computer.

In another room, Percival felt the link break and snapped his eyes open. There must have been some mistake; perhaps the boy had simply removed his bracelet to wash, placed it down a little too roughly and hit the reset button. Maybe, Percival thought, the boy had wandered too far from the house and the link between them had been lost. Yes, *that* was it. It had to be.

And yet he knew, deep within his circuitry, that it was not.

*

Jacob couldn't wait to show Phoenix to his friends, and called them all on the holophone. When they were all lined up in front of him – Kate, Zed, and Lewis – flickering slightly as a draft whispered through the room, Jacob disappeared through the door and was gone for some time.

'Do you think he's coming back?' Zed asked, not in the least bit interested, either way. He had much better things to do than hang around on the holophone all day; there was a hoverboard race over in Sector 13, and he had signed up to take part.

'Of course he's coming back,' Kate said, slightly annoyed at Zed's apparent lack of patience. 'He wouldn't have called us just to leave us standing here, would he?'

Just then, Jacob came racing back into the room. He had a massive grin on his face, and he was breathless. He looked, to the three flickering children in the centre of the room, apt to pass out. Zed was about to ask if he was okay when the thing following Jacob into the room distracted him.

'Is that a...?' Lewis started, but was interrupted by an overly excited Jacob.

'Robomate™? Yes, it's one of the new models,'

Jacob told his audience. 'My parents bought it for my birthday. Its name's Phoenix, and it's not nearly as dangerous as it looks.'

Secretly, Jacob hoped they were all as intimidated by the automaton as he had been when his eyes first met it. He knew that Zed was, just by the way he had begun to scratch at his head. It was something he only did when he was nervous, unconsciously, though Jacob and the others had noticed it even if he hadn't.

Kate, with those wonderfully inquisitive eyes that Jacob had come to love, appraised the Robomate™. 'It's one of the most amazing things I've ever seen,' she said, delighted by the sight of it.

'Well you don't go out much,' Zed spat, a hint of envy in his tone. Jacob knew that Zed pretended to hate Kate, when really his feelings were more akin to his own. They both liked her. A *lot.* They just had very different ways of showing it, and in the end Jacob hoped his methods worked more successfully than Zed's.

'Have you been linked up to it yet?' Lewis asked, breaking the awkward silence which had descended in the room.

Jacob nodded. 'My dad helped me synchronise with Phoenix this very morning.' He pointed to the glimmering silver bracelet clinging to his wrist. 'I've been teaching it already. *Watch.*' And Jacob took a few steps back and silently commanded Phoenix to do something. You see, that was all it took. A thought, a silent command from the master, and the Robomate™ would obey. In this case, Phoenix began to clap its huge, clanking hands together. The noise was like nothing any of them had ever heard. It was so loud that the holophone began to flicker so much that the images of the three children distorted, combined. There was a moment when Zed and Kate were merged completely. It looked like both of them, and yet neither. Jacob didn't like it one bit, and silently commanded Phoenix to cease his mechanical applause.

The three children returned, sharp and singular once again.

'So apart from clapping,' Zed sneered, scratching at his head as if he was afflicted with lice, 'does it do anything else?'

Jacob was expecting as much, and though he had barely become acquainted with his new companion he had prepared something special.

He smiled, turned to Phoenix, and concentrated. The automaton flinched as the instructions from its master logged. It clunked and whirred; the bright-red bulbs embedded in its face flashed maniacally, and then it proceeded with its tricks. Firstly, it lowered one hulking arm to the ground and lifted its legs up, straight up until they were completely vertical. With its free hand, it waved at the three holographic onlookers. Zed opened and shut his mouth, unable to speak. Jacob was pleased with himself, but they hadn't seen *anything* yet.

The machine flipped onto its feet once again. The not-really-there children flickered as the entire room shook, only to reappear just in time for the next trick. Jacob sent further instructions to Phoenix, who whistled and glowed. Then the robot flexed its muscles. Of course, it didn't really possess muscles, but the gesture was unmistakeable. Kate sniggered at this, and Jacob turned to watch her beautiful, enchanting face as she, in turn, watched the Robomate™ begin to dance. It was clunky – like watching a fat uncle try to master a new move – but the machine could certainly move.

'That's *amazing*,' Lewis said. 'And you managed to teach it that in just a few hours?'

Jacob nodded. 'It was as if it already knew what to do,' he said. 'It managed to get most of the moves on the first attempt. I couldn't *believe* it; it took Percival three months to learn how to do the running-man. This one is *so* much better.'

Phoenix stopped frolicking and straightened up. The way he stood – like a solider on parade – made Kate chuckle once again.

'You've certainly got its undivided attention,' she said. 'I like it, Jacob. I like it a *lot.*'

Jacob was about to speak, to tell Kate that she was welcome to come over and meet Phoenix face-to-face, when there was what could only be described as an explosion. Everything was bright, intense, and before Jacob knew what was happening he was somersaulting through the air. He crashed against the basement wall, and for a moment there was nothing but pain. The wind had been knocked out of him, and as he tried to open his eyes he fought for breath.

What was *that*?

What in the heck had just *happened*?

He finally managed to open his eye, and watched as the smoke whorled around the basement. Smoke from *what*, he wasn't sure. Had Phoenix exploded? Had Jacob broken his Robomate™ already. His mother was going to *kill* him. Yet he hadn't done anything wrong; the computer housed inside Phoenix should have been able to withstand a lot more than just a few playful commands. Maybe it was a faulty model. Jacob just didn't know.

The tendrils of smoke rose up, danced around the ceiling, around the incandescent lights. Jacob pushed himself onto his haunches and spluttered as the dust and smoke reached his lungs. He could hear Phoenix to his right; the sound of shifting metal came as a relief. It meant that the machine wasn't completely obliterated. Plus, the link between them was still established, and strong. Jacob concentrated, sent a simple command to the automaton. Phoenix must have received the order, for there came a clunking of steel, a high-pitched wheeze, a guttural voice that announced, '*Still online. Not to worry, Jacob.*'

Jacob recognised the voice as Phoenix's, and heaved a massive sigh of relief.

But he should have waited, because that was when he noticed, through the smoke and settling dust, the silhouette. A shape that couldn't have been human; a wide, bulky form that he recognised immediately.

It was *Percival*, and his eyes were glowing red.

His eyes had never glowed red, *ever*. This was very bad indeed. The explosion hadn't come from a malfunction on Phoenix. Percival had blasted the new Robomate™ in the back with a weapon that Jacob didn't even know he possessed.

And he was charging up for a second attack.

Jacob scrambled to his feet and screamed after Phoenix, but it was too late. Percival was already powered-up.

*

Kate rushed out onto the street and was almost

mowed down by a low-flying cab. Luckily, Zed was right behind her and pushed her to the ground before the flying vehicle hit her.

'Ouch!' she said, rolling over onto her front. 'What did you have to do that for?' She began to rub at her ankle, but from what Zed could see she hadn't suffered any lasting damage. A sprain, maybe. As Zed pulled her to her feet, she said, 'And what was that cab doing flying so low, anyway? Nearly gave me a haircut, it did.'

Just then, Lewis came rushing down the street. He was wearing a beige robe, and looked like one of those Jedis from that ancient movie, *Star Wars.* His feet were bare, and he was treading carefully, making sure not so step on any rocks or sharp objects.

'What happened to Jacob!?' Lewis asked as he reached them. 'It looked like he blew up!'

'Come on,' Kate said, limping a little. 'We need to make sure he's alright. I'm hoping it was just a holophone glitch, but I won't be happy until I know he's okay.'

The trio moved as quickly as they could towards Jacob's sector, though with barefoot Lewis and limping Kate, Zed didn't think they were moving very fast at all.

*

The second blast from Percival's mysterious weapon – a projectile fired from somewhere just beneath the automaton's wrist, though Jacob hardly had time to be certain – sent Phoenix crashing through the basement. Concrete and steel rained down; Jacob clambered up through the freshly-made aperture and out into the mid-afternoon haze.

Phoenix was, at first, nowhere to be seen. Jacob had the terrible notion that the shot fired from Percival's formidable weapon had obliterated it, smashed it into a thousand-and-one pieces, scattered them for miles around. He expected to come across an arm here, a leg there, a still-spinning cog that was once a very important component of the thing's heart. Behind him, Jacob could hear the other Robomate™ scrambling through the rubble – debris that it had created, and for what? Jacob didn't know how Percival was even functioning without an owner; it belonged to nobody, now, not until somebody linked with it, the way he was now linked with Phoenix.

He rushed out onto the street, aware that the antagonistic hulk of his prior servant was not far behind. That was when Jacob spotted Phoenix, picking itself up from the pavement on the other side of the street. A sky-car had been knocked from the air by the recovering automaton, its driver was dragging himself out through its roof, shaking his head in disgust at the injured robot.

Actually, Phoenix wasn't *injured*; that was not the correct term, at all. It was compromised, and the thin tendril of smoke escaping from the power-box on its back only further proved it.

The link was strong still. Jacob hadn't expected it to be so powerful, not after what his ex-servant had just done to it, not after slamming into a sky-car at God knows how fast.

'I'm okay, Jacob!' Phoenix bellowed in its calm, guttural voice. It stopped completely still as it ran a quick diagnostics check. Jacob felt the bracelet on his wrist vibrate, taking his mind off the gathering crowd of confused citizens who had started to scream questions at each other, as if they were all somehow responsible for what was happening in their own sector.

'That thing came out of nowhere!' the man from the crinkled sky-car said, checking his head for blood or any sign of damage. 'I'm supposed to be at the hoverboard race; this is terrible! I need to find out who's responsible!'

Jacob was across the street by then, wafting the smoke away from Phoenix's power-box. He would have owned up, told the poor sky-car driver that his father was very wealthy and would make certain that his damaged car was either fixed or replaced, when there came the terrible clunk-clunk-clunk of Percival's footfall. And there he was, across the street, standing the way Jacob had seen gunslingers stand in olden-day films. The only thing missing was the compulsory tumbleweed, drifting across the path.

'Is that yours as well, boy?' the man from the twisted wreck asked Jacob. 'Because I didn't know it was possible to have two of those things.'

'Get behind me, Jacob,' Phoenix said, stepping in front of the boy and shooting the sky-car driver a cursory glance that suggested he go away, before it was too late.

Just then, Jacob's parents appeared in the upstairs window of their home. They must have heard the crash, the tumultuous racket resulting from several walls being smashed through by a tonne of tempered steel. Jacob could see his mother's face – the way her mouth was curled into a horrified O as she realised that their house had been all but destroyed by warring automatons.

Yet it was far from over.

Percival chittered, as if its system had downloaded a virus. Maybe that was why it was attacking Phoenix; there were always new strains of malware going around, and since the registry automatically updated itself every three days there was a very good chance that the irate machine had contracted something nasty.

When the inscrutable chirruping came to an end, Percival said, 'Why replace? Why change? Why replace GS250 with this?' It gestured towards the automaton opposite, and although its expression was indifferent – the way it always was with Percival, as it didn't have the facial-nodes that Phoenix did, rendering him vacant and somewhat deadpan – Jacob knew what it was trying to say.

In the distance there were sirens; Jacob didn't hear them, though. He was trying to figure out what was happening, why his old Robomate™ had decided that a violent rampage was the only way to impart its feelings of jealousy as a result of its abandonment.

And then Percival began to power up again. Its eyes glazed over, flashed red, and the spots beneath its wrist started to glow an effulgent azure. In the upstairs window, his mother and father watched in amazement, too far away to help their son, too frightened to even move.

Jacob didn't know what to do. People were running through the street, trying to escape the insanity playing out in their own sector. It was absolute chaos as the sirens belonging to the sky-police neared; but they were still a few minutes away, which was, Jacob thought, too far.

He gripped the glimmering clasp around his wrist and sent a silent command to Phoenix.

He had no choice.

The automaton shuffled on the spot a few feet in front of him as the message was received loud and clear, and then it lifted its arm and shot an intense green ray of light across the street. The other robot wasn't expecting it, and shot backwards as the light slammed into it.

Should these things even have weapons built in? Jacob found himself pondering. The company behind the creations had failed to mention it on the countless advertisements. Jacob started to wonder if the Robomates™ were, in fact, child-friendly models. He certainly would have been a little more cautious with his own models if he'd been aware of their integrated arsenal.

Percival, slightly perturbed at being on the receiving end of an attack, flipped back onto its feet. Without another second's hesitation, it hissed, spluttered and began to fly though the air towards Phoenix...

Towards Jacob...

There was an almighty crash as the two metallic construct impacted; steel twisted this way and that, a sound more annoying than chalk on a blackboard or a fork on a porcelain plate. Jacob closed his eyes, managing to concentrate just enough to focus his energies on damage limitation. The two automatons were airborne, and in a moment they would crash through some unsuspecting neighbour's house in a tangle of smoking wires and frazzles circuitry. Jacob and his family would be shunned by the rest of the community; they would probably have to move to an adjacent sector just to be rid of the torment.

That couldn't happen.

Jacob concentrated, ignored the screaming of the approaching sky-police, ignored the wailing of confused spectators who were witnessing something very special indeed, ignored the faces of his mother and father in the upstairs window, and forced Phoenix to do something drastic, something that could potentially put an end to the madness.

He made him go *up*.

Now, a Robomate™ can't technically fly, not in the conventional sense. What they can do, however, is leap great heights, and it was at this moment that Phoenix slammed its feet into the ground – which was no mean feat considering they were still hurtling through the air at indeterminable speed – and pushed upwards.

The two magnificent contraptions changed course. Instead of heading for Mr. and Mrs. Rommelly's place, they were now shooting up towards the atmosphere, though they would never reach it.

A voice – *Kate's* voice – caught Jacob's attention. What was she doing here? She was with Zed, and Lewis, and all three of them looked concerned, though Zed not as much as the other two.

'Thank *God* you're okay!' Kate screamed, and then she reached him, threw her arms around him. It was so unexpected that Jacob made a strange noise – sort of a gulp, but with a whimper attached – and instantly felt extremely stupid. Zed muttered something incoherent, but Jacob had an idea that it was something nasty; Kate had her arms around Jacob's neck and was practically dangling from him. Of *course* Zed wasn't going to be happy about it.

'I'm *fine,*' Jacob managed as he reluctantly squirmed from Kate's grasp. 'Percival went *haywire.* I don't know how, but it must have felt something. *Jealousy.* It's gone crazy!' He jabbed an excited finger towards the sky, and the three newcomers glanced upwards.

'Ooooh,' Lewis said, watching the two automaton dots as they approached the atmosphere. 'This is *not* going to end well for either for either for them.'

The sirens were deafening now; three sky-police vehicles swooped down into the street, though they had no idea what they were looking for, or what everyone was screaming and running around like scampering cockroaches for. The sky-cars hovered as the doors swung up and open. Men scrambled out of the cockpits; dressed all in black, and almost identical in description, they rushed across the street and began ushering onlookers back to a safe distance. A few of them had spotted the melee taking place in the sky above, and were mindlessly moving spectators out of the way without taking their own eyes from the battle.

'Everyone, I repeat, *everyone*,' the policeman in charge said. 'Go indoors, get to a safe place and *stay* there. There is nothing to see here. I *repeat*, this is nothing out of the ordinary!'

But it *was*, and there was plenty to see. Most of these folks had never seen anything like this. Their halcyon lives had never been disrupted to this extent; this was the closest any of them were going to get to World War IV. Heck, perhaps this was the *beginning* of World War IV. Nobody wanted to miss that for the world.

And the automatons kept rising, spinning in the air like smoking arrows. Everybody knew what was coming next, but nobody spoke. They made noises – *ooohhh, ahhhh, woooooow*, as if they had just stumbled upon an improvised fireworks display – but the noises contained no words.

And then came the explosion as the warring

Robomates™ clattered into the bio-dome that encapsulated the city. It was invisible, so it was impossible to determine where the city ended and the polluted space on the opposite side of the foot-thick glass began. The automatons hadn't seen it coming...

Jacob had, and now the city sky was ablaze, a perfect dome-shaped fire spread outwards, its epicentre where the machines had impacted only a second before.

If people were running and screaming before, they were going insane now. The sky-police couldn't control the panic, and instead decided to rush back to their cockpits. If the city was about to be rained upon by fire and robot components, leaving the sky-cars where they were would be impressively stupid.

'Quick!' Jacob said to his friends. 'We need to get back to the house.' And, for some reason unbeknownst to him, he reached down and plucked Kate's hand from the air. She didn't flinch, or recoil in horror. In fact, he was pretty sure that she smiled.

They crossed the street, never taking their eyes from the tumbling fire and shimmering, steel fallout. He couldn't be sure, but Jacob thought he saw one of Percival's arms land atop a slowly retreating sky-car. There was a thud, a yell from within the cockpit, and that was all he saw because he was racing for safety, and his parents were waving frantically from the upstairs window, flailing their arms about as if they were trapped in a holophone box with a recalcitrant wasp.

No sooner had Jacob dragged Kate down into the bunker that was now the basement to his house – *God, that was going to cost a lot to fix* – there came a loud smash from behind. Lewis and Zed lunged forward, toppled in through the automaton-shaped aperture, and a cloud of smoke followed them. Within a millisecond, the basement was once again filled with debris and a thick, dusty miasma. The four children were invisible to one another, but Jacob knew where Kate was.

She was on the end of his arm; where she belonged.

And more sirens came, and the dust settled, and Jacob knew that things were going to be very different in the city from that day forth.

He just *knew* it.

*

The street was filled with intrigued and, in some cases, still-terrified people. The sky-police had given up trying to regulate the crowd, and were now only interest in picking up the debris so they could go home to their wives and children and forget all about their miserable working lives.

Jacob stood over the only remaining part of Phoenix; the panel that had once fit snuggly over its power-supply box. The bracelet on Jacob's wrist no longer thrummed or buzzed or bleeped intermittently. It was useless now, nothing more than a glistening decoration. He snapped it from his wrist and tossed it onto the smouldering casing of the automaton he'd possessed for less than a day.

'I'm sorry,' Kate said, as if Jacob had suffered the loss of the something real, a real person, a family-member.

'Don't be,' he said, forcing a smile, though it was hard. 'Who'd have thought they were capable of such *chaos*. If I'd known Percival could do that, I'd have never asked my parents for one. In a strange way, this whole mess has made me realise something.' He reached down and took Kate's hand once again, and once again she didn't wince.

'What?' she said, sniggering. Behind them, Zed and Lewis were salvaging parts for God knows what. They seemed happy enough, though, and not in the least bit interested in what was taking place between Kate and Jacob.

'It's made me realise that there can never be replacements for real friends, and why would anyone ever *want* one?'

Kate smiled. In fact, they *both* smiled, and Zed rejoiced at the discovery of one of Percival's still-glowing eyes amongst the rubble, and Jacob knew that everything would be back to normal soon.

Perhaps not normal, Jacob thought as Kate gave his hand a playful squeeze.

Maybe something *better* than normal.

Bug Boy

The spider came apart. Just like that. He didn't even have to pull it hard, not like the beetle he found in the garden yesterday. Now *that* was one tough sonofabitch. He'd almost broken into a sweat working on that beetle. At one point he'd even thought about giving in, going inside to get a glass of lemonade, perhaps slump down on the sofa to catch his breath and an episode of Star Trek. Who would have thought dismantling a bug would make a person thirsty?

This spider, though, needed no such accompaniments. He held one half in his balled-up left hand; the other in the open palm of his right. He watched as the legs continued to twitch, as warm liquid seeped out onto his hand. It was mesmerising, and *he* had done it. He had held that tiny creature in his hands and torn it apart, not because he had to, but because he wanted to. He had been afraid of spiders once, but not now. Not anymore.

He waited for the creature to cease moving before

dusting his hands free of the shrivelled remains. Its blood was smeared on the palm of his hand; he would have to scrub it off in the kitchen-sink, the way he usually did. His mother, should she notice the blood, would question him, and then he'd have to concoct some bullshit story about how he had grazed himself, or that it wasn't blood, but rust from his bike. It was easy to lie to her; she was usually out of it, anyway. She would lie on the sofa most of the day, drinking wine and smoking cigarettes. She told him that it
was normal, that it helped de-stress her, even though she didn't work and had nothing to stress about. Billy was no mathematician, nor the sharpest tool in the drawer, but he knew his mother had some sort of problem, that the other kids at school took the piss out of him when he was out of earshot.

He didn't care. They weren't friends; they were people that just so happened to go to the same school as him. Billy didn't need friends.

Billy had the bugs.

He went into the house, blinking as his eyes adjusted to the semi-darkness. The sun had been so intense outside that the house looked pitch-dark through his eyes. He washed his hands once he’d moved the stacks of filthy bowls and plates out of the way. He would have to do the dishes at some point;

his mother wouldn't.

He went through to the lounge, where his mother was watching some stupid, irreverent chat-show. The title at the bottom of the screen read: *Did I have sex with my own sister?* The host was a man called Jeremy, a contemptuous little man, and snarky with it. Billy didn't know why his mother watched such rubbish, though the way she stared at the screen, the way she was staring at it now – lifeless, disinterested, drunk – he knew that if he questioned her about it she wouldn't know *what* she was watching.

'Mom?' Billy said, slowly moving towards the chair in which she was slumped. She lit a cigarette before acknowledging him. She smiled, waited expectantly for him to continue. 'I'm going up to my room for a few hours. Do you want anything before I go?'

She shook her head, signalled the bottle of wine next to the sofa. 'I'm just fine,' she said. Her sentence was short, but she still managed to slur it.

Billy sighed and made his way up the stairs. Sitting at the top, as if frightened of something downstairs or guarding something up, was Genghis. Genghis was his mother's cat, though she did nothing to keep it alive. The job of feeding it, watering it, letting it out, letting it back in again, all fell to Billy, and he resented the cat for becoming such a fucking burden. The cat, sensing now was not a good time to get in Billy's way, stepped aside and mewled nervously.

'Fuck off,' Billy whispered.

'What?' the voice of his mother said from downstairs.

'I'm just talking to the cat,' Billy called.

'Ahhh, that's nice.'

Billy went to his room, slammed the door behind him so hard that it rattled in its frame. Genghis mewled outside the door for a few minutes before recanting, and not a moment too soon as far as Billy was concerned.

Billy wanted to do something, *anything*. Why did life have to be so boring? Why was his life much…*dirtier* than the other kids? You never heard Denis Dugan complaining about his mother, or Sandy Bayliss wishing that things were different. No, because Denis's mother was a successful lawyer – and a part-time saleswoman for some sex-toy manufacturer – and Sandy Bayliss had two swimming-pools, one indoors and the other taking up the majority of the garden. They had nothing to complain about.

Billy sat at his desk and drew. He liked to draw, and this time he did a wonderful little picture of Sandy Bayliss's swimming-pool filled with bugs. When he was finished with that, he put it to one side and drew a hilarious picture of Denis Dugan's mother, but instead of hair she had centipedes dangling down, partially covering her face. In the picture she was screaming, and Billy thought that if it was real, if it *did* actually happen to her, she would scream just as much. He didn't hate Denis's mom; in fact, there was something quite attractive about her. She had a big chest, like the girls in the magazines he sometimes found lying at the side of the rail-track. Those pictures made him feel dirty, but most of the time – and he didn't know *what* it was – he liked the way he felt after reading them. Some of the stories were a little far-fetched, but that didn't stop his dick from getting bigger as he read them.

Was that *normal*? He didn't want to make a big deal out of it, and there was nobody he could ask, so he just accepted that there was nothing wrong with it, that it happened to everyone.

Denis Dugan's mom made him hard. Not like the girls in the magazines, though. This was something else. He often wondered whether he loved her, but he knew he wasn't capable of love and quickly dismissed the notion.

He put the pictures in his drawer and went to sleep. He wasn't tired, but he planned to go back out later, after dark, after his mom had passed out from too much wine. Better things happened at night. That was when the best insects came out.

In his dream, Denis Dugan's mom was naked. Her hair was made of centipedes, like he'd drawn her, and they trailed down her body, covering her chest, squirming and flailing over her. Billy began to pull them away, snapping them into pieces, just so he could get a good look at what was underneath. She was screaming at him to help her, to get them off, and he did. He snapped every single one of them in half, and when he was done, she leaned down and kissed him on the lips. Her tongue slipped into his mouth a little bit, and...

He woke up to find that his room was dark. It was night; he must have slept for hours, though he didn't feel any better for it.

He pushed himself up from the bed. The curtains were still open, and the street-light across the road poured in. He didn't have to get dressed, so he slipped out through the bedroom door and quietly made his way down the stairs.

He was almost at the bottom when he trod on something. There was a terrible screech, and then Genghis ran across the room, disappearing into the kitchen.

That fucking cat was trying to kill him; at least it felt like it.

On the sofa, his mother adjusted her position. The cat's sudden noise had failed to wake her. Billy was glad.

He went out through the back-door, cursing Genghis with a whisper as he passed him.

The night was *glorious.* It was still warm, but there was a gentle breeze – something that had not been present during the daylight hours. As Billy made his was to the back of the garden, he breathed in the freshness, the cool, comforting scents of his surroundings.

In the corner of the garden was a shed. Billy used it to construct things in, objects that his mother didn't know about. If she found out he was carving wooden arrows, or trying to figure out how to make a bomb from bleach and batteries she might have started to pay a little more attention to what he got up to during the day.

He didn't go to the shed now, though. What he was looking for came to him.

A moth flickered through the air, not a few inches in front of his face, and as if he had been trained in some sort of formidable martial-art he quickly whipped out a hand and snatched it from the air.

'Come to Billy,' he said, trying not to squeeze too hard, not straight away. There was no fun in that; part of his enjoyment came from the anticipation. He liked to sit and watch for awhile first, to see the tiny creature struggle. He liked to think that the insect was talking to him, begging for mercy in a voice that he was unable to hear.

He sat on the grass, which was damp with dew, and placed the crippled moth between his legs. It couldn't fly away; he'd done enough to maim it beyond repair. He watched as it staggered forward, tried to leap into the air, came back down with a gentle *fpppp*. He smiled.

Night-time was definitely when the best insects came out.

*

He decided to go to school the next day, not because he wanted to – he hated the place, almost as much as he hated Denis Dugan and Sandy Bayliss – but because he knew that they were onto him, that a letter was probably already being written to his mom, that truancy was now punishable by a monetary fine or even jail-time. His mother had no money, and jail would finish her off completely. It was like his grandmother once told him: *Sometimes, Billy, you've got to man up and do things you don't want to.* She was a daft, old cow, and said silly things like that all the time, but most of the time she was right. Billy had cried when she died, though nobody ever found out about it. He'd saved it for his bedroom, where nobody would see him sobbing like a little baby. Crying in public was for women and pussies. That was one of his own little adages, one that his grandmother would have probably disagreed with.

He managed to get through to lunch-time without any trouble, a personal-best. It was 12:42, and he was sitting on his own, minding his own business (which was just the way he liked it), when Denis Dugan, Kevin Marsh, and Leroy Brown – *Mad, bad Leroy Brown*, as Billy liked to call him, though not to his face, of course – decided to shake things up a little. They approached him with their usual curiosity. *What's mad Billy up to? Sitting there, all on his lonesome. He must be doing something fucking horrible.*

The truth was, Billy was thinking about last night's moth, and how it had finally exploded in a puff of dust as he brought his fist down onto it. He was quite happy with his reverie, and it would have seen him all the way through lunch, had he not been interrupted by the annoying trio.

'Hey, Billy,' Leroy said, holding his hand out for a low-five. Billy never went along, though. Leroy would wait until their hands were almost touching before pulling away. That was what he did, and his puerile little companions would chuckle aloud, as if it was the funniest thing they had ever seen.

Billy nodded, but that was all. He wanted to be

left alone with his thoughts – *whack, pfffttt, end of moth* – but he knew that the chances of that were slim, now.

'You killed anything weaker than you recently?' Denis asked. His friends laughed surreptitiously behind him, stifling their chortles – but not completely. They wanted him to feel small, to feel like a little kid who didn't know any better. 'C'mon, Billy. Tell the guys how I saw you pull the wings off that butterfly.'

Billy *wanted* to tell them; that had been a good day. Last summer, a hundred-degrees in the shade, and Billy had managed to catch a rather recalcitrant Red Baron. He knew it was a Red Baron because he had a book about insects – his bible – and he looked it up as soon as he managed to catch it. Sitting in the front-yard – which was a lot less private than the back garden, and allowed everyone to see what he was up to – with the insect bible open to the correct page next to him on the lawn, he'd pulled one wing off first. Then he'd placed it on the ground, watched it spin in sporadic circles until his stomach hurt from laughing. He'd eventually got bored and pulled the second wing off, and that was when Denis had crossed the street, chasing a ball that had got away from him. The look of disgust on his face when he realised what Billy was doing was almost as hilarious as the listless butterfly. Without uttering a single word, Denis had retrieved his ball and was crossing back to his side of the road, casting disconcerted glances across his shoulder as he went.

'Tell them how you tortured that pwetty little butterfwy,' Denis said in a mock-child's voice. Leroy and Kevin were laughing so hard it was unreal. Billy wanted to punch all three of them, tell them to leave him the fuck alone, but he decided to remain calm and let it fly over his head.

The bigger they are, the harder they fall, the voice of his dead grandmother said in his head. At first he thought she was really there, it was so clear, but then he realised it was just a memory of one of her foolish aphorisms.

'Nevermind, then,' Denis said, sniggering. Behind him, Leroy and Kevin egged him on, as if there was some important reason for this little palaver. Billy wasn't interested; he just wanted them to go away, drown in a ditch somewhere. When Denis reached into his jacket-pocket he knew that something was about to happen. 'I told the boys, here, that you were willing to do anything for money. Ain't that *right*, Billy-boy? Just like your mom used to when she was a bit younger.'

Billy didn't know what Denis meant by that, and decided not to push it by asking.

'So I found you a little present, and I'll make it worth your while,' Denis sniggered. He held his hand out. Sitting on his open palm was a snail. Not your average garden-variety snail; this was slightly bigger. Its shell almost glowed in the midday haze, and it began to edge slowly forward towards Denis's trembling fingers. 'I'll give you *all* the money in my pocket if you eat it.'

Leroy patted Denis on the back, laughing heartily, as if he couldn't believe that his friend had just made such an unrealistic deal.

'But you have to eat *all* of it,' Kevin said, grinning so hard that his braces looked ready to fall out. 'None of this chew, chew, spit. You have to swallow it all, *and* keep it down.'

'Yeah, you have to keep it down,' Leroy added.

Billy sighed. This was so childish, and yet he was intrigued. How much money did Denis carry with him? He didn't eat the school-dinners; Billy saw Denis head down to the store at the end of the street almost every day. When he returned, he always had a big bag of sweets and soda. Since lunch-time had only just started, Billy knew that Denis hadn't been to the store yet, which meant that whatever money he was planning to spend was still in his pocket.

'Give me the snail,' Billy said, holding out a steady hand.

The boys erupted with laughter. They couldn't believe what Billy was about to do. Billy, on the other hand, had done it before, many times, and snails were the easiest bugs to eat because they were slippery. He'd gagged like a sonofabitch trying to swallow an earwig; snails were simple.

'Remember,' Denis said, carefully placing the snail onto Billy's palm. 'You have to eat it all. I want you to open your mouth when your done so we can all check it.'

Billy sighed again. If it meant they would leave him in peace, he would have eaten an entire plate of them. They did in France.

With three pairs of eyes anxiously watching, Billy threw his head back and tossed the snail in as if it was nothing more than a giant gobstopper. The instant it hit his tongue, Kevin and Leroy began to laugh and dry-heave. He crunched down, and they all heard the noise as the snail's shell shattered into a hundred pieces between Billy's teeth. Leroy was doubled over, trying not to be sick. It made Billy start to laugh, and a few shards of shell escaped through his open-mouth. After about ten chews – and when the snail was suitably mushed – Billy swallowed. The whole thing slipped down in one. It was *so* much easier than earwigs. If Denis had brought him an earwig, he might have had to politely decline the offer.

He opened his mouth for all to see. Denis dropped to his knees and grabbed Billy's head on either side. Tilting this way and that, he searched inside Billy's open mouth before climbing back onto his feet.

'Fucking *did* it,' Denis said, no longer so sure of himself. 'What kind of a sick bastard eats a *snail*?'

'That's gross,' Leroy said. 'You ain't fucking right.'

Billy smiled. Pieces of snail were wedged between the gaps in his teeth. All three of the boys recoiled at the sight. He held his hand out, as if to receive his payment, and wasn't surprised when Denis started to shake his head.

'I wasn't *really* gonna pay up,' he said, his eyes still bug-wide. 'I just wanted to see whether you'd do it.' And with that he began to walk away; Leroy and Kevin were hot on his heels. All three of them were mumbling as they disappeared amongst the rest of the lunchtime crowd.

Billy went back to what he was doing, a little disappointed about the non-payment, but not enough to let it ruin the rest of his day.

*

He walked into the lounge to find his mother unconscious. Next to her, in a long haphazard row, were empty bottles. She had made the most of her day once again. On the table to her left was an overspilling ashtray; the room was stale from cigarettes. Next to the full ashtray was a small bottle. Billy knew it was his mother's medication. She took three tablets, twice a day. Without it she was liable to go crazy.

She was, on occasion, so drunk and out of it that she would forget to take her pills. Billy always tried to stay away from her when she did. She was nothing like herself without the pills – or perhaps she *was*, and the pills were only shielding the real her from him – and was liable to say revolting things to him, unwarranted. The one time she had told him to invite his friends round so she could have a play with them, said it would be fun and they would fucking love it. Thankfully, she remembered very little about that particular occasion, and they never spoke of it, though Billy thought she might recall the offer, and was just too embarrassed by how fucked up it was.

He couldn't see her face now, as she sat slumped on the sofa, pointing in the only direction she ever faced: the TV. She was watching – or had been before she passed out – a home-shopping channel. A woman was trying to offload a pair of fake-diamond earrings, said they were the best reproductions she had ever seen. To Billy they looked cheap and tacky, and unsurprisingly, as the numbers at the bottom of the screen suggested, still out of his mother's price-range. He didn't know why she liked to watch such bullshit. Maybe she was just too exhausted, too out of it, to reach for the remote-control and change the channel. Perhaps she liked to feel normal, do what normal people do. Home-shopping was her only option, really. She hadn't left the house in months, *years* even. Billy could count on one hand the amount of times she'd managed to gather herself up from the sofa. Most of the time she would meander listlessly into the kitchen, grab an unopened bottle of wine from the rack, and make her way back to the lounge.

Who even bought her the fucking booze? She had tried to get Billy to do it for her, and the shopkeeper had simply laughed at him, told him to try again in ten years, and even then he would need identification.

No, she must have made her way to the store while he was at school. It was amazing, Billy thought, that she could drag her ass out of the house for booze, but not for anything else. He knew that she had missed her last three doctor's appointments; the slowly-growing pile of letters on the mantel was a constant reminder.

Billy didn't try to wake her. His day had been eventful enough without a fight with his mother in a drunken stupor. He made his way up the stairs, no need to tiptoe, and came to the landing where Genghis was purring to himself.

If he had the chance to explain what he did next, he wouldn't have been able to. Something took control of him, something not quite right. He felt himself reaching down for the cat, slowly, slowly, slowly. Genghis purred louder, pleased that he was finally going to get the fuss he deserved. Billy grabbed the cat around the throat and squeezed. For a few, long seconds Genghis didn't do anything. It was as if the cat had frozen. Billy thought about releasing him, letting him run down the stairs to the safety of wherever it was that he went. He *thought* about it, but didn't. Instead he squeezed tighter.

And that was when all hell broke loose.

Genghis began to thrash around. Fur filled the air at the top of the stairs; a sound came from his throat that was like nothing Billy had ever heard the cat make before. It clawed at Billy's tightening grip, drawing blood with scratches that wouldn't be sore until much later on that night. Billy clenched his teeth, ignored the onslaught which would be the cat's last, and continued to apply pressure to its throat.

Downstairs, Billy's mother didn't flinch.

When it was over, the cat lying in a lifeless pile on the landing – almost like a stuffed toy that had been in an unfortunate battle with a Doberman – Billy finally exhaled. Genghis was dead; he'd killed him. It had not been the same as killing a bug, and as he sat there Billy decided that he much preferred the torture of insects to what he had just done to the cat.

After composing himself once again, he slipped in through his bedroom door and closed it behind him. He had pictures to draw. In his head he could see the Medusa-Dugan, naked and begging for help. It made him hard. As he created what he thought was some of his best work, Genghis began to stiffen just outside his door.

*

He slept a troubled sleep for three hours, waking to complete darkness and feeling slightly disorientated. At first he thought that the whole thing had been a terrible dream, but when he opened his bedroom door and saw the lifeless feline body at the top of the stairs he realised that he wasn't so fortunate.

He stuffed Genghis into a pillowcase and carried him out into the garden. His mother was still unconscious on the sofa, in exactly the same position she had been in when Billy had returned home that afternoon. He thought about waking her, but decided against it. Now was not the time; he had a body to bury.

He dug a hole – just large enough for the corpse – at the side of the shed. Every now and then he paused, took a look up at the neighbour's windows. He would have loved to have seen a face, staring down at him, wondering what the fuck he was up to digging holes in the middle of the night. He imagined Mrs. Barber – batty old cow and nosier than a Parker – looking out on him, a deeply disturbed expression painted on her sagging face. If she'd been there he would have flipped her the bird.

There was no law against burying a pet. It was a sad moment for him – or at least that's what he would tell the old bag if she questioned his actions.

He dropped the sack into the hole and began to scrape the dirt back on top of it. When he was done, he patted it down, like he used to do with sandcastles on the beach as a toddler.

He said a little prayer, though since he didn't have much – *any*? – faith it was all pretty much for show. If Mrs. Barber *was* up in her window, at least she would see him make the faux-cross next to the grave. That would have to jangle even the hardest of nerves.

On his way back to the house something happened, something that took the edge of what he had just done. A swarm of fireflies appeared, floating around the garden in perfect unison. Billy couldn't move as he watched them, rapt. It was the most beautiful thing he'd ever seen, and yet he knew he couldn't allow it. They weren't dancing *for* him; they were *mocking* him.

He cursed, span and headed back to the shed. He knew he had insecticide somewhere. He didn't like to use it, normally, but there were too many of the little fuckers, and they were mocking him, laughing at him because he just buried his stupid cat.

He found the tin – Raid Ant and Roach Killer, though he guessed it would work just as well on fireflies – and headed back down the path, towards the nuisance display. They parted as he walked through them, and then he went to town, spraying, shooting streams of insecticide in every direction like an infuriated Mafioso. They began to drop, landing on the path with satisfying clicks. As they fell, he brought his foot down on them, crunching them. It wasn't like treading on snails; they had their own special sound as their shells splintered. It was more like treading on bubble-wrap, only more gratifying. When he was done, and there were fading lights all around him on the path and lawn, he prayed for more of them to come. *Come and see mad Billy and his marvellous spray of doom…*

He waited a few minutes, but no more came and so he headed back into the house. It hadn't been the most pleasurable of evenings, but the firefly incident had made up for having to bury the stupid cat.

He went to bed; sleeping on the pillow without a case didn't make him feel anything akin to guilt for what he had done.

*

'Haven't seen him,' Denis Dugan said. '*Nobody's* seen him for a week.'

Mr. Jacques couldn't believe that he had only just noticed the absence of Billy Coombs, though he was the kind of kid that just sort of faded into the background. He never had anything constructive to add to a lesson, and so Mr. Jacques tried not to involve him unless it was absolutely necessary.

'You might want to try the local loony-bin,' Leroy Brown said, prompting a huge roar from the rest of the class which took a full minute to die down.

Mr. Jacques knew that it wasn't normal; he would have been informed if the boy was ill or having trouble with something that required him to remain at home. Jacques didn't know him well enough to make any assumptions, but he looked like the kind of kid who had problems, the kind of kid who listened to satanic music and masturbated to the sounds of a screaming woman. He had an unnerving stare, too; Jacques always tried to look the other way if he knew the boy – Billy – was looking at him. There was something in his eyes – something unnatural – that caused the hackles to rise on the back of Jacques's neck.

'Do you think he *died?*' Denis Dugan asked, feigning concern. The class erupted once again, and only shut up when Mr. Jacques – who was not the tallest of teachers but was quarterback-wide – told them to stop being so childish and concentrate on the work in front of them. When they were silent and working he slipped out and headed for the office at the end of the corridor.

Something was a little off, and he wouldn't feel right until he found out what.

*

Jacques and Porter – the head of the school – stood outside Billy Coombs's house waiting for someone to answer the door. It was raining, and neither of the men had had the foresight to bring an umbrella. Jacques's hair was painted down onto his forehead and he had to keep pushing it away so that he could see properly; Porter had no hair, apart from the fluffy protrusions from his ears, something that Jacques had been in awe of for years.

'Doesn't look like anyone's home,' Porter said, stepping back and taking a look up at one of the first-storey windows. 'Little shit and his mom must have gone on holiday somewhere.'

'*Or*,' Jacques said, a little annoyed at his colleague's tone, 'they're in there and just don't open the door to unannounced visitors.'

'Whatever,' Porter said, shaking the rain from his dingy brown coat. 'I'm not standing here all day. Try once more and then we're gone.'

Jacques sighed. He reached up and knocked, this time loud enough to shake the door in its frame. They waited; Porter turned as if to make his way back to the car. Jacques knew that something was amiss, and before he knew it he'd reached down and pushed the door-handle. Hearing the click of the opening door, Porter span on the pathway. He looked annoyed, but didn't speak. After a second passed between them where they simply questioned each other with their eyes, Porter held a hand out. *Go on in, then...*

As soon as Jacques stepped into the house he smelt it. A putrid tang in the air that brought bile up into his throat. Porter – who was a few steps behind him – looked confusedly at his heaving colleague. It was only when he stepped in through the front-door that he realised what all the fuss was about.

'Holy *shit*!' Porter said. 'What the fuck is that *smell*?'

Jacques knew exactly what it was, and the thought

of what they were about to discover terrified him. He pinched his nose between his thumb and forefinger and turned into the hallway. There were photographs hanging on the wall of a much younger Billy. Billy on a swing here; Billy at the beach there, and none of them were recent shots. The thick coating of dust on each picture signified what Jacques had already assumed.

This was no ordinary family.

Jacques walked cautiously through the hall. Porter remained two steps behind, gagging and rubbing at his streaming eyes with fat knuckles.

When Jacques opened the lounge-door, the smell increased exponentially. No amount of nose-pinching could prevent the putrefaction from creeping up his nostrils. He doubled over, fighting back dry-retches that would ultimately ruin his stomach. When he straightened up, he saw the cause of the stench and almost screeched. Behind him, Porter had already realised what was going on, and it was too much for him. He vomited. Some of it landed on Jacques's heel, though he didn't notice, and even if he had he wouldn't have given a shit.

Sitting in the centre of the lounge was a woman. She had, judging by the state of decay, been dead for quite some time. Her marbled skin was moon-pallid; her lank hair covered the one side of her face completely.

Jacques wished it had covered both sides.

But the dead woman wasn't the most horrific part about it. He'd *expected* to find a body as soon as they stepped into the house. The stench had been unmistakeable.

The most horrible thing about the dead woman was the little boy sitting on her lap. Billy – the despondent student that Jacques tried to have nothing to do with – was just sitting there, his one arm wrapped around the corpse's neck, the other reaching up and catching maggots as they fell from between her shrivelled lips. When he had one between his fingers, he popped it before wiping the tiny viscera on the front of his dead mother's blouse. As Jacques watched, Billy did this over and over, popping maggots, wiping his fingers, popping maggots, wiping. When Jacques thought he might go crazy from what he was witnessing he turned and ran for the front-door, passing the heaving Porter and leaving him hunched over in the hallway.

Yet even outside he could hear the sound of maggots popping. And the soft rustling of flesh rubbing against cotton as he cleaned his fingers up.

Jacques fell to his knees, hoping that Porter had the good sense to call the police, and fast.

Pop, pop, pop.

The little bug-boy popped maggots until the cops finally arrived an hour later.

Pop.

What's She Got That I Haven't?

Gladys huffed, pushed her chest out until enough of her cleavage was revealed to hide a pack of cards in. *How dare he?* she thought? *How could he?*

"It's not a problem, is it?" Daniel asked, proving just how stupid he was when it came to reading Gladys's body-signals. "I mean, you used to be best of friends, and I thought it would be nice to get the old gang together. This barbecue will go down in history as one of the most epic ever held in this neighbourhood."

Oh, it certainly will, she thought.

"You're right," she said. "I *love* Debbie." *Not as much as you, you conniving prick*, she thought but didn't add.

"Then it's settled. I'll give her a call, makes sure she's free this coming Saturday."

Gladys knew, deep down, that he had already squared things away with Debbie. He'd worked late three times that week, and all three times he'd returned home stinking of some cheap tart's perfume. She didn't know what Debbie's brand was, but she'd had a helluva time getting the bitch's tangy musk out of Daniel's work shirt.

Off he went to call his bit on the side. Gladys tried to regulate the heat rising up inside her, though it was hard. She could call him on it, *sure*. She could rant and rave and divorce the sonofabitch, but what would that accomplish? She could murder him in his sleep, but then she would have a body to dispose of and digging holes in the back garden would do her eight-hundred quid manicure no good whatsoever.

No, there were ways and means of dealing with the situation. Somebody – a clever fucker, no doubt about it – once said that dessert was a dish best served cold. Gladys, in that moment, was the ice-queen, and by the time Saturday rolled around she would be just about ready to freeze the bitch.

Daniel returned with a shark's grin spread across his stupid face. "All sorted," he said. "I'll call a few others, make it into a bit of a party, and then I'll pop to the supermarket and get some food and drink."

Gladys smiled; it hurt her face. "You do that, Dear," she sighed, and as he turned and practically danced out of the room she jabbed two fingers in the air, silently cursing him in a display that would have made Tarantino blush.

On the morning of the barbecue, Gladys made herself as beautiful as she possibly could, which was the easy part; hiding the knives in a corset that left very little to the imagination – now that took some skill. Her right tit had suffered various cuts and scrapes as she'd stuffed a small roll of barbed-wire down there, but somebody – an idiot, and no doubt about it – once said: no pain no gain.

Daniel was in his office smoking a cigar, preparing himself with aftershave and moisturiser. For him, this was quite a coup. His wife and his mistress at the same cookout would go down in history amongst his colleagues. He would be the talk of the water-cooler; they would toast him with plastic glasses of icy water and he would indubitably provide them with a merry little dance. Then there would be cheers of adoration for the man that made a mockery of his marriage right in front of his oblivious wenches.

At least, that was how he was probably imagining it. Gladys, who had spent four days planning and conspiring like some clandestine despot, envisioned a completely different scenario, one where her husband stood at the water-cooler nursing a sore head while his colleagues took it in turns to approach and offer their sincerest condolences. A few of them would ask him, *"What the fuck were you thinking? Your wife and your mistress at the same fucking barbecue? Are you completely and utterly retarted?"* Daniel would fall to his knees, a sobbing wreck, stripped of his former confidence, filled now with nothing more than regret and sorrow.

Gladys laughed, found somewhere to hide the tazer, and made her way downstairs.

The guests began to arrive shortly afterwards. Daniel's best friend, Alec, stepped across the threshold whilst clinging onto his trophy wife – a Russian lady he'd recently purchased with the aid of a dial-up connection and a Mastercard – as if she might float away should he accidentally release her.

"This is Svetlana," Alec proudly announced as Gladys led them out to the garden at the rear of the house.

"What a lovely name," Gladys lied. It sounded like something you contracted on an 18-30 holiday to Magaluf. "Help yourselves to drinks and snacks. My darling husband will be out shortly. I believe he's tending to his scrotum. Such a hairy fellow." With that, Gladys left them to it, withdrawing to the house to locate Daniel.

He wasn't, as she'd informed the guests, pruning; he was stalking back and forth across the office, sipping thirstily from a large glass of scotch.

"Everything okay, Dear?" Gladys asked upon entering.

Daniel stopped pacing and refilled his glass. He was trembling ever-so-slightly, as if on the verge of expiring completely. "Of course," he said. "Just *excited*, that's all."

Excited and shitting bricks, Gladys thought.

"Alec's arrived with that Russkiy of his."

Daniel glanced at the clock on the mantelpiece. "He's early."

"Must be the Eurasian time-difference," Gladys opined. "Are you coming outside? The sun's shining, the grass is green, and the rest of the guests will be here shortly."

He sank the contents of the glass in one before slamming the empty down on his desk. "Can't keep my fans waiting," he said, feigning a smile.

Your fans are in for the greatest show on earth, you deceitful bastard.

She returned the smile but ended up wearing the countenance of a cat about to vomit. "Mustn't keep them waiting," she said.

Half an hour later and the garden teemed with people. Several of the neighbours, who Gladys certainly hadn't invited, had gathered over by the vegetable-patch. She was keeping a close eye on

Martha Moore, who would see nothing wrong in pulling her knickers down and pissing on the carrots.

Daniel was doing his best to feed the masses, though there were an awful lot of them and only two cows' worth of meat. At the rate they were going, the salad sitting on the patio-table would be all that remained.

The doorbell chimed to the tune of *Greensleeves*. Gladys watched as her flustered husband dropped the sausage he had been expertly turning and yanked the apron off quicker than she'd ever seen him move before.

"Are *you* going to answer it?" Gladys asked, but Daniel was already slipping in through the back door.

She grinned.

When he returned, with that faux bimbo at his side, Gladys realised that the scent of meat in the atmosphere had been immediately replaced with that tangy musk – the stink that had coated her husband's shirt so wholly on several occasions the previous week.

"Everyone, this is Debbie," Daniel said, smiling. Gladys watched the faces of the other guests, gauging their interest. If any of them knew of the affair, they did a pretty good job at concealing it. "Debbie, this is everyone."

She waved, squeaked something along the lines of, "Hi, everyone." Gladys had lost interest by that point. Plus, one of the throwing-knives in her knickers was starting to dig into her thigh.

People continued to have a fabulous time. The barbecue was a resounding success and, with the real fun still to begin, Gladys felt a sense of satisfaction.

Now was as good a time as any.

She waited for Daniel to finish tossing out paper-plates before tapping the edge of her glass with her wedding-ring. The irony was not lost on her.

Faces turned to her; Daniel, who had no idea what was happening, looked on with apprehension.

"I'd just like to thank you all for coming," Gladys began. "It's been a wonderful afternoon, and what splendid *weather* we had." She gestured towards the sky and a collective hum of approval sounded from all four corners of the garden. "And now I'd just like to say one more thing to my husband who, frankly, is getting off lightly today."

She winked at him. He shook his head in confusion. Mutters of, *"What's going on?"* and, *"Is she hammered?"* filled the otherwise awkward silence.

Gladys could take no more.

She reached into her corset, pulled out a knife with one hand and the coil of barbed-wire with the other. Everyone gasped. Those within spitting distance took a well-advised step back. They were in no danger, though. Gladys had eyes for only one person, and judging by the expression on Debbie's face, she knew it was her.

"Excuse me," Gladys said before launching herself, full-on lunatic, towards the blonde bimbo leaning against the bird-table. The noise that escaped her throat as she realised what was about happen was barely human; she sounded like a shocked meerkat.

Gladys hit her so hard that the bird-table uprooted and landed in the fish-pond. Women screamed, men grunted, Daniel realised that his game was up and Martha Moore saw this as the perfect opportunity to tinkle on the parsnips.

"YOU BITCH!" Gladys screeched, pulling the barbed-wire taut around the mistress's neck. "You couldn't get your own man so you stole *mine*!"

"Kkkkk-cough-cough…" Debbie said, which did her case no good, whatsoever. Blood began to pool around her exposed breasts from the opening wound in her throat. Gladys pulled tighter, and was almost through to the spinal-cord when the bitch back-kicked like *Buckaroo!*

The barbed-wire was no longer tight, which afforded the mistress just enough to scramble to her feet. Her head was almost off, but she didn't seem to care; nothing a bit of concealer couldn't fix.

"If you'd taken care of him, I wouldn't have *had* to," Debbie spat. The shocked onlookers unleashed a collective gasp.

"You WHORE!" Gladys said, yanking her skirt up and removing four throwing-knives. She threw them as hard as she could towards the mistress. One thumped into her stomach but the other two went wide, ending up in various guests and – Gladys was pleased to see – a crouching Martha Moore.

Debbie plucked the knife from her abdomen and tossed it back, hitting Gladys in the shoulder. "If you'd only given him head once in a while," she said, "he wouldn't have looked elsewhere."

Gladys rushed towards the mistress, almost tripping over somebody's wandering child. Debbie braced herself once again. This attack was going to hurt.

As she slammed into the mistress, they both flew backwards, landing with a splash in the fish-pond. The water covered them both entirely. Fish dove out of the water in a half-hearted attempt at escape. As they flapped around, gasping on the edge of the pond, the women battled inside it. The guests gathered closer, wandering if either of the rabid women would survive the afternoon.

Daniel remained shell-shocked over by the barbecue, nibbling on a cob of corn.

After the events of the final minute or so, everything seemed impossibly silent. The splashing from the pond ceased, and with it came only mumblings and mutterings from the anticipatory crowd. A row of cats and several birds had taken up position along the fence-top and were watching just as intently as the humans.

"Are they d—" somebody began, but an arm shot out of the pond to answer their question before they had a chance to finish it. The arm was followed, as expected, by a shoulder, and then the rest of a woman.

Debbie.

In her hand she gripped the head of Daniel's wife. Wires and biomechanical viscera trailed from the stump of her neck, sizzling and sparking in response to the combination of water and electric. Sodden, Debbie walked across the garden, dropping the head on the path as she went. Her own wounds were superficial; she would need to be seen by a cyborg doctor, but she would be out by the end of the day, unlike Gladys, whose days were clearly numbered.

Suddenly, the severed head in the middle of the garden sparked into life. Gladys's mouth fell open. A robotic voice, nothing like it was a moment before, asked, "*What's she got that I haven't, Dan…Dan…Dan…DaDaDa?*" As it repeated itself over and over, buzzing incessantly until somebody had the gumption to hoof it over the fence, Daniel threw his arms around his mistress.

The obvious answer to Gladys's question would have been: A head.

Mad World

The woman shuffled along the street, her head lowered to one side as if her neck was broken. She was singing to herself in an annoying high-pitched falsetto. At the end of each line of lyrics, her head swung across to the opposite side, her chin nestled on oversized breasts. The river of litter and sewage at her feet was nothing but a mild hindrance to her, slowing her down as she went about her day. She was clearly crazy, infected with the lunacy that had wiped out most of humanity.

Those that hadn't killed themselves as the madness enveloped them had turned, gone bad, and killed others. At first, people didn't notice; they just thought a few random acts of insanity were commonplace, and in the world they lived in, at that time, they might have been right. It was a world where a person throwing a newborn baby onto a railway track was considered evil, but expected. How often did you hear the words "Gunman" and "High School" in the same sentence? Madness became something of a cliché. So when people started acting crazy, nobody took a blind bit of notice.

At *first.*

Then, when more and more people started killing – either themselves or those closest to them – everyone stood up and started to take notice. The government told everyone to remain calm, to stay at home and keep all doors locked, but in the end that wasn't enough.

The panic, the strain of madness that affected ninety-nine percent of the population, didn't stop at closed doors. It would seep in through window-frames, through letterboxes and keyholes. There was nothing to keep it out. Martial law was put in place, for those few soldiers still uninfected and unaffected by the madness, but within weeks even they had succumbed. The problem was: they had guns, lots of them, and enough ammo to take out a small city. It didn't take long for the massacring to start, and even less time before bodies were piled up in the street, either lying where they fell or dragged out of their houses by armed lunatics and executed.

When there was nobody left to kill, at least nobody in clear sight, the soldiers smoked cigars, drank their way through the city's alcohol supply, and blew holes in their own faces with shotguns, handguns; one guy even stabbed himself repeatedly with a bayonet until his face was a bloody pulp.

And this happened *everywhere.* No government would take responsibility for the virus, which led to wars and individual attacks upon each other. It was petulant, but deadly. A few countries dropped nuclear bombs. Moscow had been eradicated thanks to North-Korea. In retaliation, Russia unleashed hell, and that, as they say, was that.

The woman stopped, picked up something that had been nestled in amongst the rubbish at her feet, and shoved it into her mouth. There was an audible squelch as the rat's head came away from its body and a horrible crunching sound as she chewed camel-like on the miniature corpse. It had been dead for a while; the way it jutted out of her white-knuckled, gnarled fist suggested it was either frozen or at the peak of rigor-mortis. She sucked the meat off its bones, her popcorn teeth moving up and down as she savoured its rotting flesh.

She was mid-chew when the arrow pierced her chest. The thick, muddied coat that she wore did little to prevent the projectile as it slammed into her heart. For a second, she glanced around the street, as if looking to see who would do such a thing. Her knitted eyebrows lifted up, a sorrowful sight, and she continued to chew on the mangled rat as her mind tried to work out what had happened.

Then she dropped to the ground, and was almost entirely swallowed by the mire of filth that had become Grange Street. The comical way in which she fell would have, if there was still such a thing, tickled audiences worldwide. Where she came to rest amongst the debris of collapsed buildings and skeletal remains, the only thing visible was the protruding arrow, pointing up to the bleak mid-afternoon sky like a flag on a golf-course.

'Nice shot,' Jen said to the man with the crossbow as they emerged from behind an industrial-unit. 'But you went for the head, *right*?'

Sam grinned. 'If I'd gone for the head her brain would be splattered all over that wall.' He pointed across to a single line of bricks; the rest of the building was decimated. Hanging on the wall, miraculously, was a bullet-pocked steel sign that said: *Curfew in force. Anyone out after 7pm will be shot.* It seemed like forever since that curfew had been enforced, not that anybody had had a chance to pay it any heed.

Sam stood over the twitching corpse of his latest kill. 'She looks like you,' he joked. 'You didn't happen to have a sister, did you?'

Jen flipped him the bird, and then watched in silence as he retrieved his arrow from her chest. It came free, eventually, and Sam wiped the blood off onto his fatigues. Glancing down at the body, Sam was sickened to discover she was already crawling with maggots. She had a wound on her neck, as if sliced partially open with a large knife or machete, and the bloated larvae were already at home deep within it.

'No wonder she went fucking mad,' Jen said. 'That would drive me crazy.'

They left the woman lying there, amongst the rubble and wind-strewn litter. Neither of them gave her a second thought that afternoon. If the world had been on the verge of insanity back then, five years ago, before the outbreak, it had certainly toppled over the edge now. As uncertain as the future was, they were guaranteed one thing: every day would be a fight for survival, if not from the mad, then from the gangs of marauders haunting the wastelands. In a world where money had no value and possessions meant very little to anyone but their owner, bandits wanted only one thing; to kill, to maim, to rape, and torture. It made their day a little brighter. A lot of the gangs were borderline-infected. They would ride around on trail-bikes, screeching in languages that they had created amongst themselves, and they would search and destroy. Sam and Jen had managed, so far, to remain hidden from them. There had been occasions where they had come close – too close – but as far as the scavenging hordes were concerned they didn't exist.

They wanted to keep it that way.

A few hours passed. Sam shot two more *head-cases* with his crossbow. The second guy had been running across a parking-lot, butt-naked, his erection bouncing off his belly as he ran. He was deserved of the headshot he had received as he had been rushing towards Jen, his intentions as clear as day. Jen joked about how Sam should have given the poor guy a chance, which she would have quite enjoyed for a while, but it was just a joke. The fear on her face had been palpable as the crazed nudist approached her. One arrow, *boom*, goodnight you sick sonofabitch.

They were joined for an hour by a dog that neither of them recognised. The streets were full of strays, more cats than dogs, and Jen liked to name them and talk to them as if they were her own. This one was jet-black, a white patch on its back that resembled the moon. Jen called it Midnight, said that if you squinted at it long enough you could see the stars, the moon, even clouds, though Sam couldn't.

Midnight tagged along, hoping to stumble upon food – as were they – at some point on their journey.

Jen wasn't too good with breeds, and asked Sam what he thought Midnight was.

'I'd say a Labrador,' Sam said, almost tripping over a mound of earth. A skull – human child, eye-sockets tightly packed with mud – rolled out from the dirt. Midnight nudged at it with her snout, and it rolled a few more feet. Sam didn't even notice; just continued to explain the traits of that particular breed to Jen, to which she nodded along, fascinated.

'How do you know so much about dogs?' she asked.

Sam tossed a bone – *femur*? - he had found a few metres away from the child's skull, and Midnight rushed after it, ears flapping. For a skinny thing she had plenty of life in her, which was no mean feat given the circumstances.

'I always had a dog,' he said. 'As a *kid*, I mean. When I was young, my mom came home from work with a German Shepherd. That was the best dog I ever had.' He smiled, ever-so-slightly, the corners of his lips twitching at the unexpected nostalgia. 'His name was Shine; kept me going all the way through school. Died naturally, but it didn't make it any easier when he went. I even dug the hole myself, told my dad that it was my dog, and to pass me the shovel. They were really worried about me for a while, my parents, thought I might lose the plot, or something.'

He paused, glanced around the barren nightmare that had become their lives. 'If only they could see me now, huh?'

Jen smiled. 'Whole world went to hell in a hand-basket,' she said. 'Marbles are a rarity these days. I'm just glad we still have ours.'

Sam was about to retort, to say something funny to lighten the sombre mood he had created, when the sound of a shotgun firing stopped him. Fifty feet away, where Midnight was struggling to get at the wedged bone, the earth suddenly kicked up. Shards of glass sliced through the air, one missing the dog by only an inch. Whoever had fired had meant to hit Midnight, and the dog was too stupid to even notice.

Sam pushed Jen down, tried to hide them both in the burned-out shell of what was once a German-manufactured people-carrier.

'*Shit*, Sam!' Jen gasped. 'Did you see anybody out there?'

Sam shook his head. 'They're well-hidden. I'd say from the trajectory of that shot they're high up, probably firing from up there.' He pointed through the hollow vehicle to a row of third-storey windows. The building was in pieces, but somehow still standing. A whole corner of the structure balanced precariously on a steel girder that had been wedged into the ground. A mild tremor would be all it took to bring the whole thing down.

There was another blast; more dirt and shrapnel flew into the air. This time, though, the shooter was not aiming for Midnight. The bullet ricocheted a few feet away from the vehicle Sam and Jen were hiding behind. Whoever was up there – a marauder, Sam guessed, though it must have been a loner or they would have been dead already – must have seen them crouching behind the wreckage, turned his attentions to something a little more fruitful than a stray dog.

'I need you to listen carefully,' Sam said, pushing himself against the flattened tyre of the vehicle. 'When I say run, I need you to keep up with me. There's no way I can hit them with my crossbow, not from this distance, and I'm not even certain where those shots are coming from.' Jen was looking to him with wide eyes; her mouth opened and shut as if she wanted to say something, but nothing came out. 'It's going to be okay. I promise. We need to get back to the house. As long as they don't follow us, we'll be safe there, at least for now.'

'What about the dog?' she asked. 'We can't just leave her out—'

'I'll do my best to get the dog to follow,' he told her. Another bullet tore through the car, punctured the leather on the driver's seat. They both ducked, just in case the guy had somehow forged a clear shot. 'GO!'

Jen pushed herself up and shuffled the few feet to the front of the vehicle. She wondered if her legs would move, or whether they would betray her as they often did in situations like this. As a third bullet pinged off the bonnet, she knew that it was just a marker, and that the next one would be much closer to the target.

'Jen GO!' Sam called from behind her, and she didn't know if it was the thought of a bullet ripping through her skull, popping out an eye, or Sam's yell that forced her into action, but she began to run as fast as she could, being careful not to trip over any of the debris in the street. She knew that the shooter was firing a shotgun, and he would have been loading two shells at a time, which meant right now he was pushing fresh rounds into his weapon, his adrenaline working just as fast as hers. She tried to force the thought of the shooter from her mind, for she could see where she needed to get to.

At the side of Grange Street there was an alleyway. Sam had killed three head-cases in it on the night they first met. She had been cornered, and had resigned herself to death, cowering in the corner waiting for them to reach her, to do whatever it was they were going to do before murdering her. They were on top of her, pulling her hair, fish-hooking her, dragging her skirt down and lapping at her like feral cats, when a man appeared, fired three rounds straight into them. That man had been Sam. The first two dropped away as bullets tore scalp and bone from their heads. The third one took a bullet to the neck, but that hadn't been enough. Sam had dragged the third head-case backwards through the alley, arterial spray from the guy's neck-wound shooting everywhere, painting the alleyway red. Sam must have been out of bullets by then, as he had proceeded to stamp on the third guy's head, pounding him with his boot-heel. When he'd finished there was barely anything left of the attacker's face; he looked like a joint of meat, something you would buy at the butcher's. Jen felt sick at the sight of it, but also pleased. Sam had saved her life, and she hadn't left his side since.

She threw herself into the alleyway just as a bullet exploded the bricks at the entrance. Behind her she could hear Sam trying to coax the dog towards him, but she knew that the chances of saving Midnight were slim, and nowhere near as important as saving themselves.

From where she lay in the alley, she could see the dog, bouncing around, no doubt thinking the entire thing was some sort of elaborate game designed for her. '*Midnight!*' she called, high-pitched, as if the dog would react to its newly-designated name. Jen scrambled to her feet and picked a small sliver of glass out of her leg. The amount of blood glistening on the end suggested there was nothing to worry about, and she called after the dog once again, hoping to garner its attention.

Gunshot, the trickle of solid cement down a wall, and then Sam dove into the alley, breathless and looking more frightened than Jen had ever seen him before.

He grabbed her hand and they raced for the other end of the alley. They heard a shot, a whimper, and the sound of a madman rejoicing at finally managing to hit something. Neither of them looked back as they raced for the relative safety of the house they used after dark.

*

Jen cut into a can of tomatoes with her knife. The juice spilled out, dripped over her knuckles before falling onto the carpet with a gentle pitter-patter. It was the last of their food, and they would have a quarter of a tin each, saving the rest for breakfast. Sam was sitting in the darkened kitchen tending to a wound on his arm. The shooter hadn't been far off with his last shot. The bullet had grazed Sam's flesh, leaving a wound that he had neglected to mention until they had reached the sanctuary of the house.

Jen spooned the tomatoes onto saucers – she couldn't find any clean bowls, and there was no longer running water to do the washing-up, not that they would have bothered with such a menial task – before dropping them onto the kitchen table. She began to ravenously devour hers, watching Sam as he cleaned his wound with salt and olive-oil. Since the olive-oil was no good for cooking – there was nothing *left* to cook – Sam dabbed it on furiously, grimacing at the sting of it, hissing through clenched teeth.

'Do you want me to help?' Jen asked, spooning another forkful of tomatoes into her already full mouth.

'I'll be okay,' he told her, rolling his eyes. 'Motherfucker wasn't such a bad shot after all.'

'Could've been worse,' Jen smiled, and that was Jen; ever the optimist. It was annoying most of the time, but Sam was used to it.

'Yeah,' he hissed, padding gently at the wound, 'Could've been *you*.'

When the wound was clean he wrapped a do-rag around his arm. Within seconds it was covered with tiny red blossoms, a sign that the graze had a lot of healing to do.

'Feel sorry for Midnight,' Jen said as she picked up the saucer and began to lick it clean. Between laps, she continued to speak. 'Really...liked...her. She had...a nice...coat.' She dropped the saucer down and stared at Sam, awaiting his personal opinion on the dog they heard get shot less than an hour before. He didn't offer a response. He was starving and began to eat his tomatoes, the juice dribbling down his chin.

Jen was jealous. She wanted to get up, throw herself across the table and catch the stuff that was falling from his stubble in her own mouth.

Uncouth, she thought. He would have reproached her for such animalistic behaviour, and she was in no mood for an argument, not tonight, not after the day they had endured.

'We're out of food,' she said, licking her lips, staring at the empty saucer in front of her as if it was going to magically replenish itself.

Sam swallowed, wiped the juice from the corner of his lips and sucked his finger. 'We'll have to get more tomorrow,' he said. 'I'm not going out tonight. Not with that shooter out there.'

Jen expected as much, and didn't push the subject any further. They had half a tin left, enough to see them through the night. A fresh start, a new day, was all they needed.

'I'm going to bed,' she said, standing from the table and moving across the kitchen. She turned to Sam and smiled. 'Thanks for today.'

He frowned, unaware of why she was thanking him. 'What for?'

'For saving my life, you *dickhead*,' she said. 'Or has it become so commonplace that you don't even *register* it anymore?'

Sam shrugged and licked his saucer clean. 'Go to bed,' he said. 'I'll take first watch.'

She disappeared into the darkness of the living-room, limping ever-so-slightly.

It could've been a lot worse...

*

Thump. Thump. Thump...

Sam lunged to his feet. He couldn't believe how stupid he'd been; he had never fallen asleep during his watch before, and when he saw what was making the noise at the window he knew why.

A face, bloodied and grinning, was staring in at him. It pulled back before headbutting the glass once again.

Thump.

Sam quickly loaded his crossbow and snapped it towards the hellish face on the other side of the glass.

Blood from the impacts began to drip down the window, a Rorschach-test that Sam could see nothing pleasant in.

'What's that noise?'

Sam turned to find Jen standing in the doorway, rubbing her eyes.

He shushed her, instructed her to move across to where she would be out of sight. The thing outside might not have seen them. The house was dark, and from the outside it would have been almost impossible to determine shapes unless they were moving.

Jen did as he told her. Her eyes were wide to the point of bulging, and she glared towards the maniacal head at the window from behind the wooden cabinet. Sam, from beneath the window, took aim at the face, knowing that he only had one arrow. He should have carved more, but the day had somewhat gotten away from him, leaving very little time for appropriate preparation.

The head slammed against the glass once again. A geyser of blood and bile spewed from between its sneering lips, but it didn't move; its expression remained exactly the same.

And Sam knew why.

The head had no *body*. It was being held up by somebody, pushed against the glass as part of their sick game. Sam could now see the stump of its neck, tendrils of viscera hanging beneath it. The sneer was nothing more than a result of its death, and pointing the crossbow at it was no longer important. It was the person holding it that mattered.

The head suddenly pulled back, disappeared into the darkness. Outside, somebody laughed, a delirious cackle that caused Jen to whimper from her hiding-place.

Sam watched the window, hoping that it was gone, praying that the thing had simply been trying its luck, searching houses, and moving on when there appeared to be nothing of worth to it. From where he crouched he could see the moon, half-full, and nothing else. The head had gone, and after a few seconds Sam finally managed to breathe again.

'Is it gone?' Jen asked in a trembling whisper from her corner of the room. Sam didn't answer straight away. Instead, he cocked his ear to make sure that he hadn't missed anything.

Jen stood, pushing herself up the wall, pulling away torn paper and cracked plaster. She was trying to regulate her own breathing, by the sounds of it. Sam turned to tell her not to move until he told her to, but she was already out, eyes clenched tightly shut, and moving into the middle of the room.

Before Sam could say anything, the window erupted inwards, sending shards of glass over Sam, who could do nothing to escape the sudden attack. The blast seemed to follow a few seconds later; a shotgun being fired from close range. As the glass fell all around, Sam rolled across to the side of the room, his crossbow with him. He was too busy levelling his weapon towards the window to notice Jen fly across the room behind him, her arm a few feet ahead of her, a small spray of blood shooting from her shoulder as the bullet tore through it, splintering bone and tearing flesh. She landed with a thump behind the sofa, a fortunate bonus that concealed her from further bombardment.

When the sound returned – the blast had deafened Sam completely, leading him to believe that the thing at the window had never strayed more than a foot to the side – Sam screamed at the top of his lungs, hoping she would hear him over the inevitable ringing in her ears. *'Jen, are you okay!'*

He didn't dare to look, to see where she was in the room. To take his eyes away from the shattered window would be his final mistake, and he knew that better than anything.

When she finally answered, albeit with a distraught whimper, Sam felt the relief wash over him. He'd often thought about losing her, what it would be like to have to survive alone in a world of lunatics, but he'd never truly contemplated just how much she meant to him, not just as a survival-buddy but as a friend, as a human-being.

'I'm hit,' she screeched. 'I'm fucking hit!'

Just as Sam was about to offer some assurance – as best as he could, given the situation – the head that had previously been used to batter the window came flying into the room. It hit the north-wall and slopped to the floor, out of sight.

'*Can you move?*' Sam asked, knowing that it was a long-shot. '*If we can get you upstairs I can take care of this fucker!*'

The chilling cackle came from outside again. The thing obviously found Sam's optimism hilarious.

'FUCK YOU!' Sam bellowed, his anger and hatred getting the better of him. He needed to remain calm. Losing it in front of Jen would do little to alleviate her fears. She was already sobbing behind the sofa; he could hear her panting as she fought back tears.

'Sam?' she gasped. 'Sam, I don't know if I can move.'

He cursed quietly to himself, shaking his head. 'You have to,' he told her. 'We have to get out of here. It knows we're in here, and it'll keep on coming until—'

A figure flew through the window, and landed with a heavy thump on the carpet. The shotgun was slung across its shoulder. Sam pushed himself up the wall and trained the crossbow on it. There was a sea of material, all pretty flowers and butterflies. What had once been pastel colours were now a darker shade thanks to the mud and gore painted across the dress. When it came to a stop, Sam expected to see a woman staring at him. It was a man, toothless, chestnut beard hanging down the front of its dress.

It glowered at Sam, urging him to make his move. It yipped, laughed, made no effort to reach for its gun, which was slung so far around its neck that it was probably unreachable. Sam wanted to shoot it, and was about to when there were more moans outside, more screeches of insanity.

'*Fucking shoot it!*' Jen screamed, and Sam saw in his peripheral vision that she was standing, leaning on the sofa for support.

The thing taunted him with its tongue, licking the air like a rabid dog, and as Sam pulled the trigger it seemed to grin even more.

The thing in the dress stood stock-still as the arrow penetrated its heart. Blood spewed from its puckered lips, painting its beard a deep crimson. It grinned and grimaced in equal measure as it took its final breath and toppled backwards, hitting the living-room floor with a thud. Its head clattered against an overturned table, splitting its skull wide open and spilling grey-matter everywhere.

Outside the things were cheering, as if their martyr had done them proud. Sam rushed across, pulled the arrow out of its chest, flipped it over, and pulled at the shotgun. It wouldn't budge; it was tightly wrapped around the dead thing's neck, and Sam knew that time was of the essence.

He turned to Jen and said, '*Upstairs*!'

She moved, not with any great speed, but moved nonetheless. Her shoulder was pumping blood, spraying the carpet beneath their feet, and as she reached the door leading to the stairs Sam knew that she would be dead within the hour if they didn't tend to her wound.

He gave up on the shotgun, realising that there was probably only one shot in it, anyway, and no chance to reload for the small army of headcases lurking outside.

He followed Jen up the stairs, pushing her from behind. The madness out front was going to get in; there was no doubt in his mind.

Moving implacably forward, he cursed himself for falling asleep one last time.

*

Jen lay on the floor in the bedroom; Sam stood at the side of the large window staring down at the unfolding nightmare. He was pretty sure they couldn't see him, but they knew he was in there, knew they were both in there, sane people awaiting death.

'There's too many of them, aren't there?' Jen mumbled, barely audible over the incomprehensible racket outside. She was sweating, panting for breath and wondering how many more she had left in her.

Sam glanced down to the street. He counted twelve, nine men and three women – though it was difficult to tell in the pitch-darkness. Twelve wasn't a lot, not in the grand scheme of things. They had hidden from many more and survived. The only difference with these twelve, though, was their knowledge. They knew about the trapped meat, and wouldn't stop until they got it.

A fight broke out. Four of the men began to brawl, rolling around like drunken revellers after a night out. Sam watched as they began to crowd the weakest member, and proceeded to tear him apart.

Animals.

Wild animals in human form.

When they were done they acted as if nothing out of the ordinary had happened. The attacked headcase lay inert on the ground, blood from its jugular pumping out onto the road.

Sam turned into the room and sighed. 'I don't know what they're going to do next,' he said. 'But if we don't get that shoulder sorted soon, you're going to be in all kinds of trouble.'

Jen cough-laughed, 'Thanks for stating the obvious,' she said as she wiped blood from the corner of her lips.

Screams outside made the hackles rise on both of their flesh. They would be in soon, regardless. They would come in through the shattered window, dance up the stairs like the crazy-ass bastards they were, and find Sam and Jen cowering in the corner, pleading to have mercy, though it would do no good.

'Where's my *book*?' Jen asked.

Sam sat on the edge of the bed and began to stroke the top of her head, brushing the sweat-drenched hair that clung to her face away. He knew what she was talking about; her copy of Treasure Island. He offered the room a cursory inspection, but he couldn't see it anywhere. She must have left it downstairs, perhaps in the kitchen.

'You've read it enough times,' he told her. 'Surely you don't need to read it right *now*.'

A look of panic washed over her. It must have been the first time she'd been without it, her comfort-blanket, her bible, and the thought of not having it now, when she needed it most, must have terrified her.

Sam calmed her, stroked her head, told her everything would be okay and that he would read it to her from his own memory. The truth of the matter was, he had no idea how it went. He knew there were pirates, and one of them was Long John Silver, but the rest he didn't have a clue about.

Though he doubted it would matter. Jen was already running a temperature. He had staunched the wound as best as possible with a pillowcase, but that was all he'd been able to do.

He dropped to the carpet next to her, and they both leaned back against the foot of the bed. Jen was shaking, shuddering so badly that the sound of her teeth clattering together was louder than the racket outside.

"'There was a guy called Long John Silver,'" Sam began, rolling his eyes as he realised just how lame his opening sentence sounded. Jen didn't make a peep. If it bothered her, she didn't tell him.

He continued to tell her all about *"this guy with a peg-leg"*, and in places she whimpered with laughter. Sam chuckled too. Downstairs something crashed, but nothing mattered anymore. He kept going, his story becoming more fantastic by the second. He quite liked it, and as the sound of footfall on the stairs stopped him momentarily he couldn't help but feel like he had missed his calling in life, back when the world was normal, sane. He could have been a storyteller, one of the greats...

He pulled Jen closer, his finger tightening around the trigger of the crossbow, but he carried on with the story, because he knew she was enjoying it, and they both needed to hear how it ended.

Something – a female – screeched just outside the door, and then a deeper voice grunted, a bellowing, guttural growl that Sam thought could have belonged to Brian Blessed, though he didn't hold out much hope for that.

Sam kissed the top of Jen's head. It tasted salty, the smell redolent of an ocean tainted with bitterness. He lifted the crossbow, pushed his head next to hers, and held the arrow-point against his temple.

His story was almost finished, and Rebecca was either dead or asleep. He would make sure they both were when the door finally slammed open. Sam closed his eyes.

Screaming. Confused noises, lunatics raving just outside the door, and then it burst open. He didn't even open his eyes, for there was no point.

Sam ended their story.

7:17 FROM SUICIDE STATION

Smoke, beautiful, pungent, aromatic smoke, signalled the arrival of Der Müngstener. It was a little after seven, and the hazy, Sunday afternoon was handing over the reins to a much cooler evening. If they were lucky, Lukas Bäcker thought, it would rain a little to settle the pollen and ease his discomfort. He could only hope.

Lukas had enjoyed his day in Remscheid more than he had anticipated. The Roentgen Museum was a particular highlight, for he just adored Germanic history – so much so that his parents thought him to be a little strange. His father, especially, couldn't understand Lukas's interest in things long past, and had considered him to be, at one time, a homosexual. He wasn't, of course, but Lukas's father was not possessed of a broad mind; the simplest explanation for his son's keen (and somewhat disturbing) interest in bygone epochs would do just fine.

Lukas lit a cigarette and exhaled. Had he been paying attention, he would have noticed the elderly lady sidle up next to him, a woman for who beauty had been and gone leaving only remnants and slight hints that it had once been there. When she spoke, Lukas started, for he had not been expecting conversation with anyone before reaching Solinger.

'Nice day, wasn't it?' the woman asked, the merest hint of a smile curling the corner of her lips.

Lukas, regaining composure, turned to the woman, and was surprised to find she was of years that her voice betrayed. If he hadn't looked, he could have believed her to be no older than himself, perhaps even younger...

'It's been wonderful,' he replied, switching his cigarette across to the hand farthest away from the woman just in case it offended her. 'They say it might rain tomorrow, but hopefully that'll bring the pollen-count down.' He gestured to his eyes, which were slightly reddened from intense rubbing, and watering ever-so-slightly.

The woman, for reasons that Lukas was yet to learn, began to laugh. Though there was something remorseful about it; melancholy, almost. She reached down to her stomach and began to stroke, as if there might be an unborn child within her. 'Thankfully we don't have to worry about what tomorrow brings,' she said, the smile no longer playing surreptitiously across her lips. As if realising what she was doing, she took her hand away from her belly and glanced towards Der Müngstener. 'So, when did you first hear about this service?' she asked, barely audible over the hissing and hooting of the train on the platform.

Lukas, not wanting to seem rude – though he no longer felt comfortable in the conversation – said, 'I didn't hear about it until today. A woman at the museum, you know the Roentgen...of course you do. Well, a woman there told me about Der Müngstener, and I thought, what the *hell...*'

The woman snapped from her reverie, then, as if Lukas had told her something of import. 'Nothing like the last minute,' she said, her lips quivering as if unable to decide on what to do next. 'But you must have been planning it for some time? You've *thought* about it, about everything that it would mean?'

Lukas flicked his half-smoked cigarette down onto the tracks. 'I'm one of those type of people,' he said, 'that likes to do things on the spur of the moment. If that woman from the museum hadn't informed me of this service, I would have been doing something else. I guess it's *fate*.' He smiled; the woman standing next to him didn't.

'I've been planning this for almost ten years,' she told him. 'Ten years of procrastination. There always seemed to be something better to do, something I had to do before I rode Der Müngstener. I lost my daughter about a month ago, car accident, and that did it for me. I knew that it was time.' She glanced towards the ground, kicked a piece of chewing-gum down onto the track where it lay next to Lukas's still-smouldering cigarette. 'If it's fate that you believe in,' she continued, 'then my daughter's passing would certainly substantiate it.'

Lukas didn't know what to say. Did he offer condolences? Was she fishing for sympathy? He was not good in these situations, especially with people with whom he had only recently become acquainted. This woman *seemed* nice, but she had yet to offer her name – and he hadn't bothered to give his, either – so perhaps providing solace would seem a little strange, even though he knew it was the right thing to do.

'At least I know why I'm here,' she said, thankfully filling the awkward silence before it had time to grow roots. 'And I hope, for your sake, that you do, too.'

Lukas smiled, for it seemed right to ease the mood. 'I know where I'm heading to,' he said. 'That's enough for me today. Tomorrow's another day, as the old adage goes...'

The woman chortled nervously. '*Again* with this talk of tomorrow,' she said, almost sneered.

Lukas was about to respond when Der Müngstener screeched; a plume of steam hissed out from beneath it. A voice announced that the train would be departing in five minutes and people alighting should now begin to do so.

A thick crowd of people – who had been standing back on the platform, witnessing the splendour of Der Müngstener from a few feet away – stepped forward and slowly boarded through the left-hand side of the train. There were three doors, and each of them now had a queue. Lukas was partially annoyed that he had allowed this woman, this poor, strange woman, to distract him so thoroughly, for he now had to join a queue that he would have fronted had he been paying attention.

'Well,' the woman said, gesturing to the nearest door. 'I guess this is it.'

Lukas hoped that she didn't decide to sit next to him for the journey; he didn't think he could take it.

Once boarded, Lukas shuffled carefully down the carriage; there was nothing more annoying than having your elbow knocked by an inconsiderate passenger with no spacial-awareness. The woman remained at his heels, whispering manically to herself. Lukas thought that she might have been praying, and didn't deem it appropriate to interrupt, but for God's sake she was annoying.

The carriage was wonderful, and helped to take his mind from the misery accompanying him. Red, velvet curtains framed the windows, and there were wine-glasses and a choice of red and white sitting proudly upon each table. Lukas, for the first time, realised why the ticket had cost him so dearly. He would have been satisfied with a seat at the rear, assuming this was first-class and the rest if the monetarily-deficient passengers were in a different carriage completely.

It was too late now, though. Ticket had been bought; might as well enjoy it.

Spotting an empty table, Lukas edged forward and propped his backpack next to the window. He slid in next to it as the river of people in the aisle continued with their search for comfort. The woman – had he assumed any different? - was already seated opposite him, glancing out of the window, pulling the velvet curtain across so that she had a better view of the journey.

Lukas sighed. This was *not* how he had imagined his evening at all, and for obvious reasons he silently cursed himself for not bringing a book. Surely the woman sitting opposite would have taken the hint had his nose been buried in a thick tome; even if he wasn't really reading, even if it was to delude her...

'Margerethe Weber,' she said, extending a hand across the table, almost knocking aside the wine-glasses sitting there.

Lukas shook it fastidiously, as it might sprout legs and scuttle off down the aisle. 'Lukas Bäcker,' he said, wishing almost immediately that he had provided a non de plume, although he couldn't say why. 'Pleased to meet you, Margerethe.'

She smiled, poured a glass of wine, and began to sip at it whilst peering over the top of the glass towards Lukas.

That book, he couldn't help thinking, would have been most welcome right at that moment.

He turned and watched as people continued in their search for a table. A man, perhaps twenty, with a reddish beard; a woman, mid-fifties but with the appearance of someone in her twilight; a nuclear family, the children no older than ten. They all looked so miserable; Lukas found the palpable sorrow in the carriage most discomforting, and yet *why*? Why did these people look so unhappy? Was Solinger such a terrible place to visit? Had there been some kind of funeral, to which each of them had been guests? As an elderly gent nodded to him, as if they were of the same understanding, Lukas turned his gaze back to Margerethe, the woman who was still watching him, rapt.

'So what did you do?' she asked. 'For a job? Before you decided to ride Der Müngstener?'

What a very strange question, Lukas thought. The way in which she used past tense, frivolously, suggested she was of ill education, and yet she didn't look it.

'Well, erm...actually I decided to do a bit of sight-seeing,' he told her, pouring himself a very large glass of red in the hope that it might dull the inevitable pain to come. 'I recently split with my partner, and after a few months of kicking around the house alone...God, I *hated* that silence, so I decided to do something with my life, to get out and see a few things, the things that had not interested Dierdre.'

Margerethe was nodding, as if it all suddenly made perfect sense. 'So it's a woman that brings you here,' she said, not a question. She gestured around the carriage, haphazardly poking her taloned hand in the direction of men, strangers. 'I bet if you ask a lot of these men why they're here, they would say it was a woman's doing.'

Lukas shifted nervously in his seat and took a long, hard gulp of wine. It was warm, but not disagreeable. It would, for all intents and purposes, do just fine.

The train screeched one last time before slowly pulling out of Remscheid, a trail of smoke and steam in its wake. Lukas watched as sobbing relatives and friends waved their loved ones away. He smiled, thinking to himself how ridiculous it all was; that they should be so miserable. It was as if they would never see them again.

'So, Margerethe,' Lukas said, finally mustering the courage to ask a few questions of his own. 'What do you do for a living?' He knew that there was a possibility she had already retired, but it would have been rude to assume such a thing, and even ruder to suggest she had joined the ranks of the useless out loud.

'I was a photographer,' she said without making eye-contact. She swilled the wine around in her glass and watched it as it sloshed first one way, then the other. 'I did a lot of work for the newspapers. They didn't pay me very well, but what else could I have done? My daughter relied on me, for her father had abandoned both of us when she was just four.'

Lukas suddenly felt very stupid for inviting such misery upon himself. His question hadn't been intended to invoke painful memories; it had merely been a polite way to pass the time.

'Have you ever heard of Die Politik?' she asked.

'Of course,' he said, though he hadn't.

'I did a lot of work for them; they would call me and ask me to attend functions where there might be a very special guest, and I would go, try to get some decent photographs. Like I said, it didn't pay too well, but it was enough to raise my daughter, to keep us both happy.'

Lukas didn't believe that this woman had ever been happy, though the death of her daughter might have altered her so drastically. For all Lukas knew, Margerethe was once the funniest, most charming woman in all of Germany...

The aisle was now almost empty, apart from a few standing passengers near the door. Lukas tried to listen in as a man and woman – his wife, perhaps – began to argue about something. Something about who was going to go first...whatever it was, it made no sense, and Lukas suddenly felt very uncomfortable for even trying to eavesdrop.

'Does anyone know that you're here?' Margerethe asked, refilling her glass with a trembling hand. When she signalled for Lukas to hand over his glass, he did so without question and watched as she went about filling it.

'I told my *parents* I was coming,' he said. 'But that's about it.'

Margerethe hissed and sucked air in through her teeth; teeth that were so perfectly white that they had to be false. 'The parents, huh? That must have been *terrible*. How did they take it?'

As conversations went, this was one that Lukas

didn't feel entirely part of. He answered Margerethe, anyway, in the only way he could. 'They didn't want me to come alone,' he said, thinking of how his mother had complained that he might go missing, that backpackers were always going missing, that there was some kind of Bermuda Triangle where all the missing backpackers now resided. He'd laughed it off, of course, telling her that it would be fine, that he would telephone every day. His father was probably just happy to get rid of him for a few weeks.

'Ahhh,' Margerethe said. 'They *understood*, but they were loath to let you do it alone. That's commendable of them. You're a very lucky boy.'

Lukas sat back, trying to push himself into his seat, hoping that it might open up and swallow him completely. The wine was good, but not good enough to block out Margerethe Weber, who looked apt to torment him for the rest of the journey.

The nuclear family sitting three tables along the carriage were praying, which Lukas found incredibly odd. Were people still so terrified of rail-travel? There hadn't been a fatal crash for years, at least not that Lukas could recall. Though, if the family were so ecclesiastical, he guessed that any time of the day was a good time to pray, at least for *them*. Being on a train was not going to prevent them from their daily worship, and he had nothing but respect for them and their complete disregard of surroundings.

Margerethe turned to see what had Lukas so thoroughly consumed. 'It makes you wonder,' she said, glancing across to the young family, 'just what made a perfect family like that board today.'

Lukas wanted to tell Margerethe that perhaps it was nothing more than a lovely family-outing, a picnic, a trip to the museum – and what a *beautiful* museum it was, too – but he didn't. The woman seemed intent on only discovering negativity, and Lukas no longer wanted to play along with the charade.

He reached across to the table and poured himself another large glass of wine. Margerethe held a flat palm across her glass, though Lukas had had no intentions of topping her up.

'I noticed that you smoke,' she said. 'Back there at the station, you were smoking.'

Lukas didn't know where she was going with it, but humoured her anyway. 'Twenty-a-day for ten years. My parents still don't know.'

Margerethe laughed. 'I don't suppose they'll ever find out, now,' she said, and then continued laughing as if it was one of the funniest things she'd ever heard. When she was finished – Lukas had necked the glass of red and was pouring another – she added, 'Now would be a good time for a cigarette. I don't think they mind if you smoke aboard Der Müngsterer.'

Smoking on trains, Lukas thought, was a thing of the past. 'I'll wait,' he told her, wondering why she was suggesting something that could ultimately see him arrested. 'I'm good until Solinger.'

She stopped laughing; the corners of her eyes shrivelled up, a hundred crow's feet that had been absent only a moment before. 'What do you mean?' she asked, so serious, so affected for some reason.

Lukas didn't know whether he had said something out of turn, or if the woman was simply playing games with him. If the atmosphere had been palpably disturbing before, it was uncomfortable to the point of madness, now.

'I don't need to smoke until *Solinger*,' he said, sitting back in his seat, his sweaty palms fighting to cling to the stem of the wine-glass. 'It's a bad habit, but not to the point where it's necessary to break the law.'

And then, Margerethe sat forward, reaching across the table with both rheumy hands. 'But this train doesn't *go* to Solinger, anymore,' she said. 'Deary me, Herr Bäcker, have you made a mistake?'

Lukas glanced around the carriage; a few of the other passengers must have been listening in, for they now stared towards the table he shared with Margerethe, apparently awaiting his riposte. 'I have no idea what you mean,' he said. 'Of *course* it goes to Solinger. This track is the Wuppertal-Oberbarmen-Solinger. It can't *go* anywhere else.' Despite the woman obviously being some kind of fruitcake, Lukas suddenly felt very uncomfortable. And the way she was staring at him – or *into* him, as it seemed – only served to frighten him further.

'It would have once taken you through to Solinger,' she said. 'But that was a long time ago. This train stops at Müngsten Bridge; it goes no further.'

Lukas didn't speak. In fact, he *couldn't.* Why would a train stop halfway along its intended track, and on top of a bridge, of all things? His confusion must have sparked something in Margerethe, because she sighed, dropped her head into her hands and began to shake and sob.

Lukas reached forward and gently patted her shoulder. He didn't know what else to do. People were staring, and this loon was making a scene. When she looked up, her kohl was smeared across her face, a thick black mascara-line trailed across from her eyes to her ears, and with a quivering bottom lip she began to explain just how Lukas Bäcker had made a very big mistake.

'Lukas, I don't know why the woman at the museum suggested you board this train. She should have known better, and I can only think that she must have been new to the area for her to do something so stupid. Pour me a glass of wine; I have things to tell you, things that only alcohol will get me through.'

Lukas poured her a glass – the final one of the bottle – and waited for her to continue. He wasn't sure he wanted to hear what she had to say, though, and people around the carriage were now party to the conversation, cocking their ears towards the table, making sure the woman got every detail correct.

'This railway had a history,' she began, 'and it is this history that brings us here today. The architect, a man by the name of Von Rieppel, was said to have thrown himself off his own bridge. Died on impact, which is what you would expect from a three-hundred and fifty foot drop. But the architect was merely the first in a long line of suicides at Müngsten. Over the years there have been numerous accounts of people taking their own lives. The government decided to do something about it, and as with any good government, they figured that there was money to be made, money that Remscheid needed, money that would make a difference to the people who lived – and wanted to *continue* to live there. So, Der Müngstener was still functioning as well as she ever had, and if people wanted to go off to the bridge and kill themselves, they still could. Lukas, this journey is one way for me, for them, for *all* of us.' She stroked the back of his hand, as if this might somehow make everything better.

It had to be a joke, some kind of cruel prank that the other passengers were in on. Lukas gazed around the carriage and was surprised to see that everyone, the family, the arguing couple – *I want to go first, we talked about it, I'm going before you* – the man with the rust-coloured beard and salt-and-pepper hair, they were all looking to him as if he had just been handed the worst possible news and none of them knew what to say.

'This is *ridiculous*,' he spat. 'Margerethe, have you *escaped* from somewhere recently?'

She shook her head, but didn't speak. The nuclear-family's father did, though, in a guttural voice, solemn and trembling, he said, 'She's not lying to you, son. This train stops atop Müngsten. None of us go any further than that.'

Lukas opened and shut his mouth as if to speak, but no words would come. His mind was moving in so many directions it was impossible to focus on one thing. And people were staring...gawking at him with open mouths, and whispering to one another, clandestinely, though he could hear their every word above the rattling train, above the hissing brakes.

'Poor, poor boy...'

'What a mistake to make...'

'Is there nothing we can say...?'

Lukas couldn't tolerate it any longer. He pushed himself up from the seat, and it was then that he realised the train was slowing. 'I have to get off the train,' he gasped, suddenly wishing he hadn't taken the proffered wine. It had not merely been a gesture, a gift extended to all in first-class. It was the last supper; something to make the experience easier.

Margerethe stood, glanced down the carriage. Had she been expecting the guards to appear? They did. Three men, uniformed in identical blue suits, badges pinned to their lapels, though they were too far away for Lukas to read.

'There is only one way off the train, Lukas,' Margerethe whispered. 'Those men are paid to make sure that passengers don't lose their nerve. It happens, and when it does they are called upon to...help things along.'

Lukas knew exactly what the woman was telling him, and his heart leapt up into his mouth. He could taste nothing but bile; terrible, acidic helplessness that threatened to immolate him where he stood.

'They can't *throw* me off the train!' he screeched. 'That's *murder*!'

A few of the other passengers were growing tired of the unfolding panic. The children of the nuclear family gazed up at Lukas, their parents' hands covering their ears to block out the objecting man's pleas. Though Lukas could see the sorrow in those miniature faces, faces that had already grown accustomed to the notion of death. Lukas wanted to scream at them, to ask them why they were on Der Müngstener, but he couldn't. The children, the family, had bought tickets knowingly – he had not.

The three guards watched from the end of the carriage. Lukas could see they were carrying guns. Is that what they used to help those unfortunate mind-changers? Murder. It was murder!

The train slowed even more. Brakes hissed beneath them, and Der Müngstener hooted, a jolly hoot that seemed somewhat out of place considering the circumstances. Passengers began to clamber out of their seats and into the aisle, a steadily flowing queue towards the door, where the couple had managed to ascertain just who was to go first.

A hand – Margerethe's hand – gently brushed Lukas Bäcker's forearm, and he turned to face her. She said, 'Rumour has it that the last rivet to go into the bridge was made of solid gold.' She smiled, uneasily; Lukas felt sick. 'Isn't that a lovely thing to believe in?'

Through the window, Müngsten Bridge approached. A place where suicides were rife, a place where good people went to die, for whatever reasons they deemed necessary.

Lukas thought about Dierdre, about how she had cheated on him and left him for a schweißer, and it helped, it helped a *lot.* He edged out from the table, glancing one more time at the nearing bridge. Stepping in behind Margerethe, he placed a hand upon her shoulder and thanked her. It was the least he could do.

A Small Matter of Transmutation

In a recent article compiled by the Pall Mall Gazette, the number of species on earth amounted to something in the region of seven million. There were several references to Darwinism, of which I'm loath to mention as there are many Christians – most of whom I am extremely fond of – who would argue his theories. What I must explain, before I continue, is that this article might not be wholly accurate in its summations. I am referring to a very intriguing case that presented itself to me less than a week ago, one which I deemed worthy of recording, as I am wont to do.

The case in question walked into my office in the shape of a beautiful woman. Slight in stature, and yet somehow utterly intimidating, she entered with such confidence that, for a moment, I believed myself to be in some sort of trouble.

"My name is Charlotte Porter," she told me, placing herself somewhere equidistant to me and the door. "I'm in dire need of help, and I have no idea what for."

It was the kind of thing I'm accustomed to hearing. As a physician, and if you permit to me add, a very sought after one, I am met daily with strange cases of bizarre and implausible. If I can delve suitably into the symptoms, and thus discern a reasonable diagnosis, I send the majority of my patients to an apothecary, satisfied with the service that I have afforded them. However, from the countenance of Ms Porter, I could tell I would have no such luck with her case.

"Please, take a seat," I said, gesturing to the large, leather armchair in front of my desk. "Can I offer you a glass of water? Perhaps tea?"

She declined, and proceeded to seat herself with the caution and reserve one might expect of a single lady of perhaps seventeen. "I'm not sure how to begin," she said, which was – I find – usually the best way to begin. "I'm not even sure if I'm ready to tell you what…what I fear I've become."

Now *that* intrigued me. The fact that this young lady feared that she had *become* something suggested she had a story to tell, one that would challenge and confound me. I thrive on such cases, though at that point I didn't realise quite what it would mean.

"In your own time," I said, trying not to sound too eager. Pressure would do nothing to aide Ms Porter's account, and I – despite being highly sought after – had all the time in the world to absorb her yarn.

"I believe…no, I'm *sure* that I've begun to go through certain changes."

I held up a hand, perhaps a little too soon, to stop her. "If you're referring to menstruation, and the banes of womanhood, then it is perfectly—"

"I'm *not*," she gasped. Her coyness dissipated at the mere mention of such ailments. "I'm referring to the fact that I woke this morning in Hyde Park, bereft of clothing."

Ahhh, it was music to my ears. Not that this poor girl had found herself in such a predicament, but that this was not merely a simple case, easily explained. I urged her to continue, promising not to interrupt again.

"Well," she said, "I can recall nothing from last night other than taking myself to bed at around nine. I knew I would need a lot of sleep, for I had a very important interview this morning with the McKenzies, who were seeking a nanny for their two young hellions. Needless to say, I missed the appointment. I was too upset to face them, and much too confused to feign smiling." She changed her mind and requested a glass of water, which I poured while she continued. "When I woke this morning, at first I thought I'd been abducted, that someone had taken me in the night and…well, you know what might run through the mind of a young girl. Anyway, I covered up my modesty as best I could and ran all the way home. Thankfully, I woke early otherwise I might have been arrested. I don't know if I was seen, rushing through the streets at dawn, but I would hate to think people believe me to be a dollymop."

I assured her that she would have looked like no such thing, if only to alleviate her despair.

"Once home, I looked in the mirror, and it was then that I noticed the blood. At first I thought it was mine, a result of being stolen away in the night and beaten by the perpetrator along the way. On closer inspection, I realised that I had no cuts, no bruises, no signs of harm or damage inflicted upon me. The blood was not my own."

I was now perched precariously upon the edge of my seat. I could have offered Ms Porter an array of feasible explanations for the blood upon her personage, but chose to remain silent while she continued with her account.

"This peculiar, and for me, terrifying, occurrence comes less than a month after I was attacked in the very same park." She looked apt to cry, but didn't. I was strangely proud of her for managing to control her emotions, inasmuch as I needed to hear the end of the story before I exploded with anticipation. "I had been walking along, as one does, when all of a sudden a man attempted to snatch my bag. Rotten scoundrel almost tore my arm off trying to grapple the bag from me, but I'll have you know that I'm made of tougher stuff, and managed to fight him off until a passer-by chased him into the trees."

She placed her hand flat upon the desk between us. Four lines could be determined upon her flesh, the marks of a jolly good raking. "And these are only a few weeks old?" I asked, for they were well-healed and completely free of infection.

"One month, perhaps," she said, doing the mathematics in her head. "I tended to the wound myself."

"You appear to have done a remarkably good job of it," I told her, knowing that no matter how well she had nursed the claw-marks upon her hand, they should not be anywhere near as clean and advanced of healing.

"Am I going mad?" she asked, pulling her hand away from the table as if it were liable to bite. "People don't just wake up without a tog on in the middle of the park, not without something being amiss."

"I'll need to examine you more intently," I said. If the wound on the back of her hand was anything to go by, I was almost sure of finding something else aberrant. "Though I doubt I will be able to make an adequate diagnosis on the state of your mental health without several intense sessions of evaluation."

At the mention of probing her mind, she recoiled. "I don't want to be placed in an asylum," she said, biting on her bottom lip to prevent herself from sobbing. "I won't go."

I assured her that I would not allow her to be institutionalised. Besides, we tend to only do that in the most severe of cases, and as far as I was aware at that point, she had merely shown signs of somnambulism. As much as I wished for a different conclusion, the majority of what she had told me could lead me to establish it to be a simple case of sleepwalking.

As reluctant as she was for me to further examine her, I'm pleased to say that she did, and disappointed to add that nothing of supplementary oddness was discovered. She left the office no wiser than when she had entered it, and I – with all my years of wisdom and training – was a little crestfallen that such a promising case had drawn such a simple diagnosis.

Somnambulism, I decided, and nothing more.

However, a week ago I was delighted when Ms Porter once again made herself a guest in my office. She had suffered no further bouts of sleepwalking, however she was distraught at the discovery of a local dog, which had been reported missing upon the very morning she first came to see me.

"The blood around my lips," she said, sobs wracking her body. "It must have been the dog's. They found the poor creature, half-buried less than a hundred metres from where I wakened three weeks ago."

Did I believe that this girl was possible of such a brutal deed? Not really, but I had to entertain the possibility.

"I understand you're upset," I told her, "but the dog's sudden appearance and location could be purely coincidental."

"It was in this morning's paper," she pressed. "The author suggested the creature had been chewed apart by some wild animal. I told you, remember, that I felt different, that I had become something else."

I recall nodding in that moment, yet I remained silent.

"I know, now, that for one night, that night almost three weeks ago, I was not wholly myself. I became something repulsive; something animal." At this, she broke down, and once again I was expected to console her, which I did most effectively. When she had calmed enough for me to continue, I said:

"Do you fear that this might happen again?"

She paused, looking at me through her tear-drenched fringe. "I fear it will happen on the next full moon. I can already feel it inside me, with yet a week remaining. Can you offer any explanation for why I've suddenly sought meat – *any* meat – so fervently? Why I wish the birds would fly just a little lower so that I might pluck one from the air and stuff it into my mouth? These are not normal thoughts, and I'm beginning to frighten myself by merely having them."

This was exactly what I'd wished for, and with the sobbing girl standing before me – all confused and terrified – I felt like I was exploiting her for my own personal gain.

"These feelings are certainly not normal," I said, trying not to scare her any more than was necessary. "I would like for you to return to me next week, before the moon rises. We will ascertain whether the lunar-cycle has any sort of relevance in this matter, and one way or the other I will offer you a diagnosis."

She agreed, and left the office in the same state she entered. Petrified.

Now this is where things become somewhat confusing, and that article I mentioned in the Pall Mall Gazette is no more accurate than I am a dentist.

The girl, Ms Porter, returned to me this afternoon. Once again, her fears were visible upon her countenance. I assured her that nothing would happen, and that I – being the renowned and revered physician that I am – would take care of her for the duration of her stay. She placed her trust in me, and we spent the best part of the afternoon discussing items of banality, just to pass the time.

"I still feel it," she said, interrupting one of my more jocular monologues about the science of death. "Like a wholly different beast behind my own eyes."

I assured her that it was the anticipation of the moon making her feel a little odd; was it not possible that the expectation of a mysterious change could lead to all kinds of nonsensical thoughts and feelings? She accepted what I told her, and allowed me to continue with my scientific tales.

Now this is where I need to be very specific with my words, for they should not be misinterpreted by anyone who finds this account.

Ms Porter is a maniac. Yes, that is what she is. She is currently locked in the storeroom at the back of my office. I have contemplated leaving her there, for my own safety, but I fear for her, though now I'm certain she was right about becoming something otherworldly.

I'm writing this account for one purpose. That is to say, if I don't make it through the night – and I can hear her beating her bloodied and inhumanly elongated hands against the door – I would expect somebody to write a strongly worded letter to the Pall Mall Gazette informing them of their mistake. There are species out their beyond our grasp; some we will never discover, some we should hope never to stumble upon. Ms Porter, the man who raked his dirty fingernails along her hand in Hyde Park last month, and no doubt countless others, fall into the latter category.

I will sign off this missive with one last piece of advice. If I fail to survive the night, and Ms Porter is nowhere to be found upon entering this office, I would suggest leaving her to her own devices. And should she appear to any of my esteemed colleagues seeking help in the weeks following the date at the top of this account.

Respectfully decline.

Yours Faithfully

Dr Edmond Sewell

Damage Limitation

My name is Marcus Wayne, and I died almost three days ago. I was attacked, mutilated, partially devoured by one of the undead, which isn't the most annoying part of my predicament. If that had been the end of it, enough to send me either up or down – I'm still not sure how decent a human being I was – then I would have been able to accept it and move on. The thing is...I am a spirit, or *something*, it's difficult to explain, and I wish I had the words to describe what I am. I can tell you what I remember, though, and it hurt like a sonofabitch at the time.

The outbreak started a few weeks back; I'd managed to survive from what I had been told by the people on the TV and radio. Stay indoors, barricade all windows and entrances, ration food, the usual bullshit. After a week or so, though, it became a pain in the ass. I had to get *out*; I was going fucking stir-crazy, staring at a television that no longer broadcast, eating cold mince out of a tin. I could see the corpses out of my upstairs window – slow, awkward, nonplussed – and I knew that if I was careful, if I really prepared myself, I could make it to the store and back without getting my ass bit or scratched. After tooling up with what I had – a baseball bat and more kitchen-knives than I could carry – I made my way out for the first time, and it felt good. The air was clear, not stale like the house had become, and even though the cadavers were shambling about like the lumbering bags of putrefaction that they were, the streets tasted like pure heaven to me.

I made it to the store, grabbed enough supplies to last for a few weeks – although the store had been looted already, which left me with mainly jams and a few bags of overlooked tortilla-chips – and headed back to the stinking house in which I was now a prisoner.

The corpses couldn't catch me; it had been almost fun, a little game I had created for myself. See how many of them I could slap in the face before I reached the house. I was really good at it – who knew? - and by the time I got back I counted thirty, thirty slaps for thirty rotting zombies. Once home, I celebrated with a carton of fruit-juice and a bag of chips, which tasted all the better for what I had survived to get them.

After that, I got cocky. I was out more than I was in, either collecting supplies, searching other peoples' houses for things to keep me entertained, or just playing my little slap-a-zombie game, for which I now had a scoring system. Five points for a skinny corpse, ten points for a fatty, and twenty points if I could sneak up on it before it had time to growl at me. Like I said, I had to make my own entertainment now that the world had gone to shit. I didn't see another living soul, though, not while I was out playing my game and collecting edibles. I prayed that I wasn't the only survivor in the street, but it turned out to be like that. I saw a few neighbours, all chewed up and clearly infected. Mr Patterson from number eight took a particularly painful slap from me; I always hated that prick since he borrowed – and broke – my lawnmower last year.

So, everything was going well, or at least as well as could be expected post-apocalypse, and then, in a moment of madness on my part, it all went tits-up.

I decided to leave the comfort of my own street and go further afield in search of survivors. If I didn't find somebody to talk to soon I was going to lose it completely. I was sick and tired of beating myself at chess, and there was only such much masturbation a guy could fit into a day.

I was carrying my usual weaponry – a few knives

and my trusty baseball-bat – and I had a few days' food in a backpack, just in case I decided to keep walking, or maybe I would find somebody and spend the night with them, I really had thought of everything.

And it would have been fine if I had not decided to cut through the park. I could see through the rails, and there hadn't appeared to be many of them, but once inside I realised my mistake and tried to run. There was no time to play slap-a-zombie, no time for anything, and before I knew it I was scrambling through a thicket, hoping that I had lost them, but I hadn't.

That was when I got my first scratch, which would have been enough to infect me anyway. The ones that followed, and the multiple bites I received from three extremely hungry cadavers, were just the icing on an already-dead cake. I knew, as I lay there being chewed and disembowelled, that I had made a terrible mistake. All that remained, now, was death, and I prayed for it to come quickly as, like I said, it hurt like a sonofabitch.

So that was how I died, lying in the middle of a park being nibbled and gnawed, and I remember it so vividly now, because I was *there*. No, let me explain; I saw it from a distance. I saw my body as bits were torn off it, I saw the three creatures going at me like an all-you-can-eat buffet, and I remember thinking how fucking *wrong* it all was. How was this *possible*? Was I a ghost? Was I dreaming, and in reality I was seeing what my brain wanted me to see? Was that bitch wearing a wig? She *was*, one of my apparent diners was wearing the most ridiculous blonde toupee and it was half-on, half-off her head, which kind of made me laugh, but I was in no real mood and soon stopped.

So I had watched, and watched, and two of them – the wigged woman and one of the men, who was wearing a basketball vest and not much else – decided that they had had enough and dispersed through the trees. The third corpse, a fucking fat thing who looked like he could finish me off all on his lonesome, continued to feed for another hour. I even struck up a conversation with the lard-ass. *"How do I taste, you sumbitch?"* and *"I hope you fucking choke, you goddamned bag of maggots!"* were pretty much all I could manage, but it was a pleasant change to be speaking to something other than myself or pictures in magazines.

When fatboy finally waddled off, ass shaking and man-boobs wobbling through his vest, I decided to stick around, see what happened to my own corpse.

You can imagine just how pissed off I was when my body decided to get up and join the rest of the fucking horde. I was *livid.* Most of my – *its* – arm was chewed off, and guts were on the outside when they should have quite clearly been on the inside. I looked a right mess, and yet I was up and about, one of the gang.

The first few days were the worst. I had to watch my corpse search for something to eat, someone to devour, and since there was nobody left on the block to eat, it became frustrating for the both of us. I knew that I couldn't just stand by and allow my zombie-self to go off a-wandering, to attack some poor schmuck, but there was very little I could do about it.

At one point, the zombified version of me joined a group of Scouts. I couldn't believe it; there I was, a fully-grown adult hanging around with a bunch of cannibalistic kids. I was almost ashamed by what I had become. I was no longer just a walking corpse; I was now a walking corpse trying to collect fucking badges and start fires, or at least I would have been if I still had any senses.

The fourth day after my dead body decided to get up and wander listlessly around, I watched my corpse make its first kill, although I have to use the word loosely. A budgerigar – I shit you not – was squawking away in one of the long-abandoned houses, and my corpse, the sadistic sonofabitch that it was, left the Scouts outside and headed off in search of the racket. It was around this time that I realised I wasn't completely helpless; I could have sworn that my zombie counterpart sensed me, or maybe even saw me. I had watched that fucking thing for days, and this was the first time I actually saw its eyes focus on something.

Me.

But if it *did* see me, it had the attention span of a toddler and continued towards the birdcage at the back of the house. I'd like to say that the budgerigar hadn't suffered, but I would be lying. That goddamned bird couldn't have *been* more unfortunate; at one point, its head was neither completely on or off, but it didn't matter. My rancid friend – that was how I saw it, now. It wasn't me, it was just some cunt that I used to know – bit down, chewing the bird's head and some of its body, and yet it was still alive.

Anyway, needless details, and I really don't have time to digress. Let's move forward to today.

I know now that it can see me, as it had just before the budgerigar massacre a few days back. Yesterday, it tried to chase me, and not because it thought I was edible – which, of course, I'm *not* – but because I was cramping its style, or something. I even ran for a while, just in case it didn't go right through me when it tried to get a hold. In the end, it gave up and went about its day, simply accepting that I was not going to give up and that there was nothing it could do to stop me from lurking around.

I wouldn't stop until it was dead, until *I* was dead, *properly.* I'm still of the opinion that the maggot-infested twat walking around in my dead body is the reason why I'm stuck here, and the longer it goes on, the more time I spend around the cursed bastard, the harder it's going to be to kill it.

Oh great, it's back with the fucking *Scouts* now, and one thing I've learned is that, nobody farts more than a group of undead twelve year-olds. It's enough to drive a person crazy, if I wasn't already ninety-nine percent of the way gone. The main culprit of the group was a ginger-haired, freckle-faced, one-eyed, no-teethed asshole, the kind of kid whose own mother refuted all knowledge of his existence. That little carrot-top was the smelliest one I had ever had the misfortune of haunting. I wished I could touch things, because as I stood on the street, smelling that dirty, pitiful creature, I found myself suddenly yearning for a round of slap-a-zombie.

I watched as my cadaver lumbered aimlessly around; occasionally it gave me a reproachful glance, and I just smiled and gave it the finger. What was it going to do? *Kill me?*

It started to wander off, away from the prepubescent clan that it had hooked up with. I followed, no longer worried about what it would – or *could* – do to me. I just knew that I had to somehow finish it off. There had to be a way.

It reached the end of the street and shambled right, onto Westacre. I know this street quite well, mainly because I used to fuck a girl who lived at 242. I wonder if she's one of them, now, bumbling around like a drunken ape. I'd like to think so; at the end of our relationship – if you could call it that – she hated my guts.

Ahhh, there she was, falling all over the place in the middle of the road. I watched, laughing, trying to figure out what she was trying to do. Turns out, nothing in particular. Staying on her one remaining leg was difficult enough for that bitch.

My zombie-avatar, or whatever the fuck you want to call it, didn't even give her the time of day as it nonchalantly ambled by. In that moment, I found myself proud with...well, *myself*. She'd treated me – *us*? - like shit, so let the legless bitch roll around in the road like a fish out of water. It was the least she deserved.

As I passed her, she didn't growl, didn't snap at my ghostly ankle. I don't think any of the others can see me. Just the one that I used to reside in. I wanted to kick Cindy – that was her name – in the face, but it wouldn't work, and I knew it. My foot would go straight through her half-chewed head, and I'd feel like a complete tool. It didn't warrant a second thought.

Zombie-me was heading towards the railway-station, for some reason. I was about to shout and ask it why when a trio of fighter jets split the sky overhead. The thunderous roar as they whipped through the air was deafening, and even though I was dead, in more ways than one, I had to cover my ears.

Where did they come from? What were they up to?

I wanted them to drop a nuke, or any bomb as long as it was on my rotting corpse's head. I was quite disappointed when they disappeared into the distance, and the sound of their roaring engines faded into oblivion.

I followed the creature down into the station, and marvelled at the way it fell down three flights of stairs and lay in a crumpled mess at the bottom for a few seconds. Just when I was about to cheer, to celebrate the coming of the white light and the tunnel and all that malarkey, the sonofabitch got back up and carried on along the platform.

I knew I had to do something fast. It was starting to get on my nerves, even though they were no longer functioning as they had in life.

My corpse was grunting at a vending machine. I couldn't believe my fucking eyes. How shit a zombie *was* I? Most of them were out there, hunting human flesh and devouring the corpses of young children; mine just wanted a packet of chips and a chocolate-bar. And then, if things couldn't get any more surreal, something happened which made me realise just how crazy the world was now.

At the end of the platform, watching zombie-me and licking its lips, was a tiger. At first I thought it was some sort of mirage, a strange vision that dead people like me sometimes get. I didn't know, did I? There wasn't a rulebook for people in my situation, though that *Handbook For The Recently Deceased* out of Beetlejuice would have been pretty fucking handy right about now.

When the tiger didn't move, I started to believe it was one of those statues, you *know*? The ones where you pop a coin in for charity. Yes, it had to be one of those; it was a prime location.

And then, it prowled forward a few feet, and I banished all thoughts of charity-statues and visual trickery. This was real, and zombie-me didn't even have a clue it was there. It was too busy bashing a bloody fist against the glass of the vending-machine in a vain attempt to break out the milk-duds.

So, there we stood, on a railway platform that

hadn't seen a train for weeks; me, *zombie-me* and the tiger. I knew that I was safe, that the approaching beast couldn't even see me, but my corpse was about to take a lesson in how to devour meat, and I had the best seats in the house.

To say that I was upset wasn't quite right. It had been a strange experience, not what I had imagined from the afterlife at all, and in a way I pitied the zombies. If skulking around, hitting busted vending-machines until their hands were nothing but a bloody pulp, was all they had to look forward to, then I'm glad I'm not a part of it.

The tiger lunged, roared, licked its lips all at once.

I sat on the bench at the far side of the platform and waited for heaven.

Nyogtha of the Northern Line

Goodge Street Station, as was its wont on an early Monday morning, swarmed with people. Intolerant commuters shoved indecently past each other in an attempt to board the train currently sitting on the platform, momentarily disremembering that another exactly like it would be along in a few minutes. One would imagine the lack of etiquette – and sheer savagery they afforded – suggested that the workers enjoyed their jobs, when in fact most of them would rather be doing anything other than boarding that train.

A woman, frail and rheumy and wearing a silken scarf over her head, was almost crushed beneath the melee as the doors to the train swished open and the crowd surged forward. She, unlike these wage-slaves, had no deadline for her destination. Her working days were over; she'd paid her dues and was enjoying life as much as she possibly could with the little benefits the government granted her. Not that money was important to her; she had plenty of it. It was just that the world had become accustomed to leeching, and to decline a pension was tantamount to boasting.

Stepping aside to allow the suited businessmen a clear run-up to the train, she inhaled and wiped the mirrored sunglasses perched upon her nose as best she could without taking them off. The air was thick with the scent of a thousand perfumes and aftershaves, commingling to create something barbaric. Her eyesight wasn't what it used to be, and her hearing had gone the same way, but she could smell shit if it drifted beneath her nostrils, and that was what the amalgamated stench reminded her of.

Shit. Coming soon from Paco Rabanne.

The commuters fighting for entry through the myriad doors soon realised they would all make it on, although it did nothing to tame them and they proceeded to elbow, nudge, knee, shoulder-barge and – in one instance – head-butt fellow passengers. The head-butted man simply shrugged it off, as if being clobbered in the face by another man's face was perfectly acceptable, especially at such an ungodly hour on a Monday morning. Later that evening, the man would peer into a mirror at the purple egg formed on his forehead and devise an elaborate ruse in which he would get his revenge on the nut-job who'd clouted him. He would also, once ready to take his revenge tomorrow morning, chicken out. Instead he would locate the head-butter and silently curse the man, who would have no idea how close he had come to receiving his comeuppance.

The elderly woman shuffled forward, shaking her head with dissent at what she had just witnessed. *Animals*, she thought, nothing more than primates in suits, and that was being unfair to primates, who she surmised would act in a much better fashion given an Armani two-piece and an Oyster card.

She boarded the train cautiously. A punk – *that's what they call them*, she thought as she looked at his orange-tinged spikes – grimaced at her. The nose-ring dangling from his septum chinked like a cow-bell as he moved an inch back to allow her suitable room. She could tell he wasn't pleased with having to move for an old dear such as she.

"I'm terribly sorry," she said, and then – somewhat snidely – added, "It's a little early for a Halloween party, isn't it?"

A few of the passengers within earshot snickered. The punk, an upper-class rebel whose birth-certificate named him as Cedric Carter-Bowles, grunted something indecipherable. Knowing that his parents would hit the roof if they found out he'd been disrespecting his elders once again, he followed up the grunt with an apology.

"That's quite alright, young man," the geriatric gnome said, satisfied with herself. Next to her, a businessman glanced impatiently at his watch. He clicked his tongue and sighed heavily before roughly straightening his tie. The elderly lady offered him a smile, which he chose not to return. Instead, he glanced once more at the golden monstrosity coiled around his wrist. He was clearly running late and was eager for the train to start moving. The old lady felt no sympathy for him, nor did she envy him. Time was no longer significant to her the way it once had been. What mattered was the remaining years. She had had a long and fruitful life, filled with suffering and delight in equal measure. She had nothing to grumble about, no regrets, nothing she would change given half the chance. And the man nervously stepping from one foot to the next beside her made her realise how fortunate she had been, how lucky she now was.

Just as the doors were about to shut, three men appeared. They were virtually identical. Her first thought was of clones, genetically created copies of a single source, but knowing that science hadn't quite reached that point yet she pushed the thought away and settled on something a little more plausible.

Triplets.

The men embarked the train. The punk sighed, grunted, apologised once again. The lady pushed herself back as far as she could before realising she could go no further. The men seemed to fit their combined forms into the tiny space, regardless. As if they were liquid, capable of shape-shifting to accommodate their dozen limbs. They had an insect-like quality, what with their slender countenance and pitch-black suits. Spiderlike, almost. But those heads, perching precariously upon spindly stalks which could barely be called necks, were perfectly hairless. If there ever had been hair atop those heads, there was no sign of it now.

The doors hissed shut and within a second the train pulled away from Goodge Street. Its forward momentum caused everyone on board to lean towards the back of the train. At the back of the train, a tiny man named Paul Jacoby tried desperately to push back on the throng, but it was of no use. His face was smooshed against a window, and even after he'd exited the train at Kennington his face would peer out from the glass for quite some time. One child, a little girl with beautifully plaited pig-tails and a face peppered with cutesy freckles, would draw a dick on his head.

The three men standing in front of the elderly lady began to whisper. Their respective bald heads bobbed and dipped as the train surged onward through the tunnel. The lady cocked her head so that the scarf covering her ears lowered ever-so-slightly. She caught the tail-end of their murmurings.

"…wgah'nagl fhtagn."

As a travelling lady, she liked to think herself well-versed in the multitude of foreign languages she'd chanced upon. Yet, for the life of her, she couldn't place the language these three baldies were using. It was more a series of throaty clicks and misplaced vowels than any language she had ever encountered.

Must be some sort of idioglossia, she thought. A language created between the three that could only be understood by them. She'd heard of such things between identical siblings, but never witnessed it first-hand.

"…ph'nglui mglw'nafh…" the one on the left said.

"…Cthulhu r'lyeh…" the one in the middle added.

"…wgah'nagl fhtagn…" the third bald-pated fellow concluded.

"I say, that's terribly rude," the lady interjected. "I mean, would you like it if we started talking in some foreign language? Hmmm? For all we know, you're terrorists about to set off a device."

The passengers around her gasped. "Terrorist" was still one of those taboo words, especially on public-transport. The mere utterance of it was apt to get you swamped with bodies or arrested at the next station. Somebody near the front of the train begged to be let off, but since the tubular tin moving at forty-five mph was deep beneath the ground – and equidistant to Tottenham Court Road and Goodge Street – it was highly unlikely the driver would make such an allowance.

One of the androgynous men turned to face her while the other two remained facing forward. He sneered; curling his lip just enough to make the perplexed old lady wish she'd never opened her mouth. "Mnahn'," he said. "Mnahn' gof'nn." And then he laughed. A sound emanated from deep within him, an incessant drone which suggested he'd skipped the regular breakfast of cereal, toast and sundry jams and opted instead for a hornets' nest.

Whereas the rest of the passengers were happy to let it slide, the old lady folded her arms resolutely across her chest. "See, there you go *again*," she said. The man was at least a foot taller than she; she found herself arching her neck to make eye-contact as she reproached him. "This is Great Britain, is it not? We are in London, are we not? I'm pretty sure I saw a large sign outside that said we were." She glanced around to check that the rest of the passengers were still with her, if they ever had been to begin with. They were looking in all directions; anywhere but towards the strange bald trio and the apparently racist old lady giving them a right earful.

"Mnahn' hrii, kadishtu," the man said.

"Bless you," the old lady replied.

The man grunted; she could see she was going to get nowhere.

"Maybe you should leave it be," the Rolex-sporting businessman whispered to the old dear, clearly afraid of what might unravel should the gangly triplets decide to ruck. "This is a free country, and we'd all like to—'

The lights went out. It was so sudden that screams literally leapt from throats. Somebody near the front of the train began to pray aloud. A dog began to bark, which made the entire experience all the more unsettling for those who had a phobia of small, whiny animals. Then, the train began to slow. Light flooded in through the windows as the platform appeared. People, once again, began to breathe. For some, the episode would be worthy of a mention upon arrival at work; for others, it was already forgotten, and as the train pulled to a halt and the doors hissed open, people continued to go about their tedious lives relatively unscathed.

However, the busy commuters failed to notice – upon alighting Tottenham Court Road – the missing triplets, the scarf-wearing old ninny, the punk and the businessman. It was as if the darkness had swallowed them up wholly, leaving nothing behind but a slight tear in the fabric of time and space, which would slowly stitch itself back together as the next horde of humans clambered aboard.

*

It was all very surreal. In the first instance there was only darkness, confused cries, a mangy dog doing its very best to burst eardrums. Something had coiled around her arm, constricted like one of those impossibly large snakes she'd seen in National Geographic documentaries. Then there was silence, and a silvery buzz, like television static pumped directly into her mind. Something very abnormal was happening, but it was all so sudden that she could do nothing to stop it.

The intolerable thrum inside her head dissipated, leaving her crouched upon a tiled floor, head between her arthritic knees, wondering what the hell had just happened.

"What just fucking happened?" a voice said. "Is this some kind of joke, 'cos if it is it's not funny?"

She lifted her head to find the businessman – though now he looked a little like a vagrant who had stumbled, somewhat fortunately, across a designer suit – pacing frantically across the deserted platform. The punk was sitting cross-legged on the solitary bench; he looked terrified, which didn't suit him.

The businessman glanced around the platform. The battered and rusty sign hanging upon the wall announced the station as KING WILLIAM STREET, which was a new one on him. He threw his hands up and began to pull at the greying hair; the internationally recognised gesture of panic. "This can't be happening," he said with a tremulous voice. "No *way*. This can't be real. I've got a meeting in…" He glanced down at his watch, or would have if it was still there. His eyes widened, his mouth fell open as if his jaw had decided dislocation was a great look for him. "Holy shit! I've been *robbed*!"

The punk stood, checked for his wallet. Gone, along with his nose-bar and the twenty-two other piercings. He felt lighter, somehow. If it wasn't for the terrible, ominous sense of impending doom weighing him down, he would have felt like his old self again. Reborn. Like the old Cedric that mother and father approved of, the one who collected beanie babies and drew delightful pictures of unicorns and fruit-bowls.

"No, this has to be some kind of prank," the businessman opined. He scanned the abandoned platform for clues, any signs that what they were going through was pre-empted. But there was nothing; not even a security-camera. "This doesn't make any fucking sense. We were just on the train. You were about to get yourself into a scuffle with those foreign maniacs." He jabbed a shaking finger towards the elderly lady, who had picked herself up from the tiles and was in the process of brushing herself down.

"Yeah," the punk said, suddenly growing a pair. "You were being incredibly rude to those men. Then everything went dark."

"Are you seriously suggesting that my being rude somehow resulted in...*this*?" She gestured to the empty platform.

The businessman jabbed his accusatory finger at her. "He's right. The first rule of subway travel is not talking to strangers. You broke the rule, *lady*, and now we're in some...some sort of *purgatory*."

She couldn't help it, but a giggle escaped her. She'd heard some things in her incredibly long life, but this was a statement worthy of note. "That's priceless, that is," she said, pulling her head-covering around and tying a fresh bow. "So what you're saying is that by reprimanding those men for their insolence, we've been shifted sideways through time and space and placed in some sort of holding cell for the obnoxious?"

When she put it like that, the man realised how insane it sounded. "Well, *I* don't fucking know, do I. One minute we were on the train, the next…the next we're on King William Street…is that even a station? I don't *think* so."

"It used to be," she said, pacing casually across the platform. "It closed a long time ago, from what I can remember."

"Well, colour me impressed," the businessman sneered. "What are you, a history teacher?"

She didn't deem his question worthy of a response and decided to ignore it. "What's fascinating," she said, "is that the three of us are here."

"Yeah, why *me*?" the punk asked, though he could barely be called a punk, now. He was a preppy with spiked hair and a leather jacket.

"We were the three closest to those men," she continued. "The men speaking in tongues." It was the only way she could describe it.

"Something grabbed me when it all went dark," the businessman said. "I felt it. Wrapped around my throat like a giant dick, only cold and wet."

"Yeah," the punk said, as if the businessman's recollection had suddenly ignited memories of his own ordeal. "I thought something was crawling on me, and then I passed out. At least, I *thought* I did."

The old lady smiled, though if you were to ask her why she wouldn't be able to tell you. "Those three men weren't men at all," she said, nodding her head as if the words passing her lips made any sort of sense.

"I don't believe in ghosts, lady," the businessman said, shuddering – which was a contradictive reaction considering his words. He glanced across his shoulder, suddenly aware of their surroundings and the impossible manner in which they had arrived at them.

"I'm not saying they were ghosts," she said. "But I don't think they were human, either."

"Oh, great," the punk sighed. "Demonic triplets. All we need now is a spider-clown and my nightmares are complete."

Something rumbled overhead, followed quickly by the screeching of brakes. The echoes travelled along the tunnel on either side of the platform. It was genuinely unnerving, like a thousand voices groaning and hissing all at once. The punk didn't make a big deal of it, but he suddenly felt the urge to urinate.

"We're beneath the other stations," the businessman said, staring fixedly on a spider-web crack in the ceiling. "Which means that we're still in the real world. We just need to get back up there."

The punk was already on it, checking for doors, windows, anything he could fit through or throw himself at. The lady and the businessman watched as he frantically searched the platform, neither wanting to interrupt, neither willing to tell him that his searching was fruitless.

It was clear there was no way out. The one door to the platform had been welded shut, perhaps years ago. The steps to the left of the platform led up to a solid brick wall, as if the architect had been drunk at the time of its creation. The place was sealed tighter than a gnat's chuff. The tunnel running through the station was cordoned off with orange bollards and neon-yellow tape. It was like a crime-scene.

"Nothing!" the punk breathlessly announced as he returned to the platform. "Whatever this place is, there's no way in *or* out."

"Then how the fuck did we end up here?" the businessman said, tugging at his tie as if he'd suddenly discovered it was a salamander. After a few seconds of failed tugging, he gave up and tore it off completely. He was beginning to ooze sweat; a thin film of panic and despair coated him. The old lady wouldn't have pegged him as a claustrophobic. Maybe he was in the closet about it. The thought tickled her insides.

"We were teleported here by those fucking men," the punk said. "That's the only way to explain it."

"Not *men*," the lady corrected. "I knew it the moment they stepped on board."

"Well, you should have stuck one of your gnarly, old feet out and waited for the doors to shut in their face," the businessman snapped. "We wouldn't be in this mess if you had."

The lady sighed. "Yes, well, it's too late now. We need to figure out how to get out of this place."

"I know this might seem rude," the punk said, which usually meant that what followed would be exactly that, "but would you mind taking those glasses off? All I can see is two of me, bobbing around. It really is distracting."

The woman thought about – even went as far as lifting a hand to oblige – then said, "I'm afraid I can't. Cataracts."

"Look, can we forget about the old lady's optical affliction just for a minute," the businessman somewhat unceremoniously interjected. "She'll be telling us about her piles next, and we don't have time to…"

That was where he stopped. His eyes bulged from their sockets, threatening to drop out and roll along the platform. His mouth quivered as he fought to find the words that would not come. He lifted his hand

and pointed across the station. The punk and the old lady turned to see what had spooked the businessman so effectively.

Standing beside a single stanchion, the trio of spiderlike men gazed towards them. There was something in their eyes – those infinite whirlpools that had seen universes implode and civilizations fall – which suggested they weren't here to ask the time or discuss economic growth in the banking sector.

"This can't be good," the businessman said.

And it wasn't. A sudden torrent of wind whipped through the station; ancient dust and brown paper whorled up into the air creating a grotesque miasma. Rats squealed – where the hell did the rats come from? – as they were forced to join the ever-expanding tornado of debris. The triplets took a step forward, away from the stanchion holding up the Northern Line in its entirety. As they touched, they began to merge, a liquefied mess replacing what had only a moment before been limbs. Their heads distorted, melting into the singular, cyclopean ichor. It was, the old lady thought, really quite revolting.

"We're gonna die down here!" the punk screamed as he threw himself down onto the tracks. A rat slapped him in the face as it whizzed through the air to join its brethren. The tornado of rodents and century-old litter was now circling the expanding blackness. Occasionally, a rat wall fall out of orbit and dissolve amongst the mass. Such was life…

"What the hell *is* it?" the businessmen yelled, though it was barely audible over the tumultuous din of the cosmic anomaly.

The old lady didn't know. Why *would* she? Why would this fool even ask her opinion?

The viscous blob rushed suddenly forward, scooping up the punk from the tracks. As it washed over him, flesh peeled and burned. The thing was consuming him, but there was no way it was doing it raw. The punk's skin charred and bubbled for a moment, and then he was gone. As the floating ichor rose up into the station's atmosphere, the old lady glanced down to where the boy had been a moment ago. A carbonised outline of the punk was all that remained; his orange Mohawk hair floated up, luminous porcupine quills, and joined the tempest.

The lady staggered back, trying to distance herself from the approaching form. This was not how she had expected to die. A simple stroke would have been quite acceptable. At a push, she would have envisaged a nasty fall – perhaps when the gritters failed to suitably take care of the small avenue in which she lived, as was usually the case – resulting in a fractured hip, six weeks in hospital and a nasty bout of MRSA, which would certainly do the job.

Being swallowed by an inter-dimensional deity was something one could never seriously entertain, at least not in this particular part of London.

"It's getting *biggerrrrrrrrr*!" the businessman astutely pointed out as he forced himself back into the platform's central stanchion. The old lady was grateful he'd chosen that moment to speak, for the ichorous mass suddenly turned to him, forgetting, for the time being, she was present.

"Oh God, *no*!" the man screeched.

The darkness moved towards him; as it did, the businessman's suit tore from his body, leaving him standing against the bollard in nothing but a pair of Superman briefs. The Armani two-piece did three laps of the form before being sucked into the obsidian conflagration. The man appeared more shocked at losing his favoured suit than he was by the malevolent being.

Overhead, a train soared through its tunnel. Passengers going about their daily grind were blissfully unaware of the terror unfolding beneath them. The cowering lady wondered how often this occurred, how many innocent souls this aberrant demon had enveloped. Missing people reports that remained unsolved suddenly made sense; the cases involving city-dwellers failing to reach their destinations had been solved. You could close the book on hundreds of London citizens' mysterious disappearances. It was just a pity that nobody would ever know the truth.

The businessman screamed as the mass of swirling rodents began to pick flesh from his naked torso. Bits of him flapped loosely as they feasted. The blood floated from him the way it would from a suicidal astronaut – in one solid, crimson globule. His screams turned to gurgles; his gurgles turned to inaudible whimpers as his lips were chewed away. The rats were making a right old meal of him, and as the meaty chunks were stripped from him the tarry being sucked them in. The colossus had expanded exponentially. As the blood and flesh disappeared into it, it sighed and groaned as if in pleasure.

It was quite possibly the most disgusting thing the old lady had ever seen, and she had dined with the royal family…

As the thing swallowed the final morsels of businessman, his Superman briefs flew across the platform and landed in the old lady's lap. Disgusted, she hooked a trembling finger into the leg-hole and flipped them away, shuddering at the sticky texture.

The thing turned on her. It had no eyes, not to speak of, but she could feel its stare boring into her, delving into her thoughts and plucking from them the things that terrified her the most.

It paused. Rodents fell from its orbit and scurried down onto the tracks and into the dark tunnels. Their distended bellies prevented them from making a hasty exit, though they did their best with what they had to work with.

The old lady clambered to her feet. She was tired, sapped of energy and barely able to stand, but she knew she couldn't just sit there and let the thing engulf her the way it had the punk and the businessman.

More rats toppled from the rotating miasma as the darkness contemplated its next move.

The lady grinned. Her teeth were not as clean as they once had been, but they were still all her own. "You weren't expecting *me*, were you?" she asked. Despite feeling her age – which was closer to three-hundred than it was to two-fifty – she knew she had the upper-hand. The thing knew she had the upper-hand. The thing also knew that she knew she had the upper-hand, which was why more and more bloodthirsty rodents dropped from the air and scuttled off into the tunnels.

"You're an abomination," she said. "You should be damned ashamed of yourself, feeding off these innocents like this. It wasn't like this in my day. *Noooo.* We had to keep a low-profile, try not to piss of the…" she poked a skeletal finger upwards. "Things have changed around here, *that's* for sure. That Lovecraft fellow has a lot to bloody answer for."

The creature growled, though it was an uncertain noise, as if it was not quite sure how the rest of the day would pan out.

"That's *right*," she said, stepping tentatively towards the floating blackness. "You're one of his, aren't you? One of old HP's? I should have bleedin' well known it. Where are your tentacles? Huh? Don't tell me he forgot to give you tentacles? What, so he spent all that time and effort on Cthulhu and made you a giant ball of black? No wonder you're angry."

The Nyogtha snarled, for that was its name. Now that it considered it, Cthulhu had a ring to it. It rolled off the tongue…*Cthooo-looo.* Not like its own name. Nyogtha sounded like something you ate with cheese and pickles at Christmastime. It was ridiculous.

"So while he's out there, living it up on R'lyeh, you're in London feasting on these poor saps? I must say, seems a little unbalanced to me. Talk about favouritism."

The old lady was really starting to grate, but there was something about her that prevented it from attacking, something it'd seen inside her mind that told it, *'No, best not…'*

"Well, I'd like to say it's been a pleasure," she said, "but it hasn't, so if you could just put me back up there, you savage little git, and I'll forget we ever had this little meeting." She straightened her glasses, which had slightly skewed on the bridge of her nose.

The silence that followed was fairly uncomfortable; more distressing than watching a man stripped to his underpants get eaten by floating rats, she surmised.

She knew, in that moment, that the creature had made a decision. As the orbiting rats and dust gathered speed once again, she sighed. "But you read my mind," she said. "You *know* what I'm capable of."

The low thrum became a deafening groan once again. The time for talking was over. The Nyogtha meant business, and despite what it had seen inside her, what it had witnessed inside that fucked up head of hers, it was pretty sure that she was an old lady now, incapable of things she had once so easily managed.

"Fine," she said, whipping her glasses off to reveal two silvery orbs. The Nyogtha lunged across the platform towards her, leaking mice and rats – and somehow a possum – as it went. Passing the central stanchion, it was relatively confident of reaching the old bag in time. It hadn't counted on her preternatural speed.

Her hand was a blur as she unpeeled the silken scarf from her head. The Nyogtha managed another foot before freezing.

Snakes. Hundreds of coiling, writhing snakes sat atop her head where one would usually find a nice, tight beehive or a plaited bun.

There came a crackling sound as the black ichor began to solidify in mid-air. Even the rats turned to stone, and as they did they landed on the platform tiles, shattering into millions of rocky shards. It was a shame, for this Gorgon had a particular affiliation with animals that was rarely seen.

The floating ichor tried to outmanoeuvre the stone creeping up from its bottom. It spilled out over the top, like the remnants of toothpaste from a fast-emptying tube, only to find itself hardening along with the rest of it.

It groaned, moaned, hissed and said, "*Ftagn…*" before gravity finally won and it toppled over the side of the platform and onto the abandoned tracks. She expected it to break up, the way the rats had, and so was slightly disappointed when it rolled onto its side in one piece the way an elephant might snuggle in for a nap.

"Well, *that* wasn't part of my plan for today," she said as she covered her serpentine hair and tied the scarf securely. She pushed the mirrored shades onto the bridge of her nose and sighed.

"Well, something to tell the grandkids I suppose," she said as stepped down onto the solidified Nyogtha and then onto the tracks. Rats raced away into the darkness, either scared of her – which was understandable since she'd just made paperweights of their siblings – or willing her to follow.

"After you," she said, ducking under the bright yellow cordoning tape and stepping into the darkness of the eastbound tunnel. She hoped it wasn't too far to the exit. She wasn't as young as she used to be.

The Nucleus Note

The cloaked figure ambled along at a leisurely pace, kicking things along the ground and stopping occasionally to either take a rest or mutter something incoherent. He looked to be intoxicated, which the man watching him knew could not be true; alcohol, in all its forms, had run out years ago. No, the cloaked figure was simply injured, limping ever-so-slightly, and only appearing to be under the influence of a substance long gone.

The observer flicked a switch; the screen in front of him flickered momentarily before the cloaked figure was gone, replaced by two women. He edged closer to the screen to get a better look, and was surprised to discover that one of the women, the blonde one, was in fact a man in drag. He made a disgusted sound in his throat before settling back into his chair. What were they doing out there? Salvaging? There was nothing left, not since the world fizzled out over five years ago. People, for some strange reason, were actually trying to survive. But *why*? He couldn't understand it. For him, it was different. He was part of the in-crowd, one of the creators of The Nucleus Note. For him, life was a completely diverse affair to that of the vagabonds beyond the fence. He had luxuries, a life worth living. He smoked three Cuban cigars a day, ate food that didn't have maggots crawling through it, and washed it down with vintage wines from around the world. He was one of the fortunate ones, the ones who had decided, when the outbreak began, that containment was not an option.

The damage was done, even if the uninfected people weren't aware of it. So he, Julian Graves (a nom de plume, not that anybody *cared*) and eight others, scientists and academics just like him, had decided to put their project to the test.

Needless to say, it worked. It worked very well, indeed.

The Nucleus Note was designed as a neat and effective way to euthanize the infected. An inaudible note, somewhere up in the frequency of thirty-thousand hertz, it renders everyone in its vicinity dead within a few seconds of hearing it. The problem was, it could not be trained to only kill the infected, those unfortunate victims of the pandemic commonly known as François *Flu*, named after the first person to have contracted it. No matter what, the only way to prevent the virus's spread, to keep those fortunate enough to know about the Nucleus Note safe, was to utilise it – to great effect – on the populace. Entire cities were wiped out in moments as the note was played over loudspeakers and Tannoy systems. Bodies had fallen in the street, infected or otherwise, and most of them remained in the same place now, for the clean-up operation was so vast that it would take years to accomplish thoroughly.

'Anything out there?' a voice asked. Julian started, not expecting anyone to be awake at this time of night. He was, however, relieved to discover the voice belonged to Doctor Evelyn Waugh. She looked tired, as if she had been asleep but was now struggling to return to it.

'Just a few stragglers,' Julian said, jabbing a finger towards the black-and-white flickering monitor sitting on the desk in front of him. 'I don't know why I bother watching them, anymore,' he continued. 'They all look lost, and there's nothing we can do for them.' And why would they even bother? They, the people within the compound, were the safest humans on the planet. If the virus was still out there – and Julian was pretty sure it *was*; the majority of the people staggering onto his monitor in the preceding weeks seemed to be afflicted with *something* – then it was eventually going to get to the remaining civilians. Ten years, twenty, fucking *fifty*, one day they would be rid of it, and then they – or their children if the latter time-scale applied – would reclaim the earth. In the meantime, they must continue doing what they had been doing all these years.

Making sure.

'Why don't you just press the button and go to bed?' Evelyn said. Julian wished, though it was never going to happen, she had instead used the term "*come* to bed," but she didn't, and Julian sighed.

The button she referred to was the tiny, red toggle next to the monitor. It was the same switch he depressed every night, and a few times during the day, should the monitors become a flurry of activity.

'You think we're ever going to be able to forgive ourselves for what we do here?' Julian asked, though he didn't know where it came from, and immediately regretted it the moment it passed his lips. Evelyn thought silently, contemplating her riposte. He considered telling her to forget it, that he was just being silly and sentimental, that fatigue had simply crept up on him and now not only was he feeling the effects, he was speaking them, too.

'No,' she said, just as blunt as that, and Julian knew that she was right, that he had merely sought to confirm his own suspicions. And now that he knew she was in agreement with him, he didn't feel so bad about it.

'Why don't you go and try to get your head down?' he said, forcing a smile. 'I'll be going to bed in a little while myself, I promise.'

She patted him gently, yet without affection, on his shoulder before turning and disappearing through the door. Julian couldn't help staring at her ass as she ambled slowly out of the room; something else he would never experience.

He turned back to the monitor, the grainy greyscale images of desolation that he was required to watch in twelve-hour increments. The two women were riffling through an industrial bin, the kind that restaurants and bars use for empty bottles and dismantled cardboard boxes. One of them found something to eat, and they began to fight over it. Julian used the dial on the monitor to zoom, and was unsurprised, yet still sickened, to find they were brawling over a dead rat. One of the women had the head in her mouth; the other was pulling on the tail, to no avail, and slapping the woman upside the head with her free hand in a frantic attempt to release the rotting rodent from the other woman's jaws.

Julian had seen enough for one night. Evelyn was right; he should be in bed, for tomorrow he had to do this all over again.

He pressed the red toggle next to the monitor, and turned to the screen.

The women, who were so animated just a second ago, were now frozen solid. The half-devoured rat hung listlessly from the jaws of the one lucky enough to have had a final supper; its tail swung deliberately in the night breeze, a sign that *rigor mortis* was either yet to attack or had already passed.

And then her nose began to bleed. Julian wasn't offered the scene in all its chromatic glory, but when you had seen it happen as many times as he had, the blood being pitch black didn't detract from its intensity.

And then, as quickly as it had started, it was all over. The two women fell forward, bouncing off each other – almost in a final embrace – before landing in a heap beside the industrial bin at the edge of the street. The dead rat fell from the first woman's lips and lay motionless, and headless, between them.

Julian leant in and flicked the monitor to make sure everything had gone as...yeah, there he was, the cloaked man who had been limping along as if inebriated, only now he wasn't limping anywhere. He had died on his feet, taking a piss against a six-foot aluminium railed fence. Somehow his wrist had caught up in the rails and he was wedged, prevented from dropping to the ground, where he would have remained until the clean-up crew got around to shifting him. They would have to disentangle him from his aluminium restraint. Until they did, he was going nowhere.

So that was how The Nucleus Note worked; it really *was* that easy. The compound where Julian and the others resided was soundproofed, impossible to penetrate. If there *was* such a thing as a higher-frequency note than that of the Nucleus – and there *wasn't* – then it would still be unable to affect the people within the perimeters of the compound. A great deal of time, work, and money – despite being useless – had been used in ensuring the safety of every man and woman on the inside. They were the only true survivors of François Flu. Sure, the few stragglers shambling aimlessly around on the outside were immune, otherwise they would have succumbed to the virus's effects years ago, but they were just as dead as those who contracted it initially.

They just didn't know it yet.

Julian pressed the switch on the monitor and it flickered a few times before blinking off. He yawned, stretched, and headed for bed, hoping that Dr. Evelyn Waugh, in a strange turn of events, was waiting for him beneath his sheets.

*

Julian had been asleep for an indeterminable amount of time, but he knew that it wasn't long because he couldn't recall suffering any nightmares – as was his wont – and the pillow beneath his head was still dry. He lay motionless in the semi-darkness; something had woken him, it must have.

After almost a minute of listening in silence, he noticed that he had ceased breathing. He slowly allowed air back into his lungs, being careful not to make a sound. Not only did he believe that something had brought him out of his unconsciousness, he sensed eyes upon him, eyes that, despite the almost impossible darkness in the room, could see him just fine.

And then something grasped onto his wrist, and he was being yanked from the covers. Another hand – sweaty, *salty* – slapped down over his mouth so hard that a tooth cracked. What would have been screams for help turned into nothing but incoherent mumbles. This hand, however, belonged to another, which meant that he had at least two attackers.

A voice, deep and guttural, said, 'Be careful with him,' and Julian wanted to thank the possessor of kind words, although he knew that ultimately his days were numbered.

What was happening? Who were these people? They had

to be insiders, people that he had lived amongst for the preceding ten years...

They dragged him across the room, still in the cloak of darkness, and began to bind his wrists and ankles together, being ever-so-silent as they ripped through the tape. He knew, in that moment, that there were at least four men in the room. Two were holding him down while another made sure he couldn't move for shit. A fourth man spoke from the edge of the room, and it was the possessor of the kind words, the man who had urged caution in man-handling him from his bed.

'Make sure he can't warn the others,' he said. 'We've come too far to fuck this up, now.'

It wasn't the way in which the man spoke that frightened Julian; it was his words. They confirmed that this whole operation – for that was what it was – had been premeditated, planned to within an inch of its life. That was what made Julian Graves (not his real name, of course) sit up and take notice while his bowels relaxed beneath him.

Suddenly, a radio crackled; a voice said, '*We're in position. Everything okay your side?*'

'Everything's smooth,' the voice across the room replied. 'Just make sure that nobody gets hurt. He wants to set an example here, *remember*?'

'*They're all cooperating like we said they would*,' the

crackling radio-voice said; there was the tiniest of sniggers following his statement, a sign that these people – *whoever* the fuck they were – seemed to be enjoying themselves.

One man who wasn't enjoying any of it, Julian, could hardly breathe through the twisted tape jammed between his trembling lips. He blinked tears and sweat from his stinging eyes, and all the time thought of Dr. Evelyn Waugh and her almost-perfect derrière. Quite *why* he pictured her, walking away from him, leaving him sitting at the monitor as she ambled off to bed, was beyond him, but it took the edge off an otherwise unbearable situation. He knew that things were about to go tits-up, not that they hadn't already, and if this was to be his final night on a godless earth, then he was going to go out with some semblance of a smile painted on his face.

'Right,' the voice said, determined and somewhat eager. 'Take him to join the others. If he gives you any shit, you have my permission to knock him out.'

As they hoisted Julian up from his cowering position, the last thing on his mind was to give these maniacs any shit.

*

Sixty-eight people, all in night-gowns or whatever

garb they had been wearing when they had retired for the night, were placed in the centre of the main hall. A few of the women – especially the younger ones; the elder women knew that it was fruitless – were trying to scream through their gags.

They didn't have to scream, though. Their eyes, wide orbs that suggested sheer terror and confusion, said it all.

Julian was led into the room, and as soon as he saw the ensuing chaos – people being clouted across the back of the head by masked men dressed all in black; children also gagged and bound as if to prove there was no prejudice in what this group were trying to achieve – he knew that things had nosedived drastically.

The men dressed uniformly in black were armed, though not with guns. Each of them carried a blade of some description. A machete here, a Bowie-knife there; blades that glimmered beneath the incandescent lighting, shimmering with each movement of its employer. Julian was mesmerised, and yet as he was forced through the hall, between scampering children and hysterical adults, he searched for the one person who could possibly make this transition into death passable.

'All of you need to calm the fuck *down*,' the man, possessor of kind words, bellowed at the top of his lungs. 'This will all be over shortly, and we will be gone just as quickly as we arrived.'

Was that supposed to be comforting? It meant nothing to the people gathered on the cold, hard floor of the main hall. Julian, especially, was aware of its connotations. They said they would be *gone*, but that didn't mean anyone would be left alive when they were.

People, seemingly sensing that there was no point in struggling further, began to fall silent, and when they were suitably hushed, the balaclava-wearing speaker at the edge of the room gestured towards the door.

Now, there were two men at the doors, and each of them grabbed their respective handles and pulled inwards. Julian, still struggling to breathe through the gag which was starting to cut away at his top lip, thought this was a little over-the-top. He half-expected the President to walk in, or at *least* the Queen of England. When a little man, the only one of the group sans-balaclava, strode into the main hall – flanked by a further two uniformed men – he felt somewhat cheated.

The man paced confidently into the centre of the room, stepping over cowering people as if they were minor inconveniences. His two guards remained with him until he waved them away, to which they duly obeyed.

Julian couldn't help but stare at the strange, little man. He didn't look like a mercenary, or anything of that ilk. He would have been more suited, perhaps, to office-work, or telling at the local bank. There wasn't an ounce of muscle on him; and why would he need it? *His* muscle was scattered haphazardly around the room.

'I'll bet you all have a thousand questions you want to ask right now,' he said, surveying the miserable room. 'Which is why I'm going to give one of you the chance to speak. Since you're hardly in the position to nominate your spokesperson, I'd like one of you – *anyone*, for what it's worth – to raise your hand slowly. One of my men will come to you and remove your gag. Is that clear?'

There were mumbles and hisses, though Julian didn't think anyone would put themselves forward for such an act. Which was why, for some reason, his hand slowly edged into the air as he leaned back on his haunches. At first, the little guy in charge didn't see him, but the guard behind Julian coughed to grab his attention.

The man turned to Julian, nodded to the guard stood behind, who proceeded to remove Julian's gag, albeit forcefully.

'I would like to take this opportunity to tell you,'

the man in charge continued, 'that should you scream, or become unruly, one of my men will be ordered to decapitate you where you kneel. Is that understood?'

Julian nodded. As the gag was yanked from his mouth, he spat blood onto the floor in front of him. He glanced around the room, dry-swallowing, and noticed that all eyes had fallen upon him. He was their only hope now, and yet he knew that no matter what came to pass in the next few minutes, it would make very little difference to their chances of survival. In truth, he wasn't sure why he had volunteered to speak in the first place; he was just as – if not *more* – frightened than the rest of the room.

'You may ask,' the man sneered, gesturing in a manner that caused the blood to boil inside Julian, who was completely helpless and yet speculating just how quickly he could rush the barbaric little scrote and tear his fucking throat out with just his teeth.

Julian asked the first question that came to mind: 'Who *are* you, and what do you want?' He could taste the blood on his tongue; that metallic bitterness which is neither offensive nor tolerable.

The man sighed, closed his eyes as if in deep thought. He started to speak with exaggerated clarity, almost patronizingly. 'We are *people*, just like you. I don't suppose you recall what it's like to be an equal. While you were all holed up in safety, we had to fight.

None of us became infected; that piddly fucking virus was nothing to some of us, and yet we were executed just the same as if we carried it.' A pause as the man kicked the nearest person – which just happened to be an elderly gent by the name of George Simms – in the side of the head. The rest of the room gasped in horror; women and children began to sob once again. 'You have no idea what it was like out there. I watched most of my family fall ill, suffer as the flu took them, and then die. But the ones who didn't die, my brother, my uncle, my niece, they were taken by your infernal Nucleus Note.'

For the first time since the man began to speak, Julian became aware of something cold and sharp at the nape of his neck. The guard was holding his blade to Julian; and now he *was* terrified.

'You took it upon yourselves to finish off what the François Flu started, all the time cowering between these very walls like the cockroaches that you are. There is a place in Hell for you and yours,' the man said as he lit a rudimentary hand-rolled cigarette. 'For all of us, ultimately. We're the people who you've been killing, picking off with your silent poison. How does it feel to be helpless, to know that nobody will help you, to know that people want you *dead*?'

Julian could tell him exactly how it felt; it felt like *shit*, but he managed to hold it down long enough to ask his next question. 'How did you get *in* here?' There came an audible revolt from the cowering hostages, who couldn't quite figure out why Julian Graves was being so tenacious. The difference between them and him was, *they* could still envision a way out of this; *he* knew it was all over. The tone of his questioning might hasten the execution, but that was all. The one thing he was certain of was that there *was* going to be an execution tonight. These people, the women and children and men with whom he had shared quarters with all these years, would hopefully come to realise it while they still had a chance to pray.

'We've had a lot of time to plan,' the man said, crouching beside a squirming woman, who recoiled as his warm breath danced across her face. He stroked her cheek, and Julian suddenly realised that the man – that evil *bastard* – was not just taunting any woman with his touch; he was stroking the face of Evelyn Waugh. 'Trust me, out there on the street, with all those maniacs running round losing their marbles, you find a few good men, people that still have a bit about them. It's survival instinct. Pick the biggest man in the room and stand behind him until the trouble's passed.'

Julian wanted to scream at the man; how dare he touch Dr. Evelyn Waugh. She was cringing, wincing every time the man's fingers brushed her skin. Julian swallowed the blood in his mouth and was about to lunge to his feet when the prick stood up and began to move away from her.

Close.

Too close, but now he knew where Evelyn was in the room. It offered him something wonderful to focus on as the horrors played out.

'You once had a man here named Dugan,' the little man continued, scratching at his partially-formed beard. 'I believe he abandoned you when you executed three children in the middle of the city with your stupid Nucleus Note.'

Jasper didn't need to reply. This man had clearly had dealings with Marcus Dugan, which would explain how they had managed to penetrate the complex so easily. It had never crossed anyone's mind to alter the codes after Dugan went AWOL; a mistake that had now cost them dearly.

'Word of advice, not that it's of any use to you now,' the man said, a hint of a smile curling the corner of his lips. 'Never annoy your allies. So many wars have been lost that way. When Dugan gave me the codes, I had him martyred. That man handed you to us on a plate, and for that he was commended. A few of us even went back for seconds, such was the taste of his bravery and lack of honour.'

They ate him, Julian thought. *They fucking ate Dugan!*

'Which brings us here, to you, tonight, and what better way to finish off what has already been an amazing evening by personally thanking each and every one of you for your inexorable hard work in decreasing the population, infected or otherwise?'

'You're going to kill us,' Julian said. 'Wouldn't that make you just as bad as us? How does that work in your tiny little mind?' From the ground across the hall, Evelyn gave him a cursory glance, a warning of sorts.

'*We're* not going to kill you,' the man said, gesturing to the guards nearest the door. They saluted and left. 'You did that a long time ago, when you started playing God and annihilating innocents out there on the street.'

There was a clunk at the door, and the guards reappeared. They were wheeling something – a trolley, a *gurney*? - and people began to clamber out of the way as it was pushed through the room to where the unmasked man stood, grinning maniacally to himself. There was a white sheet across the trolley, which prevented the room from seeing what it actually was, and when the man grasped the cover and yanked it back, women screamed once again, men began to sob wholeheartedly as the realisation finally hit home.

Sitting atop the trolley was one giant speaker – an

amplifier that could have previously been used for some now-defunct heavy-metal band's guitars – and Julian smiled ever-so-slightly as he came to the same conclusion as the rest of the room.

The man began to flick switches on the speaker, whistling a tuneful little ditty as he went. 'We came to terms with our demise a long time ago,' he broke off long enough to say. 'Humans aren't *meant* to survive out there, not any longer. Our days have gone; we were bettered by a virus billions of times smaller than us. You should have realised that and accepted it, instead of hiding in here and delaying the inevitable. Lots of innocent people died from *François*, but not nearly as many as those killed by your unholy creation. Today, for us, is all about making sure that we take the responsible party with us. And on that note...pardon the pun...I bid you all adieu...'

He flicked the switch.

Julian glanced across to Evelyn, but she was looking somewhere else. He could see people falling all around the room in his peripheral vision. The unmasked man was the last to go, hitting the ground with such force that Julian was certain he saw the man's head explode.

He looked up to the huge, silent speaker, to the trolley rattling beneath it.

And then there was nothing.

The Incongruous Mr Marwick

He was out again, digging up his front garden with his gnarled, rheumy claws. Samuel had watched the mad old coot do this before; there was something deeply inhuman about the way he hooked his fingers into the ground, as if he believed himself to be an animal. Samuel watched, not with fear and apprehension like the rest of the kids in the street, but because Marwick intrigued him. Whilst his friends taunted the geriatric oddball, Samuel observed, a casual outsider trying to ascertain just what had propagated the man's absurd behaviour.

Samuel's father, a respected physician, believed Marwick was mostly harmless. Sure, he didn't respond well to having shit pushed through his letterbox or graffiti-tags on his front door, but who *did*?

The cases in question were both, unfortunately,

perpetrated by Samuel's friend, Kevin Jacobson. Kevin was the kind of kid who lacked boundaries. If an offer of cash-money was made in return for Kevin lopping off one of his own fingers, he would walk away with the money and a bleeding digit, without a doubt. Most of the trouble in the neighbourhood was down to Kevin, and more than half the japes inflicted upon Marwick were either by his own hand or a brainchild of his that he'd managed to offload on another impressionable fool.

The shit through the letterbox had been a mistake; Samuel had wanted no part in the caper, and had stood across the street, raptly spying. Deep down, he had been as involved as Kevin; prevention would have been the only thing to eliminate him from blame, and from across the street – where it was safe and he could get a good head-start if required – he had done nothing of the sort.

Kevin had crept along the front of the house like Fantômas. The only thing missing was a mask and a bag labelled *swag*. Samuel had wanted to call out, to tell his friend to abort the mission, that he had a very bad feeling about it.

But it had been too late. Kevin delivered the package – an amalgamation of Mrs Beetham's tabby and Roger Bernstein's Jack Russell – and quickly traversed the driveway, too scared to check across his shoulder, too excited to enjoy the moment.

If he *had* looked, he would have seen Mr Marwick fast approaching. Samuel had watched the old guy practically sprint from his house, swinging the bag of shit in that liveried right claw of his. He was completely naked – apart from a flat-cap which perched precariously on top of his balding pate – and he'd screamed in a manner usually utilised by the final girl in horror movies.

He'd chased them all the way to Birch Street before giving up the ghost and limping, breathlessly, back to his house. Kevin had found it hilarious; Samuel had felt nothing but utter shame.

'Is he pretending to be a dog again?' a voice asked. Samuel didn't need to turn to know that Kevin was there. 'Makes you *sick*, don't it? They allow nutters like that to roam free. Look at him, he's eating the dirt, now, *eurgh*, that's gross!'

Samuel couldn't avert his eyes. It was like watching a car-crash in slow-motion. He knew it was wrong, but there was something grotesquely fascinating about it. Marwick loaded fistfuls of mud and grass into his mouth, chewing momentarily before letting it all fall out again.

'I heard he tried to eat a pigeon last week,' Kevin said as he placed a friendly hand on Samuel's shoulder. Samuel, for some reason, found his touch overwhelmingly offensive and stepped aside. Kevin continued. 'Managed to catch it in one of them traps he has set out in his back garden. Lindsey Baker's garden backs right onto his, and she saw him pulling its feathers out. Toying with it, she reckons.'

Samuel shook his head. 'Lindsey Baker's house doesn't back onto his garden, Kevin. She's two doors down; there's no way she can see over his fences.'

'Why do you always have to stick up for him?' Kevin asked. 'What is he? Your *granddad*?' He laughed; Samuel could see bits of breakfast still stuck to his teeth which made him feel quite queasy.

'Why do you always have to *pick* on him?' Samuel said, knowing very well that it was because Kevin liked to think he was the cock of the neighbourhood, the funny one from down the street who always got the girls and never got caught. Truth be told, Samuel suspected Kevin would find himself in a prison-cell before he turned twenty. His crimes were small now, but the time would come when shit through a letterbox would not be enough. When that happened it would be a car through an off-license window, or a knife through an old lady. Samuel knew one thing was for sure.

He didn't want to be there when Kevin made the transition.

'He's an *idiot*,' Kevin retorted. 'Look at him. Thinks

he's a fucking cow, or something.'

Samuel finally managed to overcome the strange compulsion to watch and turned away. 'He's misunderstood,' he said. 'How would you feel if that was one of your grandparents? Would you throw rocks and spit *then*, huh?' Samuel already knew the answer. If it wasn't Marwick, if it was instead one of Kevin's own, Kevin would treat them just the same. Maybe worse. With kin you could get away with a hell of a lot more.

'He'd be in a home,' Kevin shrugged, as if it was the simplest answer imaginable. 'Somewhere he wouldn't be able to attack some poor fucker. The man's a hazard to society; anyone who eats their own front garden is.'

As far as Samuel was aware, Marwick had never attacked anyone. There had been rumours of indecent exposure, but nothing violent. And Samuel, who tried to see the good in everyone, put the self-exhibition down to the fact that the guy didn't know what day it was; it was highly likely that he didn't know whether he had pants on, or not, half the time.

'Anyway,' Kevin continued. 'Wait until you see what I've got in store for him tomorrow. He won't know what's hit him.' He burst into a fit of laughter that was more frightening than anything old man Marwick had ever done.

Across the street, Marwick snapped his head towards them. Soil and worms dangled listlessly from his puckered lips. Had he heard Kevin's threat, or was he simply reacting to the uncontrollable laughter that followed?

'Leave him alone,' Samuel whispered. He tried to look aloof, but it was difficult knowing Marwick's piercing blue eyes were watching him.

'Don't be such a pussy, Sam,' Kevin said, patting his friend on the back. Once again, Samuel shrugged him off. 'Anyway, you don't have to do anything. Just sit back and watch the fireworks. It'll be hilarious, dude.'

Samuel was about to appeal one last time when Kevin turned his back and began to walk away. Marwick, across the street, scrambled to his feet, kicking up mud and dirt, and for a split second Samuel thought he was going to chase Kevin. He didn't. He made a strange mewling sound before rushing for his front door. Kevin was cruelly laughing and pointing as Marwick slammed the front door shut. The dead wreath that hung just above his letterbox swung to and fro, threatening to fall but never quite attaining enough momentum.

Just then it started to rain. Samuel took it as an omen and made for his own house.

Wait until you see what I've got in store for him tomorrow.

Those words repeated over and over in Samuel's mind; a stuck record that turned his blood to mercury. He hoped Kevin was exaggerating, but if he knew Kevin – he *did*, and it wasn't something he was proud of any longer – he had something epically boorish up his sleeve. Samuel didn't want anything bad to happen to the old guy, but he knew there was very little he could *do* about it.

'I could tell Dad,' he mumbled to himself as he lunged through his front door and out of the rain.

He didn't notice Marwick's curtains twitching across the street, nor the dirty grinning lips beyond.

*

At dinner that evening, Samuel – somewhat laboriously – informed his father of Kevin's plot to deride Marwick the following day. Since he had no proof and wasn't sure exactly what his friend intended to do, his father responded in pretty much the manner Samuel had anticipated.

'Just don't get involved, Sam.'

That was it. There would be no heroic intervention, no phone-call to Kevin's parents to report the news of their son's perverse scheme. Sam had been warned to keep his distance, as if that would somehow make it all okay.

'Dad, I don't know what he's gonna do, but I'm worried for the old guy. Kevin can be—'

'A pain in the ass,' Samuel's father interjected. The way in which he slammed his mug down on the kitchen table suggested he was drawing a line under the conversation.

Samuel knew he was wasting his time. Marwick was going to be made a mockery of, whether he liked it or not. Standing up to Kevin wouldn't stop him. He was unyielding, the kind of kid who did what they liked whenever they felt like it. In fact, attempting to counteract would be the equivalent of friendship suicide.

No, there had to be something. Some way to keep the old guy safe without Kevin realising he had a part in it.

Samuel went to bed that night with a heavy head and a hollow heart. Sleep, or anything like it, was not forthcoming.

*

Marwick spent the morning standing in front of his own door, knocking as if there might be someone there to eventually welcome him. The door was ajar, and occasionally he would peer around it to check before quickly pulling out and proceeding to knock.

Samuel kept his distance, slowly rolling the skateboard along on the opposite side of the street. If Marwick knew he was there, he didn't show it.

It was a bright morning; people walked around with permanent squints. The usual plethora of dog-walkers marched up and down the street allowing their hounds to shit for all and sundry to tread in. Newspaper delivery-boys went about their rounds, their earphones pumping tinny garbage into their heads. Across the way, Mrs Beetham and Miss Schofield palavered over their separating fence. Samuel couldn't quite hear the conversation, but several choice words drifted across, enough for him to know they were discussing the terrible paedophile-ring that had dominated the previous week's news. They did that a lot; prattled on and on about things that were of no concern to them. Their lives were so sad and pathetic that all they had left to talk about were asinine stories plucked from whatever shitty tabloid they had the misfortune of subscribing to.

And Marwick, the poor, misunderstood man from number thirty-four, was considered the odd one.

Samuel reached the end of the street and flipped his board up, catching it adroitly in his right hand. As he began to walk back towards his house, he saw that Marwick was no longer banging at his front-door. He'd moved along the front of the house and was now peering through a window, shielding his eyes from the impossible morning sun. As Samuel approached, he could hear the old guy laughing.

Samuel often wondered what went through Marwick's mind. Did he see the world as everyone else did? Was he capable of seeing things others weren't? There was no way to know, or ever find out. Marwick was an enigma, a perplexing anomaly that no amount of psychiatric help or care would ever fathom.

His laughing grew louder, and Samuel felt a chill run the course of his spine, despite the blazing sun. He watched as Marwick did a little dance – a Leprechaun's jig – in front of his window. For a man of his years, he could certainly move; he was jaunty and lithe, as if he hadn't a care in the world, and Samuel wanted to scream across at him to be careful, to watch out for Kevin Jacobson who would be paying a visit later with his bag of tricks.

He couldn't speak. He hurried along the path, clutching his skateboard to his chest, trying to ignore the dancing eccentric in his periphery.

Wait until you see what I've got in store for him tomorrow, Kevin's voice said in his head, but it was no longer *tomorrow*. It was *today*, and Marwick was blissfully unaware that his day was about to take a turn for the worse.

That afternoon, Samuel made a point of calling for Kevin. The chances of stopping him were zero if he didn't at least know what he had planned. Kevin nonchalantly answered the door in his pyjamas; he looked like he'd just clambered from his pit.

'Hey,' Samuel said. 'What are you doing in there? Have you seen the weather?' It was a valid question but – as much as it sounded like one – not an invite. Samuel didn't want to spend his day around Kevin, and not just because his father warned him against it.

'Late night,' Kevin replied. 'Mom and Dad were arguing all night. I think my dad's been screwing his secretary again.'

Samuel snorted, then suppressed it as he realised Kevin wasn't joking. 'Shit, man, that sucks.'

'Not for my dad,' Kevin yawned. 'His secretary's stunning.'

Now Samuel did laugh, and despite Kevin's apparent fatigue, so did he. Somewhere in the house, a vacuum-cleaner whirred into life. Kevin rolled his eyes and stepped out onto the street, pulling the door to silence the incessant drone of his mother's frantic cleaning.

'She always does this after an argument,' Kevin sighed. 'I don't know whether she thinks the dirty words they call each other leaves a stain, or what. Dad's gone to work in a huff, and I'm left with old misery while she tears the place apart with a feather duster and a hoover.'

'So, you've got no plans, then?' Samuel asked. He honestly hoped that Kevin had forgotten his threat from the previous day, or that the sleepless night had taken the wind out of him. Marwick might have nothing to worry about, after all.

'Nah,' Kevin said, yawning once again. 'Video-games and low-budget horror.'

Samuel sighed; this was the best possible result.

And then Kevin said, 'Got to get my rest before tonight's main event.' His mouth contorted into a wide grin, like something you might see carved on a pumpkin. Samuel's heart dropped down into his guts; Kevin hadn't forgotten at all. He was conserving his energy for whatever twisted trick he had in store. He had probably been up all night finalising things, making sure that everything went off without a hitch. If anything, his parents arguing and keeping him awake had given him more time to get things right.

Samuel had never felt so utterly helpless in his life.

'Eight tonight,' Kevin said, rubbing his hands enthusiastically together. 'Sean and Trucker are gonna be there.' He said it as if it would somehow make the whole nightmare more appealing. Sean Rogers was an idiot, and Tommy "Trucker" Dale liked nothing more than seeing Marwick suffer, although he never got his own hands dirty.

And why would he need to when Kevin was more than happy to step up to the plate?

'You *are* going to be there, aren't you?' Kevin asked. It had never crossed his mind that Samuel would rather be somewhere – *anywhere* – else. 'Please don't tell me you're thinking of hiding in your fucking bedroom when the fun starts. *Shit*, Sam, it's gonna be hilarious. The old fart's finally gonna realise that his crazy-ass behaviour has consequences.'

He won't realise *anything*, Samuel thought. The man was vacant and so far mentally detached that it was impossible to determine just how he might react, or what he might do.

Samuel grimaced. 'I'll be there, but don't expect me to do anything. And please, Kevin, don't do anything to hurt him. He might be freaky, but he's still a person.'

'Yeah, yeah, whatever,' Kevin said as he pulled his front-door open and stepped inside. The sound of the vacuum-cleaner was gone, replaced by some shitty radio-station; Samuel could hear the rowdy voice of an overzealous sportscaster. 'It's just a bit of *fun*, Sam. Crazy old fucker ain't gonna have a coronary.'

Samuel was about to disagree when the door closed and he was left staring into frosted glass.

He had done what he could. It wasn't, by any

means, enough.

*

Samuel and Sean watched from the bushes across the street. Trucker had somehow managed to drag his fat ass up the tree outside Mrs Beetham's house. Sean held a crackling walkie-talkie in one hand; Trucker had the other. They were arguing back and forth over who would win in a fight, zombies or vampires. Samuel couldn't care less because neither were real. Mr Marwick was real, and something terrible was about to happen to him. *That* was all Samuel could think about.

Samuel had a walkie-talkie, too. His was on the same frequency as Kevin's, who was busying himself with something in Marwick's back-garden.

No doubt putting the final touches to his master-plan.

'What do *you* think, Sam?' Sean asked, snapping Samuel from his reverie.

'About what?' Samuel spat. He was not in the mood for bantering with idiots.

'A vampire could rip a zombies throat out, *right*?'

'Have you heard yourself?' Samuel said. 'It doesn't fucking *matter*. It doesn't matter who's hairiest, Bigfoot or Chewbacca. It doesn't matter if you think

Star Trek's better than Star Wars. Sean, just tell Trucker to pipe down, will you, and stop arguing over stupid things, for fuck's sake!'

Sean released the button on his walkie-talkie; the annoying hiss, Samuel thought, was nowhere near as annoying as the two boys bullshitting each other. After a moments of contemplation, Sean pushed the button in and said, 'Trucker, be quiet now. Kevin's gonna do his stuff and Samuel's on the verge of crying over here.'

Samuel shot him a reproachful glance. In the tree along the street, Trucker waved acknowledgement before turning his attention to Marwick's house.

Ten more minutes passed; the streetlights began to flicker into life. Samuel thought about radioing through to Kevin. It had been a long time since they'd last heard from him. *Too* long. But Samuel had visions of his friend stealthily approaching the house, the walkie-talkie suddenly crackling into life. They emitted a stifled hiss, but it would be enough to alert Marwick to the interloper.

Wasn't that what he *wanted*? To foil Kevin's plot? It would certainly put an abrupt end to the night's entertainment as Marwick would emerge and chase him off, an unleashed dog with the scent of bacon beneath its nose.

'Fuck it,' Samuel muttered. He pushed the button

on the side of his walkie-talkie, and before Sean could stop him he began to speak. 'Kevin, what's taking so long?'

Click. *Hisssssss.*

'What the hell are you *doing*, man?' Sean gasped. A look of utter disbelief had washed over him. 'You're gonna drop him right in the—'

Samuel shushed him and they both glanced down at the crackling transceiver. Kevin would not be happy with the interruption; they waited for the inevitable barrage of abuse to begin.

It didn't.

Samuel and Sean stared into each other's fearful eyes, jaws slack and drooping as if dislocated. Sean was about to suggest going in after their friend when the hissing from the walkie-talkie ceased. Samuel heaved a sigh of relief; Sean patted him hard on the back.

The silence, however, was not broken by Kevin's angry voice. A shrill laughter pierced the night, a cackling that Samuel was all too familiar with.

Marwick.

Samuel dropped the walkie-talkie just as the fireworks began to light up the pitch-black sky. Both he and Sean rolled away from the bush, terrified by the sudden noise, mesmerised by the explosions overhead.

So that was what Kevin had been planning. He'd set up an entire display of fireworks in the old guy's backyard. He was probably out there now, trying to get them all lit before he was chased away by the deranged resident. Across the street, Trucker fell out of Mrs Beetham's tree and landed with a thump on the pavement beneath. As he clambered to his feet he began to whoop and dance at the sight of the spectacle. Rockets and silver spinners, crackling starbursts and brocade plumes filled the night-sky; the resulting cacophony was enough to bring people out of their houses, no doubt fearing a terrorist-attack or something of that ilk.

Samuel and Sean staggered to their feet and waited for Kevin to come rushing from Marwick's backyard. They were amazed when the front door to Marwick's house flew open and Kevin ran, full-pelt, towards the street. He was completely naked, and appeared to be bleeding from his neck. Rivulets of crimson ran down his bare chest. He was howling, or screaming, or both, but the noise of the fireworks rendered him inaudible to anyone farther away than his bewildered friends.

Samuel staggered backwards, pulling Sean with him. He'd realised something, he'd seen the silver pubic hairs in the glow of erupting fireworks.

It wasn't Kevin.

Marwick stopped still in the road, illuminated in

reds and yellows and greens, and as he tore Kevin's face from his own to reveal the sickening grin beneath, Samuel could have sworn his heart stopped completely.

Kevin had been right all along. The guy was a maniac, a savage, a murderous old crone who'd had plans of his own.

The fireworks continued to explode, and Marwick continued to dance, swinging his antagoniser's face around and around until the police arrived twenty minutes later.

The Unseen

The Priestess lay the fetish amongst the ashes; a small wooden carving of a crocodile. The flames lapped around its legs, singeing the wood wherever they touched. She continued to chant, working up to a feverish crescendo. The heat was almost unbearable, and she found herself wiping sweat from her brow on several occasions during the ritual. The stench of burning wood and the Priestess's body odour would have made her gag if she were, in fact, wholly *compos mentis*. Fortunately – for her – she was a few slices short of a full loaf, and therefore unaware of any intolerable stench.

After what seemed like an incredibly intense orgasm, the Priestess threw her hands up in the air, almost slicing her eyebrows off with what you might call treacherously neglected fingernails. The crocodile fetish continued to burn beneath her; all that remained was its head, and even that was black and smouldering.

"Wees onsigbare!" the Priestess screeched. "Dood te maak hulle aslmal!"

The fire hissed; the ashes blew across the room as if somebody had sneezed on them. It was, for want of a better description, messy as hell. The Priestess looked as if she'd been rolled in flour.

As the final hunk of wood burnt to cinders, an ominous howl filled the hut. The Priestess apologised to no-one in particular and scratched her ass. Then, as the last of the ashes whirled up into the atmosphere, coating the Priestess, choking her, she toppled backwards and landed on the ground with a meaty thump.

That was the thing with Voudou. Occasionally it worked, but ninety-nine percent of the time you just gave yourself a coronary.

In this instance, though, the Priestess had done everything right. A hundred miles away, in the Democratic Republic of Congo, a dwarf crocodile blinked out of existence, leaving three of its buddies staring at one another, a look of bewilderment etched on their not-too-pretty faces.

"What the fuck!" one of them said, or something to that effect.

*

"Jesus Christ, how can people stand this heat?" Annabel said, climbing out of the boat and onto the banks of the Congo. "I feel like I'm gonna pass out."

Richard, a large, heroic-looking man with a jaw to rival Schwarzenegger, stepped off the boat. He flicked his blonde hair as if auditioning for some shampoo commercial. "Annabel, *mon dieu*," he said, without the slightest idea what it meant, but it was French, and therefore poignant. "It's going to get a lot hotter than this, babes. By the end of the day, I guarantee you'll be a stone lighter."

"Really?" Annabel said. She looked terrified. "Maybe I should go back to the hotel. I'm just not cut out for this poaching malarkey. I'm covered in bites already." She flicked frantically as something – or nothing – landed on her leg. "Seriously, Rich, this was a bad idea." She fumbled around in her purse and came out with a compact. Flicking it open, she blew herself a kiss before powdering her nose.

"You'll be *fine*," Richard said, helping Ngozi and Mbali off the boat. "Won't she guys?"

The African men glanced at one another, nodding. Truthfully, they had no idea what the muscle-bound prick had said. It didn't matter. They were being paid handsomely enough. All they had to do was escort these fools to the crocs. A simple day's work, if they could put up with the whiny bimbo currently smearing scarlet lipstick across her face and giving her the appearance of a Batman villain.

"Ah, elle ressemble à Batman méchant," Mbala said, sniggering.

Ngozi snorted. "Haha. Le Joker."

"What are you two saying?" Richard said, cocking his rifle. His French didn't extend further than *Mon Dieu*, apparently.

"He say, we catch *lots* of crocodile today," Ngozi lied. "Make pretty handbag for beautiful wife." He nodded towards Annabel, who sniggered and feigned coyness.

"That's all very well and good," Richard said, "but if I catch either of you giving my lady the eye, I'll put so many bullets in you, you'll be…" He paused to think, then smiled. "…you'll be shitting bullets."

Mbala nodded, laughing maniacally.

When Richard turned his back to suck Annabel's sweaty clown-face, Ngozi said, "What did he say?"

"No idea," Mbala shrugged.

They headed into the rainforest, Mbala leading the way as he seemed to know where he was going. It wasn't long before they were entirely surrounded by trees; a small hut with the Starbucks logo painted on it in what appeared to be guano came as something of a relief to Annabel.

"Oh, thank God," she said. "I'm drier than a camel's urethra." She ordered two caramel Frappuccinos® and, after taking a piss behind the ramshackle coffee-house, agreed to move on, deeper into the forest.

"So, what are the chances of us snagging ourselves a couple of crocs today?" Richard asked, his rifle slung across his shoulder.

"Yes," Ngozi said, wishing he knew what the giant ponce was babbling on about.

"Have you ever been bitten by one?" Richard said. "Of course you have. I'll bet you've wrestled one, haven't you? I'll bet you supplexed the shit out of it, didn't you?"

"Yes," Ngozi said, grinning a mouthful of yellowing teeth. *Keep smiling*, the voice inside his head instructed him. *Keep smiling and nodding and he'll leave you alone.*

"This is a first for me," Richard continued, surveying the jungle on either side of him. "You can have all the money in the world, and *fuck*, I have a lot of money, but you've never truly enjoyed life until you've hunted it." He laughed; actually threw his head back and laughed so hard it made him cough. "Annabel's not like us," he said, finally composing himself. "*Women*, huh. She didn't want to come out here, said the marshland would fuck up her heels. Can you believe that shit? I told her, I said, 'Babes, if you want the handbag with the matching purse and shoes, you're going to help fucking catch it.'"

Keep smiling and nodding. Smiling and nodding…

"Anyway, here we are, about to catch us some crocs. Your buddy up there does know where he's going, right?"

Time to say yes again, his inner-voice said.

"Yes," Ngozi smiled.

"That's good to know," Richard said. "I mean, I ain't afraid of *nothing*, but say, for example, your friend up there takes a wrong turn and we end up roasting on some fucking tribe's campfire, apples in our mouths and leeks sticking out of our assholes, Annabel might not cope with that none too well."

Ngozi laughed; apparently, it wasn't the right time to do so. When Richard shot him a warning glance, he nodded and said, "Yes." It might have been his saving grace.

"Crocodiles jusqu'à venir," Mbala said, holding a fist in the air, imploring the others to wait.

"What did he say?" Richard said.

Ngozi grinned. He slammed the palms of his hands together, imitating a crocodile's jaws. Then he pointed up to Mbala.

"Oooh, crocodiles," Richard said, his eyes widening, his grin almost shark-like. Ngozi smiled; this fucker was living proof that evolution could go in reverse.

"Honey," Annabel said, sucking the final remnants of her Frappuccino® through her Heath Ledger lips. "Are there any benches around here? I could really do with a little sit down."

Richard unslung the rifle from his neck and began rudimentary maintenance. *That bit looks fine…that's where it should be…oh, a fly…yeah, everything seems to be in order with this here gun.* In truth, he had no idea what he was doing. As far as he was concerned, a gun was for killing. All that nonsense about cleaning, stroking, naming, was bullshit. Point and shoot, and if you were lucky, you'd hit something, and if you were *really* lucky, you'd hit the thing you were aiming at.

"You and your toys," Annabel said, stroking his hulking arm, running her fingers around the tattoo pronouncing his love for his mother.

"Goddamn, Annabel," he said, angrily. "How many times have I got to tell you? It's not a toy. It's a shooting stick. Now give me some space before I accidentally shoot you in your lady sex-organs."

Annabel, not fancying the sound of that, took a step back.

"Il pense qu'il est Commando," Mbala snickered. Ngozi slapped a hand across his mouth to prevent the laughter from spilling out. "Stick around, Bennett," he added, and that was it. They both erupted in a fit of hysterics. For reasons unbeknownst to her, Annabel joined in.

"What's so fucking funny?" Richard said, obviously perturbed at being left out of the joke. Enraged, he lifted the gun and pointed it at Mbala. "What's so goddamn *funny* all of a sudden?"

Mbala threw his hands up in the air; Ngozi followed suit. Annabel didn't know what was happening, so she joined in, too. It was a ridiculous scenario, and one that you couldn't make up, even if you were a bestselling author with a truly remarkable imagination…

Richard barked with laughter. "Haha. I'm only joking. Put your hands down, you dummies." He lowered the rifle. "Now, let's go catch us some crocs."

"Tosser," Mbala muttered. Roughly translated, it meant, "Tosser."

They pushed their way stealthily through the trees. Annabel continued to sigh and whine, as was her wont. *How do people cope in the jungle*, she pondered, *with only one Starbucks and no sign of a McDonalds?*

Richard, on the other hand, was enjoying every moment of it. He was born for this; it was in his genes. Well, some part of him *believed* it was in his genes. He'd never hunted anything before, unless you counted pussy as prey. The only thing he'd ever caught in the wild was chlamydia.

Ngozi, walking a few metres ahead with Mbala, suddenly turned and held his hand out: the universally recognised sign for *Not another fucking step…*

"Has he found one?" Annabel asked, clinging to Richard's arm as if he was liable to abandon her if the opportunity presented itself. In truth, he had thought about it, but she had the car keys and he didn't fancy walking back to Liverpool.

Richard shrugged her arm away and sidled up to the two Africans. "What are we looking at?"

"Trees," Ngozi said.

"Jungle," Mbala added.

"I can fucking well *see* that," Richard said. "But what else? You didn't stop because of the sudden appearance of trees."

Ngozi pointed through the jungle ahead; his finger, Richard couldn't help noticing, was thinner than a twiglet, liable to break if a sudden gust of wind kicked up. He followed the emaciated digit, his eyes eventually landing on a small bask of crocodiles.

They were tearing at something meaty, something that could have been *anything.*

"Yessss!" Richard hissed, readying his rifle. "It's about time, lads. She's starting to do my head in." He gestured surreptitiously to his wife, who was flapping around trying to rid herself of a sudden influx of flies. She looked like she was attempting *Gangnam Style* for the very first time. "So, what do we do now?" Richard asked. "Do we go in there, all guns blazing, or is there some clever way to do it?"

"Yes," Ngozi said, shrugging.

"Excellent," Richard said. "Well which is it?"

Mbala patted Richard on the shoulder. "I explain," he said. "We no go any further. We point at crocodile, you kill."

"Now hang on a minute," Richard said, his thick, dark eyebrows knitting together giving him the countenance of an enraged Jack Nicholson. "That wasn't the deal. I don't know the first thing about shooting crocodiles. You said—"

"I say we show you crocodile," Mbala said. He pointed through the trees, to where the beasts feasted upon the thing made of meat. "There. That crocodile. Big green things, lots of teeth."

"You looking for a slap?" Richard said, raising his gargantuan hand. "I know what a fucking crocodile looks like. I've seen them on the TV. Now, part of the fuck…" He trailed off, took a few deep breaths before starting over. "Part of the deal was for you two to assist us on our hunt. You know all about crocodiles, don't you?"

Ngozi nodded. He wished he knew what this guy was talking about; he also wished he knew a few things about crocodiles, other than what he'd learned from Attenborough and Disney cartoons.

"Well, what if I doubled what we were going to pay you? Would that purchase your assistance in killing these things?"

"Il a dit qu'il va nous payer le double," Mbala told Ngozi.

"Le double?" Ngozi said. "Pour cela, je tuerais sa femme."

"What did he say?" Richard asked. All this French was making him nauseous.

"He say for that, he kill your wife." Mbala translated, laughing.

Richard laughed, too. That wasn't a bad deal.

With an agreement arranged (for the crocodiles, not the guy's missus) Ngozi and Mbala stepped out into the clearing, being careful where they placed their feet. They needn't have bothered; Annabel's ridiculously high heels practically churned up the ground. They might as well have approached the crocodiles with vuvuzelas.

"I want that one," Annabel said, pointing a glossy fingernail at one of the creatures. She pointed at a second. "And that one would be perfect for shoes."

Richard sighed. "How many pairs of shoes do you have?" he whispered. Now was not the time for an argument, but the amount of times he'd tripped over a pair of ill-placed Jimmy Choo's…

"I don't have any genuine croc-skin ones," she said, pouting.

"Then you shall have them," Richard said, thinking about the blowjob he would be getting later. He turned to Mbala. "Well, you heard the woman. Clobber the crocodiles so she can have some nice, new shoes."

The not-so-professional poachers stepped warily towards the beasts. Mbala clenched a Swiss army knife in one hand, proving they hadn't really thought this through. Just as they were about to attack the smallest – and least violent looking – croc, Richard howled like something from a horror film.

"What is it?" Annabel screeched, gripping her husband's arm, trying to calm him down. "Honey, is it cramp?"

Richard was hopping around on one leg, kicking and swinging at thin air. His face was contorted, his mouth agape, a sonorous grunt emanating from his throat. If Annabel didn't know better, she would have asked him why he was doing his sex-face.

"There's something on my leg!" he gasped. "It's…it's fucking got me."

Ngozi wound his finger around his ear (*This guy's a complete and utter nutjob*); Mbala nodded.

"Honey, there's nothing there," Annabel said. A second later, she was sprawled on the ground, kicked away by Richard's frantic leg.

"Aaaarrggghhhh," Richard growled. "It's…*biting* me. Something's…" That was as far as he got. His leg flew away from the rest of him. Blood spurted from the stump. Annabel screeched. Mbala and Ngozi looked around for trees to climb.

The severed leg disappeared entirely, but not before the others had a chance to watch it miraculously compacted into a ball of undulating meat, as if unseen jaws were chewing it up.

Richard toppled to the ground, screaming so high-pitched that a dog, two-hundred miles away in Gabon, climbed into its basket and covered itself over with a *Thundercats* blanket. "Help me!" he just about managed through a mouthful of froth.

Annabel didn't know what to do. She wasn't prepared for this. Who *was*? "Did it just fall off?" she screamed over her husband's pained howls. You see, that was how her mind worked. The simplest solution, no matter how ridiculous, was usually the only one as far as she was concerned. Richard's leg magically detaching itself, as if it had grown bored of him and wanted to move to London where its prospects were better, made more sense than anything else she could come up with.

Mbala was doubled over, fighting the urge not to vomit. It wasn't every day you saw a human leg removed from its owner, and it affected him in pretty much the way one would expect. Ngozi, a little more steadfast – he'd served as an apprentice in a slaughterhouse – was doing everything he could to scramble up the nearest tree. Jungle trees are shit for climbing, despite what Tarzan might tell you. He kept getting three feet up before slipping back down again.

"Nobody move," Mbala said, heaving, trying not to think about what he'd just witnessed. "Just stay very still."

Everything fell silent; even Richard, who'd gone a funny shade of alabaster. His nubbin continued to squirt blood, albeit mutedly. You could have heard a pin drop, though quite why anyone would be dropping pins in the jungle was a mystery.

Annabel couldn't believe what was happening. This was just their luck. And she'd bought Richard a new pair of chinos. What a waste of fucking money *that* was...

Just then, Richard screamed again. Mbala was about to tell him to shut up when he saw the other leg come away, a little less cleanly than the first. Strands of sinew and flesh stretched along the jungle floor. Richard, it appeared, was having a very bad day.

"Couillon!" Ngozi gasped. Translated it wasn't a nice word. At least in French it sounded like something you might add to a salad. "It got his other leg!"

Richard threw himself back. He was a sitting duck down there on the ground, not that he had much choice. Glancing down at the geysering stumps protruding from his shredded jeans, he thought, *Well, I'll never play tennis again.* It was an odd thing to be thinking, but his mind was straying, and he was surprised he still had the capacity to think *anything.* Plus, he'd never in his life played tennis. The scoring system confused him, and there was nobody he hated more than Cliff Richard.

Annabel, not wanting to stick around and watch any more parts of her husband removed, made a run for it. Her heels, six inches long and not made for sudden bouts of sprinting, prevented her from getting far, and she buckled under a twisted ankle on only her second step.

The panic in her eyes as she fell reminded Ngozi of his dead mother; she had had the exact same look in her eyes just before she was run over by a herd of stampeding elephants.

"Help me!" she squeaked, clawing at the ground as she tried to scramble to her feet. "Help…" That was as far as she got, for it is – by law of physics – impossible to continue speaking once your head has been removed.

"Yes." Ngozi said. He'd meant to say *No*, but the English language confused him greatly, and the sight of a headless woman on all fours did nothing to allay his bewilderment. The head, as with the husband's legs before, compressed and warped before vanishing into thin air. Ngozi tried to remember if he'd eaten any strange mushrooms for breakfast.

The headless body slumped; blood continued to spout from the wide-open neck.

"We need to get out of here," Mbala said, staggering back, away from the carnage, away from the thing they could not see; the thing that was hungrier than a two-dollar whore in a sausage factory.

"What is it!?" Ngozi asked. They were now conversing in African; you didn't continue to bark once the dog had left the room. "What the fuck is it?"

"I don't know," Mbala said, pulling Ngozi to his feet. "Bad magic…the apocalypse…Patrick Swayze?"

They scrambled for the edge of the clearing, forgetting, for a moment, that there were several crocodiles just milling around. By the time either of them realised it, they were knee-deep in scaly beasts. Ngozi leapt aside as one lunged for him; its teeth snapping shut sounded like something from a Looney Tunes cartoon. Of course, in cartoons nobody bled, Wile E. Coyote never died as a result of falling off a cliff, and Pepé Le Pew was never arrested and put on a sex-offender's register, but this wasn't a cartoon, and Ngozi's hand was now hanging on by the merest of threads.

"Come on!" Mbala said, leapfrogging one of the voracious beasts. They rushed back into the trees. The crocodiles seemed to lose interest. Either that, or they were frightened of something.

Ngozi was trying to put his hand (mitten?) back on when Mbala roared in agony. He turned to find his friend being swung from side-to-side, the human equivalent of a dog-chew.

"No!" Ngozi bellowed. "He owes me eighty franc!"

Mbala gurgled as blood pooled in his throat. The unseen beast must have been bored of toying with the man, and snapped down hard. Mbala fell into two pieces, neither of which was pretty.

Ngozi turned to run, but found he couldn't. Something had him by the ankle. He heard his mother's voice say, "I tole you not to go running around with women." It made no sense in the grand scheme of things, but she used to say it a lot.

He looked down, expecting to see the nothingness chewing at his ankle, and so it came as something of a surprise to discover he was being held in place by the legless husband, Richard.

"Where the hell…do you…think you're…going?" the wannabe-poacher said through a mouthful of froth and blood. His hue suggested he should be weak, but the grip on Ngozi's leg was strong enough to choke a donkey.

"Let me go!" Ngozi said, or tried to. What he actually said was, "Yes!"

Just then, the African screamed and fell backwards. As he rolled around on the floor, hissing and screaming in agony, Richard began to laugh and released Ngozi's ankle, satisfied that he wasn't going to die alone, happy in the knowledge they were *all* royally fucked.

Ngozi, however, was having none of it, and jumped to his feet, grinning in Richard's direction. After giving him the finger (of his good hand), Ngozi ran off, disappearing into the trees, screaming something or other in a language that Richard would never have a chance to learn.

"Shit," the newly-widowed wannabe-poacher mumbled. A second later, he was swallowed by the unseen jaws of the anomaly.

*

Crocodiles have good memories. Not good enough to play cards, or complete a jigsaw puzzle, but they were still talking about the mysterious disappearance of one of their own when it suddenly flickered back into existence right before their eyes. After a few hours of distrust – and a couple of arguments about perceptual psychology, chameleon principle, and Claude Rains – it was as if nothing untoward had happened. But that crocodile – *Larry*, they called him – had experienced something truly remarkable, and though it never happened again, no matter how many times he prayed to Sobek, he always remembered that day, and three of the easiest meals he'd ever received.

The Many Deaths of Private Stanhope

Reginald Whittaker glanced around the small, cold office. A large, ornate bookcase filled the opposite wall, and the desk at which he sat took up the rest of the room. Hanging upon the walls were several framed photographs of a man Reginald recognised. There was, in fact, a full platoon shot, in which the man from the photographs and Reginald sat side by side, staring towards the camera with expressions of anticipation and fear. 1913, that photo had been taken; Reginald had had a youthfulness about him, an innocence that the years to follow would wipe away completely. Reginald averted his gaze from the picture before the inevitable tears had a chance to seep from the corners of his eyes.

Just then the door opened. The elderly gentleman who had welcomed Reginald at the door fifteen minutes earlier shambled through it. He looked, to Reginald, close to death; his liveried skin suggested an ailment other than simply old age, and his gait was that of someone struggling to maintain balance. He also had the countenance of an aristocrat, which was not beyond the realms of possibility since Reginald had made a point of inspecting the house and its gardens before committing to an audience with the fine fellow.

"Sorry to keep you waiting, Mr. Whittaker," the genteel man said as he closed the door behind him. 'I'm currently up to my neck in taxes, and the paperwork is something of a rotter.'

Reginald nodded. His neck cracked, reminding him that he, too, was almost in his twilight years. "Not to worry," he said. "I've already cancelled the domino-match in which I was to partake. Have you heard of the Swan With Two Nicks?"

The man shook his head in dissent. "I'm not a drinker, Mr. Whittaker." He smiled, more out of courteousness than anything else. "Let's just say that the tipple and I are not, nor have we ever been, very good friends."

The thought that this man, this immaculately-dressed and distingué gent, had at some juncture in his life battled with the demon booze was incomprehensible, but such was the way with aristocracy. Reginald had neither the money nor the idiocy to become an alcoholic; though things might have been different if he'd been offered the chance back in the twenties, when it had been easy to be led into a debauched existence by any number of miscreants masquerading as friends and colleagues.

"I received your letter last week, as were your intentions," Reginald said. He couldn't, for the life of him, fathom the meaning of the correspondence, and if he wasn't intrigued, to say the least, he might have been a little less predisposed to attend without suitable knowledge of what he was actually turning up *for.* "I've noticed the photographs peppered around the room. Would it be presumptuous to assume that I am here regarding a certain Walter Stanhope?"

The man's lip curled up; what should have been a smile was actually more of a sneer. "You would be correct to assume such a thing," the man said. "I believe that Walter and yourself were stationed together during the First World War." It wasn't a question; the man knew exactly of their connection.

"For three years, yes," Reginald said. "We used to call him The Cat, for reasons you are probably not familiar with."

This seemed to strike a chord with the man, for he smiled genuinely, something that Reginald had not seen since making the gentleman's acquaintance that afternoon. "Oh, please, I'd love to hear how he came about such a wonderful moniker." His eyes creased, a hundred crow's feet spread across into the fellow's diminishing hairline.

Well, Reginald thought. Why not? The domino-game was already postponed, and he had very little else to be getting on with.

He requested a glass of water before starting, and the old man said he could do much better than that, producing a bottle of fine scotch. When Reginald offered the man a cursory glance, he simply smiled and said, "Just because one doesn't imbibe doesn't mean it's not on hand."

So with a glass of warm, golden heaven in his hand and a lit pipe in the other – the smoke from which the elderly gent had no reservations about – Reginald began.

"The first time it happened was 1916," he said, sipping frantically from the glass. "Messines Ridge, a *hell* of a place to be in the winter, I'll tell you . . . "

*

As they rushed for the small, German pillbox, bullets whizzed through the air. One of them clipped Tommy Russell's ear, but he didn't stop running. That would have been stupid. Reginald didn't think they were going to make it; the pillbox was a lot further away than he'd previously believed it to be, and he wouldn't have suggested making a break for it if he had known the true distance.

The gunfire was coming from *everywhere.* It was a wonder they were all still standing. The only possible explanation, Reginald thought as he leapt across a ruined trench, was the riflemens' indecisiveness over who to shoot first. There were five of them, and surely – should the shooters settle upon just one of them – it would decrease their number more successfully. Instead they were haphazardly spraying fire over the area, hoping for some good fortune.

The men reached the pillbox – which was hexagonal in construct, and barely camouflaged – and threw themselves inside. Surprisingly, Reginald was the last in; even Tommy Russell with his blood-drenched ear made it before he did. He made a mental to work on his fitness-levels, should the chance ever present itself again.

"Is everyone okay?" Reginald asked. To Tommy he said, "How's that, Private?" He extended a tremulous finger towards Tommy's sopping earlobe.

"Just a graze," Tommy said, patting the side of his head gingerly and wincing as the pain hit him. "Could have been a lot worse."

"Did anyone see the shooters?" Wally Stanhope asked. He was doubled over in an effort to catch his breath.

"I didn't know there *were* any until after we started running," Private James Croft exclaimed. "If I had, do you thin I would have done it?"

"That's exactly why I didn't tell you," Reginald said. "We all *made* it, didn't we? Most of us in one piece." He signalled to Tommy's ear.

"The trouble is," Private Sidney Walker – *Sid* – said, "we're now stuck in the middle of nowhere with lord knows how many riflemen waiting for us to stick our heads out. Not the best idea in the world, Reg."

"They've been onto us for miles," Reg reminded them. "If we hadn't found this place, we'd be out in the open and dead by the end of the night." He paused, surveyed the pillbox, then added, "No, they won't come anywhere near us, not tonight, anyway. Too scared of getting shot themselves."

After around an hour of back and forth, trying to concoct a plan of action that would get them back on the safe side of the ridge, Wally Stanhope stood, hoisted his rifle up onto his shoulder, and said, "We can't just wait here for them to figure out a way in." The other four soldiers exchanged confused glances, unsure of what Wally considered as an alternative.

"General Plumer knows where we are," Reginald

said, hoping that he wasn't lying. "Give it a few more hours and the cavalry will come rolling in. There's—"

"Not a chance in hell that Plumer's going to risk the rest of the platoon to pull our sorry behinds out of here," Wally interjected. Whatever he had planned, there was no talking him out of it.

"So, what? You're just going to walk out there and hope the riflemen are having a tea-break?" James asked. "It's *suicide*, Wally."

Walter Stanhope was not a stupid man; Reginald actually thought him the most intelligent in the platoon, which was exactly why what he was suggesting made no sense at all. "He's right, Wally. We don't even know where they're positioned, or how many of them there are."

And then, for reasons unbeknownst to the rest of them, Private Walter Stanhope smiled. "Well, I guess we're going to find out."

For ten minutes they tried to talk him out of it, but he was insistent. They were to watch for the gunfire through the front loopholes and attempt to take out the source; Wally would simply do his best to dodge any incoming fire. It was a ridiculous plan. In fact, it wasn't a plan at all.

It was *preposterous*.

Wally told the group to make sure they fired true, for his life depended on it, and Reginald told him that there was no way, not in a month of Sundays, that any of the survivors would feel an ounce of responsibility or guilt if he was taken out by the enemy.

"I wouldn't expect you to," Wally said, and then he was on the outside of the pillbox, running for the adjacent woods. Snow filled the atmosphere, fluttering in each and every direction like miniature butterflies. And then the first shot came, whipping up a white miasma as it pounded into a drift. At the front of the pillbox, Tommy, James and Sid returned fire. Tommy began to shout aloud that he had managed to get one of the bastards right in the face, though whether that was true, they would never know. At the rear of the fortification, Reginald said a quick prayer for Wally, for he didn't expect the man to return after such an ill-conceived gesture that was bordering on stupidity of the highest order.

*

"So what happened?" the man asked, leaning across the desk to fill Reginald's glass. "We both know he didn't die."

Reginald sipped whiskey, savoured the burn first on his lips, then at the back of his throat. "We couldn't *believe* it when he returned almost an hour later," he said, eyes wide open as if to demonstrate just how shocking it was. "He was covered with snow from helmet to boot. He looked like the abominable snowman, whatever one of those looks like. At first we all thought he'd been shot. There were red patches in the snow, especially around his mouth. We got him cleaned up as best as we could; Tommy asked him how he managed to avoid being shot. Do you know what his reply was?"

The gentleman chortled. "I couldn't even hazard a guess, Mr. Whittaker."

"He told us that it was easy to evade enemy-fire once you'd decapitated the enemy." Reginald shuddered as if a goose had wandered across his grave. "At the time we just laughed. Tommy said Wally was cuckoo, in a manner of speaking, but we didn't mention it again. As far as I was concerned, it was just good to still be among the realm of the living. I managed to keep a few things to myself, too; things that would have unhinged the rest of the men."

"Go on."

"Wally's coat, once we'd wiped the snow away, was covered in bullet-holes. He took me to one side and told me they were glancing shots, but there was no way so many bullets could come so close and yet miss." Reginald began to load tobacco into his pipe. He hadn't noticed until now, but his hands were shaking, as if the momentary nostalgia had put the fear of God into him. Tobacco was scattered nervously along the desk's edge, and Reginald found himself apologising before brushing the minuscule brown dregs into the palm of his hand and dropping them back into his gilt-trimmed tin. He relaxed back in his chair; the leather creaked beneath him. "The next time it happened, it was just me and Wally. We'd been in a trench on the outskirts of Arras for almost two weeks. The Canadians had secured Vimy Ridge, and when the news reached us we managed to get hold of some wine with our last pennies, and we intended to celebrate and toast fallen comrades, as was the way it was done back then. Would you believe we even managed to acquire a bottle of Crème De Menthe? Anyway, news had come from Field Marshall Haig that the chances of attaining some prime positions were good. As you can imagine, although it was frowned upon, we all embarked on a jolly good knees-up."

*

"Tastes awful," Reginald said, handing the bottle across to Wally before spitting against the trench wall. "Where did they get this from again?"

Wally took a heart slug from the bottle, wiped his lips with the back of his hand and said, "Squiffy

McNee's lot raided a bombed barracks over in Nantes. Apparently there were cases of the stuff." He drank some more; the sound of distant bombs dropping did nothing to perturb him.

There were cases of the stuff, Reginald thought, because nobody was crazy enough to drink it. His mouth felt violated, and he'd only taken a sip. He walked across to the corner, picked up the Crème De Menthe, which would at least take the edge off the wine's astringent aftertaste, and proceeded to glug thirstily from it.

They had much to celebrate, that was for sure. The Canadians had done well to take Vimy, and Reginald's platoon had a clear run at some key targets. But tonight, tonight was for drinking. The rest of the men were camped further along the trench; the sound of merriment was audible above the explosions from over yonder. Wally had suggested keeping the first bottle to themselves before joining up with the rest of the platoon; Reginald, who had tasted the state of the putrescence in the bottle, would gladly forfeit his share of the booze.

An hour later, and Reginald was still relatively sober. Insomuch as any infantryman who had not imbibed so heavily for almost two years. He had a nice, gentle buzz; the kind of mystical thrum that was both warm and welcome. Wally, on the other hand, was pissed as a newt, slurring his words to the extent that Reginald had taken to simply nodding as a retort.

It was raining heavily outside – and, to a certain degree inside – but it was met with level of felicity. The snow from the winter had taken its toll on the men, with several dying from exposure and more as a result of the subsequent afflictions. The rain had its own drawbacks, of course, but at least it didn't make the terrain impossible to traverse, the way the blizzards had.

Reginald wouldn't have even noticed the rain had it not been for Wally's removal of the trench tarpaulin. He had been blissfully in a world of his own, the effects of the alcohol bringing dancing stars to his vision, when all of a sudden he found himself getting wet very quickly.

"Jesus, Wally! What are you playing at?" Reginald pushed himself away from the edge of the trench to better his view. Wally was already scaling the side of the gorge, kicking mud and dirt down onto his scattered webbing and personal effects. Somewhere, off in the distance, another bomb exploded, its rumble almost knocking Wally off-balance. "Where the hell do you think you're going?"

But it was no use; Wally had drunk enough of the nasty stuff to knock his senses for six. He staggered up, further and further, finally managing to drag himself completely out of the trench.

"Wally, you're going to get yourself killed, you fool!" Reginald called up to him, but he paid no heed. There was a good chance he hadn't even heard Reginald's reproach or the concern tainting his tone.

He turned in to face the trench, and to Reginald he looked tiny way up there above the berm. He was grinning, though his eyes were shut tight. In the darkness, Reginald could have sworn he winked the moment before he fell inwards.

Reginald made a sound deep in his throat, the kind of noise that can only emerge when something terrible is happening. He wanted to catch the fool, to race across and break his fall, but there was no way he would cover the distance in time. Instead, all he could do was watch as Wally fell through the air, almost in slow-motion.

And then, when he made contact with the ground, caving in his bugwarm in the process, there was an audible crack as loud as the bombs falling off in the distance. Wally's head was pointing away in an unnatural direction; the top of his spine pushed out against the flesh at the nape of his neck the way a pen would stretch parchment.

Dead, Reginald thought. The barmy idiot had only gone and broken his own neck.

Dropping to his knees, with the fine yet terrible

rain peppering his exposed neck and hair, Reginald planted his face deep into the palms of his hands and began to sob. This was not how it was meant to go; tonight was in celebration, and now Reginald had a lot of explaining to do. Corporal Simmons was a fair man, but even that wouldn't save Reginald from this mess. If he wasn't shot for this he would, at the very least, be tossed in a chokey.

But Reginald needn't have been worrying himself with such silliness. The prone and twisted form of Private Walter Stanhope was moving, contorting itself back into a more acceptable shape. It was the sound of cracking – like chicken wishbones being snapped – that made Reginald lower his hands. He was just in time to see the bone from Wally's neck sink back into its proper position.

For a moment, Reginald was speechless. He sat there, paralysed, apart from his mouth, which flapped open and shut like a fish out of water. Wally seemed to be composing himself, too. He brushed the mud and grime nonchalantly from his knees and elbows before straightening his posture.

"H. . . *How*?" Reginald finally managed.

But Wally was in no mood to explain. He simply skittered backward along the trench and slumped in the far corner. Over the distant bombing, Reginald could hear the words . . .

*

"'I'm not drunk any longer'"

The man had listened to the tale raptly. He was perched upon the edge of his leather chair, his hands knitted together so tight that his knuckles were white. Eventually, he shrugged. "That's quite a story, Mr. Whittaker," he said. "Could it be that your eyes deceived you? That Walter was, in fact, unharmed by the fall? I'm no doctor – though I *could* have been had I taken more interest in my studies – but something as serious as a broken neck would be impossible to recover from the way in which you described it."

"I know!" Reginald said, almost spat. "And there were more instances just like this. I watched him fall at the Battle of Verdun, only to reappear without a scratch three days later. He'd somehow managed to drag himself along a road, into some trees, where he'd kept a low profile for almost forty-eight hours before daring to attempt a return to base. Some old comrades of mine swore blind, pardon the pun, he'd taken a bullet to the eye during Passchendaele. That was when we gave him his nickname. *The Cat.* Private Walter Stanhope had nine lives, that was for sure, and yet there was nothing any of us could do to prove just how odd it was."

The genteel man stood from his chair for the first time. He wandered across to the photographs adorning the wall and gazed, silently, at them for what seemed to be forever. Eventually, he turned; a small grin played upon his lips, and his left eyebrow was raised. "What if I were to tell you that you were indeed correct?" he said.

"Excuse me?" Reginald said, all of a sudden feeling more than uncomfortable in his surroundings. There was a palpable eeriness about the atmosphere, now. The fine hairs on the back of Reginald's arms perked up and danced around, as if the room had become statically charged.

"All those times you believed Walter dead," the man said returning to the desk. "What if I told you that you were right?"

This, Reginald thought, must be some kind of terrible set-up; and if it was, there was something deeply deplorable about the whole thing.

Reginald stood, and immediately felt better. The man in front of him was of no threat. *Sure*, they were both elderly, but the man was more advanced in years than he, and Reginald thought he would be able to get by him without too much trouble, should the need arise.

"I have to leave now," Reginald said. "This has clearly been an error on your part. I think you for the hospitality, but unfortunately . . . "

It was at this point that the man reached down for the doorknob and twisted it. Reginald believed it to be for his departure. He was shocked, and once again paralysed as if inflicted by a mild stroke, to discover a man standing between the doorframe.

A man that couldn't possibly be, and yet *was*.

"Wally?" Reginald gasped, clutching his chest as pain racked through him. His legs threatened to give way beneath him, and all the time the man – the esteemed gent with whom Reginald had rather taken a liking to, but not anymore – was smiling.

The man between the doorframe *was* Private Stanhope, and yet there was something missing. He was older, but not as old as he should have been, and his eyes were deep and dark, like chasms looking into the very depths of hell. His face was haggard, loose, as if it could be torn away from the skull beneath with the merest of effort.

"I. . . I don't understand!" Reginald said, almost choking on the foetid stench which accompanied Walter Stanhope.

"It really is quite simple," the man who Reginald had spent the best part of an afternoon recounting stories to said. "Walter Stanhope, here, has been dead for longer than you could possible imagine. He was dead before he enlisted back in 1914. Before my own mother fell pregnant with me in 1890." Behind him, Walter was snarling, drooling black spittle down the creases of his flapping jowls. "You see, Mr. Whittaker, there are things in this world that neither you and I could comprehend. If I should tell you that Walter Stanhope maintained his youth by feeding upon the flesh of German soldiers, would you believe me? Or perhaps that he would tear the throats from enemy officers in an effort to remain youthful and therefore keep this secret from you, what *then*?"

Reginald shook his head, never once taking his eyes from the aberration standing opposite. "This is impossible! Lies, all *lies*! What has he done to you, Wally?"

The man took a step back, allowing the beastly newcomer entrance to the office. "I fear we shan't be seeing each other again," the man said, slipping out through the door and into the dimly-lit hallway. "But I want you to know that it is nothing personal; merely a request on behalf of my associate."

He pulled the door shut as he exited, leaving Reginald and Wally alone in the office. By the time the screaming ceased, the man had made a pot of tea and scattered cucumber sandwiches upon a silver platter. He returned to the office to discover Walter had made something of a mess.

"Was it really necessary?" the man asked the beast,

who was becoming younger by the second thanks to the fleshy repast. "It will take forever to clean this lot up."

"Oh don't be so pernickety, Charles," Walter said. He looked like his old self again, after almost six months of inexorably ageing. *The power of the flesh*, Charles liked to call it.

"It's not as if you have anything *else* to be going along with, is it?"

Walter was right, although Charles wasn't to be outdone. "And who, pray tell, will be contacting the next one? I do believe I still have my uses."

Walter had sidled up to the photograph hanging upon the wall. He began to run his spindly finger along the line-up of soldiers. When he was satisfied, he tapped the glass. "This old boy should do," he said, his jagged teeth still covered in meaty morsels.

"As you wish," Charles said, settling down to his desk. As he wrote, he couldn't help thinking that the cucumber in the sandwiches would repeat on him something terrible that evening. Oh well. Ultimately, it was worth the pain, which was Walter's theory too. He didn't *enjoy* feasting upon veterans, men that he had pleasurably fought alongside, but they were the only thing that sustained him. And he was running out of options.

"*The Cat*?" Walter snorted, picking Reginald's head

up from the office floor and staring into its wide eyes. "How very droll."

"Indeed, Walter," Charles said, his pen darting across the paper before him. He sighed, drank his tea, and finished writing the letter.

Dear Sidney Walker,

I hope this missive finds you well and that the years have been kind to you. You don't know who I am, but I wish to meet with you to discuss something of utmost importance. My address is Bintree Manor, The Street, Dereham, Norfolk, NR20 5NE. It is with great anticipation I await your response.

Sincerely Yours
Charles Beauregard

The Sallow Man

She first saw him, the sallow man, sitting in a Parisian café. While she sipped tea from a cup two sizes too big, he watched furtively over his copy of *L'Humanité*, of which he had not read a single article. At first, she took his interest to be nothing extraordinary; she was a very beautiful lady and, as far as she knew, he was a Frenchman. They seemed to pay close attention to such attributes. There was nothing to worry about; if anything, she should have been flattered.

Yet there was something in the wetness of his eyes and the way in which he grit his teeth that was inherently unsettling. Eventually, she stood, deigning to embroil the gentleman in conversation. As she began to walk across the café, the man lowered his newspaper, as if, all along, he had known it would come to this.

As she neared, though, something altered within her, for she could see he was ill. His flesh was the colour of butter, his eyes ruby in their sunken sockets. She approached his table, no longer intending to berate him for his impertinence; her heart tightened inside her, as if somebody had gripped onto it and refused to let go.

The man, whose fingers now drummed nervously upon the table-edge, smiled up at her, and she walked right past him, deciding that the only way to avert embarrassment was with the pretence of a toilet-break. As the door closed behind her, shutting out the poorly man and the sound of his gnarled fingers a-tapping, she cast her mind back to the last time she had seen such sickness.

Her mother, afflicted by colorectal cancer, sitting at the kitchen table with her head in her hands, sobbing uncontrollably. That same yellow tinge painted on her like some foul guano; her eyes not sunken, but bulging from her face like poached eggs. Tara had been fifteen years old, and finding her mother doubled over like that, in such pain, her resignation as tangible as the disease eating through her, was enough to cause nightmares for years to follow. Her mother, who had always been so strong and brave, reduced to a crumbling tangle of a person; it had been almost impossible for Tara's fifteen year-old brain to accept.

That man, seated in the café, was suffering – or so she believed at that moment – in much the same way as her mother had in her final days. He had the same air about him; the same scent (though it might not have been as palpable as she perceived it to be) of putrefaction seeping out from his pores.

Tara washed her hands, though there was no need as she had done nothing but stand and consider her options. The reflection in the mirror stared back at her, and for a second she didn't recognise the face as her own. Only when she winked – for her own piece of mind – did she accept it as a true likeness, and yet there was still something different that she couldn't quite put her finger…

The door burst open and a woman with a young child rushed through it. Tara, feeling caught in the act even though she was doing nothing untoward, feigned inspection of her own teeth, not realising how pathetic she must have looked, grinning and snapping at the mirror, until long after exiting the room. As she did, she walked past the sallow man's table without so much as a cursory glance.

If she *had* looked, she would have found nobody sitting there, for the sallow man had made his point and left while Tara had been inspecting her fading beauty in the W.C.

The second time she saw him was the library. Tara had been browsing the romance section, hoping to discover something that would distract her suitably from the strange feeling within her, the bitter taste that had suddenly taken up residence on her tongue, the ear-splitting headaches that kept her up all night, clinging to her toes and rocking gently back and forth as the world slept around her.

As she removed a tattered hardback book from its shelf, she almost choked at the sight of him: the sallow man. It had been almost a month since the avoided confrontation at the café, but that was a wholly different country. How could it be that this man, who still possessed the countenance of a man on the verge of death, could be here, back in England, in the same library?

What was even more unnerving was that he adorned the same bistre suit as he had the last time she'd seen him, as if he was possessed of only the one set of clothes. It wasn't dirty, nor frayed, but it hung loosely from his frame, possibly a whole three sizes too big for him.

He didn't look directly at her, though she was concealed by an entire shelf of psychology books, but she had the strange feeling that he knew she was there. It caused the hackles to rise on her arms. The atmosphere was suddenly thick; she felt that she would have to swim through it to make the hasty exit she so desired.

A cough, neither her own nor the sallow man's, startled her, pulling her back from the terrifying reverie that she had unconsciously succumbed to. The librarian sidling up alongside her, replacing various volumes of erotica that she was loath to look at as she worked, said, "Sorry. Got a hell of a cold coming."

Tara nodded, smiled, and made her way toward the exit without the book she had been so intent on borrowing. She reached the double-doors and turned, but the sallow man was nowhere.

Nowhere.

Over the course of a year, the man appeared to her on numerous occasions, never speaking, acknowledging her only with a bowed head or forced smile. Tara never once responded, for her fears were too great. A harmless and sickly fellow he might have seemed, but there was something powerful about him, a strange vigour that suggested he was nowhere near as weak and stricken as he appeared.

As many times as she saw him during the day, he appeared again at night, in dreams so vivid that Tara wakened in films of sweat, gasping for air, sometimes screaming, seldom wary of her surroundings. In the dreams he was far worse; his bistre suit was damp, decaying, spilling maggots from its buttonholes and sleeves. His face, more jaundiced and loose on his skull, wobbled from side-to-side as he chittered at her in a language that she neither understood nor cared to learn. More often than not, he would creep up behind her, placing a gnarly hand upon her shoulder. Then would come the hissing – and the sickly-sweet putrid breath like honey and death combined – that would send shivers through her. Sometimes she was lucky enough to wake at the sound of the *ssssssssss*; others, she suffered in much the same way that her mother had in her final hours. A tortuous night filled with incomprehensible garble on the lips of the sallow man was enough for Tara to seek medical assistance.

The drugs they prescribed helped her to sleep, but they also prevented her from waking, which left her at the hands of the sallow man for the entirety of whatever he had planned for her. After three nights – so bad that she had wished herself dead – she emptied the pills into the toilet and flushed.

Vanquishing the real sallow man, however, was not so easy, as once again she found herself faced with him, this time whilst visiting her mother's grave. She had barely placed the fresh flowers into the urns either side of the headstone when she noticed him shambling ahead. His gait was somewhat disorientated, as if he had forgotten which foot went where, but Tara knew it was a façade, a cabaret intended to conceal the truth from her.

She ignored him long enough to set the grave back into some sort of organisation, but by then she was seething. She could feel his eyes upon her and, although he was some way off, she could smell the disgusting reek that accompanied him everywhere, a stench that was worsening with every passing encounter.

Mustering up what little courage she could find, she paced across the cemetery toward him. He stood, stock-still, awaiting her with – she felt – excitement. Time stood still all around. With the emergence of Tara's valour came the cessation of birdsong, and anything else that had – up until a moment ago – been audible.

Hssssssss.

She heard *that* just fine, though. The sallow man was hissing, sucking her in through discoloured teeth. The rows and rows of headstones between them lessened; the sallow man grew, both in size and dominion. Tara found herself wondering what she might say when she reached him; whether she would speak calmly, or if the anger would spill forth, an irrepressible torrent of abuse.

A second; that was all it was, a second that she took her eyes off the man, and when she looked up he was gone. She collapsed atop some Elvis Presley fan's grave, sobbing until her chest hurt. The notion that her opportunity to palaver with the sallow man was forever lost was too much for her to accept, but she convinced herself that he would return.

He always did.

Though she hadn't predicted the brevity of his absence, and a voice from somewhere to her left hissed, "*Taaaaraaaaa…*"

She choked, spluttered, glanced past the scale bust of Elvis Aaron Presley, and watched as the sallow man took a seat on the rotting, wooden bench beyond the grave. The smile upon his face was somewhat incongruous; his yellow teeth reminded her of cinema popcorn.

"Who are you?" Tara said through staccato sobs. "What do you *want* from me?"

The man scratched his chin; as he raked his skeletal fingers down there was a sound like sandpaper on a disintegrating door. Tara wondered whether the man would simply blow away if a moderate gust of wind kicked up.

"You *know* who I am," he said, now sneering. "You know, I remember you when you were but a child. Thirteen, I think, when I first laid eyes on you, though of course it wasn't you that interested me back then. Not like now, of course. Only got eyes for you now, baby." His face contorted, like liquid tar, and the red lines around his pupils began to dance.

Tara thought back, trying to place the man, but she couldn't. "I don't know you," she told him, sounding more defensive than she had expected. "The café in Paris; that was the first time I ever saw you."

"You and I go farther back than that," he said, a throaty chortle rattling through him like a misfiring motorbike. "Your mother knew me *very* well."

There was something grotesque about the way he said it; she suspected he'd utilised that breathy tone purposely, as if to invoke her rage for some reason.

Perhaps it would make his big reveal all the more dramatic…

"I don't…"

"Look at me, Taaaaraaaa," he hissed, gesturing down at the bistre suit hanging listlessly from his frame. "I'm death, I'm expiration, I'm everything that your mother feared, and I'm coming for you."

Tara should have been terrified; that was what he'd intended by dropping the mask and revealing himself. Whether it was because she was already kneeling, or that she had known all along that she would succumb, in much the same manner that her mother did, to the cancer, she didn't know, but all she felt was intent, a strength that may have escaped her mother but would not manage to do so with her.

The sallow man sneered. "You think you can beat me?" It wasn't a question, and he spat upon the ground next to her as if to confirm so. "Your mother couldn't, and she had more time to prepare."

Tara leant back on her haunches and, using Presley's stone head to steady herself, climbed to her feet. "I should've known what you were," she said. "I recall your stench round my mother. You made me sick so many times."

"Oh, not as many as I *intend* to, Deary," he snorted.

Tara nodded, accepting the sallow man's challenge. "You want me," she said, determined and stolid. "Come and fucking get me."

As she turned and walked away from the Elvis Presley-themed grave, the sallow man, and the foetid stench enveloping him, she didn't glance back, not once, for she could feel his fear as he watched her leave. If she turned, it would only confirm what she already knew.

The sallow man was powerful, capable of the cruellest death, but unconquerable? He'd been beaten before, *thousands* of times, and Tara – leaving the cemetery with the knowledge of a battle yet to commence hanging heavy over her – would give him a fight he would never forget.

As the girl shrank into the distance, the sallow man shrivelled into himself, choking on thick, viscous phlegm caught in his throat. Things were changing; these people were no longer afraid the way they once were. Another one slipping through his rheumy fingers; so many souls surviving his assault. His desiccated bones threatened to give way inside him. He staggered across the cemetery, glancing down at the headstones of people he'd taken. The wind crumbled flakes off him as if he was made of parchment, the power stripping from him like ancient varnish. Eventually he would disappear completely.

Flatwoods

Beverly coughed, waking herself from the only sleep she'd managed in days. The stench almost immediately returned, reminding her of the terrible encounter with the thing in the woods. Whether the fetor was tangible or not, she didn't care. It instilled fear in her, and she sat bolt-upright, glancing around the room.

"Mother?" she whimpered. Her eyes fought to adjust to the darkness, and as they did she saw shapes everywhere, forming from shadows, reaching for her like the limbs of a tree. When her mother didn't respond, she breathed deeply and relaxed.

That nice man, Gene – who had arrived on the farm earlier that evening and announced himself as a guardsman – had told her that the thing she'd seen was just a man, and that an arrest had been made over in Gassaway. There was something about the way in which he spoke – with an assuredness she should have found comforting – that suggested he was lying to appease her. It must have really affected him, seeing a young girl like Beverly so upset, and she was sure that played a part in his decision to placate her rather than tell her that yes, she had seen a ten-foot creature with a heart-shaped head, wearing a skirted dress. *Everyone* had seen it; some had not lived to report it.

Thinking about the thing caused her to shudder. She had been the closest to it out of the three of them, though not through choice. It had just appeared amongst the trees, slowly oozing out, as if it was a dark aqueous gloop rather than a physical being, Bobby Brewster and Tom Hicks had tossed a few rocks at it, but they were too terrified by its sheer size to do anything else.

Beverly, realising that the thing was reaching for her with clawed hands, had run as quickly as she could towards the boys. They had hollered at her to get away from it; Tom had called it the 'Lizard Monster', which had only served to make her run faster. She'd once watched a documentary about lizards, and the thought that a giant one was pursuing her across the field turned her legs to jelly.

The rocks being catapulted at it by the boys must have kept it at bay, for it had stayed along the tree-line, not venturing any farther than was safe. As

Beverly ran, she'd choked on the putrid stench accompanying the creature. It had assaulted pretty much all of her senses; she was almost blind from the tears rolling down her face, and she had barely been able to breathe. The only thing she could hear in that moment was Bobby Brewster telling her she was going to be okay, that the Lizard Monster had slunk back into the trees.

She'd kept running, though, and hadn't stopped until she'd reached the edge of the field. It was there that she had collapsed, with the boys' concerned faces hovering over her. The last thing she had heard before the darkness took her was Tom Hicks. "Do you think that was it?" he'd asked. Bobby might have nodded, or shook his head with dissent. Beverly had fainted and would never know.

That was three days ago, and the guardsman's unexpected visit a few hours ago had done nothing to alleviate her fears. If they *had* arrested a man, then they had made a huge mistake. What she and the boys had seen had not been human. Sure, beneath the strange, pleated skirt it was bipedal, but that didn't make it hominid. Besides, they weren't the first to see it. Sherman Pickering swore blind the thing had eaten his spaniel. How true that was, Beverly didn't know, but recalling the thing, towering over her – those short, stubby arms reaching for her; the talons on the end clicking with excited nervousness – she was pretty sure it could manage a whole pack of dogs and still have room for dessert.

She pushed herself up from the bed. The sheets clung to the parts of her flesh that weren't covered by her gown; she was sweating profusely. The terrible nostalgia had reignited the horror she'd felt three days ago as she raced to escape the 'Lizard Monster.'

She'd seen its face – up close and personal, as it were – and could recall two bulging eyes penetrating her soul. They could certainly be mistaken for reptilian eyes, but the thing's face had been bright red, like the head of a matchstick. Lizards, Beverly thought, were for the most part green. She'd heard about yellow ones, and blue ones, and red ones, but they were the venomous species, not indigenous to West Virginia. There was the red-headed skink, but Beverly hadn't heard anything on the radio about one walking around all pissed off with the world and scaring kids half to death.

She climbed out of bed and walked across the room. She lifted the window, and was instantly soothed by the breeze as it brushed past her, ruffling her nightgown and prickling her sodden flesh. From her mother's room there came a cough and that, combined with the relaxing draft from the open window, calmed her. The stench of the thing – *Lizard*

Monster? – was no longer present, if it ever had been. Beverly wondered what the boys were doing right now, off in their respective houses. Tom would be sleeping, she was certain. Bobby was a night-owl, from what she understood. He said it was because he liked astronomy, and *"There ain't a helluva lot of stars out in the damn day."* She thought he had an affliction, something that prevented him from sleeping. Her mother was a big drinker, and managed to knock herself out most nights. Maybe Bobby should try *that*, she thought, and then sniggered as the picture formed inside her head: Bobby lying on his bed, holding a bottle that was almost the same size as him.

Her mother coughed again, almost choking this time. Beverly wished she wouldn't drink so much. All over Braxton people talked; she was ashamed by her mother who was, for the most part, loath to admit she had a problem. She spluttered again, made a horrific noise that sounded somewhat like it might be her last. Beverly turned back to the window, ignoring the tumult across the hall.

"What are you doing right now, Bobby?" she whispered. What stars he must be watching through the telescope his father had given him for his twelfth birthday; what splendorous universes he could see through its lens.

She was so bewitched by the thought of Bobby stargazing that she didn't notice the cessation of her mother's coughing. The house was silent once again, eerily quiet. It was almost three minutes later that Beverly noticed it. With it came a sense of oppression, as if the air had been sucked from the room and replaced with something considerably denser.

Beverly closed the window. The breeze had dried her skin, but had also left her chilled. And now this silence…something was not quite right.

She turned and walked across the room. She yearned for her mother to break out in another breathless and wheezy fit, if only to ease her own discomfiture. But there was nothing. Nothing but the steady *hush-thump* of blood in her ears, a sign – at least – that she hadn't gone deaf.

Then, the door slowly opened. Beverly gasped, fell back onto the bed. Her mother would never enter her room at night; she rarely made an appearance during the day. Here she was, though. Her nightgown was stained at the front – possibly vomit – and she was hunched over, as if either still drunk or sleepwalking.

Beverly stood, patting her chest with an open palm to slow her racing heart. "Mother," she said. "You're…you're *sleepwalking*." She didn't know why she was whispering. Wouldn't she be more successful at rousing the drunken old fool if she spoke with more ardour?

She was about to speak again when she saw the hard shell either side of her mother's waist. It took her a moment to realise what she was looking at in the semidarkness.

Claws. *Talons.* The hands of the thing she had encountered on the edge of the woods.

Beverly realised that her mother's feet were an inch above the floorboard, listlessly dangling. The stain on her nightgown was not vomit, after all. It was already blossoming outward; a hellish bloom that darkened with every passing second.

The thing lifted Beverly's flaccid mother and tossed her across the room. It ducked beneath the doorframe as it entered the room. Huge eyes bulged from its glowing red face; Beverly was almost certain it said her name.

Lizard Monster, the boys had called it, but this was no lizard. It was a devil; it was something that had escaped Hell; it was *Death.*

And it had come for her.

She slumped to the floor, closed her eyes and wept. The putrid stench swamped her, and she gagged and choked as the thing's talons wrapped around her neck. She heard a snap – louder than anything else she had heard in twelve years of life – and then everything buzzed for a while.

Stars momentarily danced in the space between her eyes and eyelids.

Keep watching the skies, Bobby, she thought. And then the stars disappeared, leaving only a pitch dark void that would forever be her home.

Brotherly Love

As Tom looked into his brother's jaundiced eyes, trying to comprehend what he was being told, he realised that things would never be the same again. If Jason was telling the truth – and he had no reason to lie – then Tom would have to do something about it. How could he *not*?

'I *had* to tell you,' Jason gasped, barely audible over the incessant beeping from the machine at the edge of the room. Tom loathed the machine; he would be hearing that fucking noise all night long, as was always the case after long periods of visiting. Perhaps it was the pitch of the thing, but whatever it was, Tom would find it difficult to sleep as it inexorably reverberated around in his head.

'And this was going on all the time?' Tom finally managed. 'When we were building the tree-house? When we went camping in the woods? You could have told me then. Fuck, Jason, I'm your *brother*.'

'I could never tell you,' Jason said; the congealed

spittle around his lips cracked and fell onto the sheet. He sighed. 'I was too ashamed, Tom. I'm *still* ashamed.'

He started to sob, but there were no tears. Jason was all dried up; just an empty, desiccated shell waiting to die. They had both come to terms with it; the funeral was arranged, and exactly as Jason wanted it. Time had passed them by, and it seemed like only yesterday that Jason had been diagnosed. Tom had made certain of his brother's final wishes, and it should have been so simple . . .

But now *this*.

'I'm not scared anymore,' Jason said, and Tom could see, in his brother's eyes, that he was telling the truth. 'But I couldn't take this secret to the grave with me, Tom. I had to tell you before it was too late.'

Tom couldn't bear to look at his brother, his best friend – the guy who'd taught him how to make paper sail-boats, and how to skateboard without falling on his ass. For twenty years, Jason had kept this from him. Tom couldn't understand why. Their mother had died three years ago; if there had ever been a perfect opportunity to reveal this dirty secret, that would have been it.

But no. Jason had waited until his own life had seeped from him, until there was nothing left but a yellowing husk lying, bones protruding from parchment skin, on his deathbed.

They sat for the remainder of the afternoon in what could only be described as morose silence. Tom had nothing to say; he was too busy contemplating his next move. And Jason, well, he'd used up what was left of his energy to impart the horrendous nugget of information that his brother would never be able to forget.

And the machine in the corner of the room went *beep, beep, beep* . . .

*

When the telephone rang at half three, Tom knew exactly who it would be. Jason had been weak when he'd left the hospital, drained of life and information. Perhaps he'd known this was his final chance, his last night on earth. Maybe he'd sensed it, which was why he'd wasted no more time.

Tom hated him for what he'd concealed. How could a person go through life with such an overbearing burden hanging around their neck? How could anyone live as if nothing was wrong? The shame was one thing, but the knowledge and memories alone would surely be enough to drive a man insane.

Or to vengeance.

'Tom?' the voice on the end of the line said as he pushed the phone to his ear. It was Philip; Tom liked Philip, usually, but not tonight. Tonight Philip was a cunt, and this cunt was about to tell him Jason had finally expired.

'I know,' Tom said, pre-empting the bad news. 'I saw it coming this afternoon, Philip.'

There was an audible sigh of relief on the other end of the line. Had Philip been expecting an argument, a fierce exchange in which Tom accused the hospital of gross negligence? Tom was pretty sure it happened, from time to time.

'It was peaceful,' Philip assured him. 'I wasn't there when he went, but Casey was reading to him and . . . well, she said he was smiling.'

That's Jason, Tom thought. Smiling all the way to the fucking grave, despite what he went through, despite living for twenty years knowing what he knew.

Tom thanked Philip for notifying him and promised to be at the hospital first thing to collect whatever possessions Jason had amassed over the last few months. Philip, by the end of the conversation, sounded as if he might cry. Perhaps, Tom thought, Philip isn't such a cunt after all. Not even tonight.

*

A week later, Jason was buried in Commongate Cemetery. A few friends attended, but that was it. Family, or what remained of it, had either moved across the country or decided not to show. It was a nice service; short, Tom thought, which was exactly how Jason wanted it. Neither of them had any truck with religion, and so it was more of a tradition than a personal choice. In truth, Jason would have been just as happy stuffed into an old *Pringles* tube and tossed into the Pacific.

Tom went straight home after the funeral. A few of the guys wanted to go out and get drunk, but Tom didn't see the point. It would only mask the anger, the pain, the sheer hatred he felt, and tomorrow morning he would wake up with a sore head, a dry mouth and no memory of what might have happened.

No, he went directly home, much to the chagrin of his now-distant buddies.

He had some planning to do.

*

'You fuckin' cheatin' sonofabitch!' Terry Dermot said, clambering drunkenly to his feet and pointing himself in the general direction of the refrigerator. 'Ain't no way you coulda got three fuckin' aces two games runnin'!'

Sid grinned a mouthful of popcorn teeth. 'Them's the way of the cards,' he said as he lit a cigarette. 'And this is my fuckin' house, so don't be disrespectin' me none, you hear? I'll put you out on your fuckin' ass quicker'n you can say sorry.'

Terry returned to the table with three beers, one for each of the players. When he spoke next, he did so with some trepidation. Sid was not the kind of guy he wanted to piss off, and although they had been friends for more than thirty years he knew there would be no hesitation if Sid truly wanted to strike out. 'I just think it's an awful lot of luck for one guy to have, is all,' he said, handing Sid a beer.

'Sid's always been a lucky sumbitch,' Marcus said as he started dealing for the next game. He sniggered. 'He's the only guy I know who could fall into a barrel of dicks and come up eatin' pussy.'

They all laughed at that; Sid nodded along as if in quiet agreement.

'What you all need to remember,' Sid said, sucking long and hard on his cigarette, 'is that I've been around the block a few times. Ain't much I don't know. Shit, when I remarried, God rest her soul, I shoulda known better. Especially since she had those fuckin' kids.' He paused as if deep in thought. 'Ain't much you don't learn about life after what I had to put up with all those years.'

'Best thing that ever happened, her dyin' on you like that,' Terry said. 'You changed some while you were with her. I ain't meanin' no disrespect or anythin', but y'all went off the grid for a few years.'

It was true. Sid had spent eighteen years with Paulette, and ten of those had been miserable. The trouble with Paulette, Sid thought, was that she never knew when to stop running her goddamn mouth. She could jaw-flap with the best of 'em, and nine times out of ten Sid would have to clock her one just to shut her up. And those kids of hers were little shits – little bastards that needed straightening just as much as their mother, half the time. And Sid had done his best to straighten all of them.

'I ain't never been happier,' Sid said, shovelling peanuts into his mouth as if they were going out of fashion. 'Now let's see if I can't take all your money before you decide to call it quittin' time.'

Terry stood from the table. 'Y'all play this one without me.' He patted his crotch. 'I got a lizard needs drainin'.'

Marcus almost choked on his beer. When he could speak, he said, 'Old Mrs Docket reckons it ain't more'n a worm.' He exchanged a high-five with Sid; both of them were in hysterics. Terry, on the other hand, looked decidedly perturbed.

'Yeah . . . well, I didn't hear her complainin' when I

was givin' it to her,' he stammered as he backed towards the door.

'Whatever you say,' Sid laughed. 'Hey, *tell* me somethin', hoss. Was she an early riser?'

Terry didn't know what Sid was going on about, but he shook his head. 'Naw, man. Bitch liked a lie-in. Why?'

Sid winked at Marcus before saying, 'Because I heard that "the early bird catches the worm".' *That* did it; cards went flying, beer was spilled, nuts toppled from their precarious position on the edge of the table and rolled across the already-stained carpet.

'Fuck you, man!' Terry said as he turned and left through the door, mumbling to himself as he went.

By the time he reached the bathroom – after getting lost in the dark on the way thanks to the copious amount of high-volume alcohol they'd imbibed – he was still stewing over Sid and Marcus's comments. They could say what they liked about his weight, or the fact that he'd fucked a lot of things that nobody else would touch with a bargepole, but when they started mocking the size of his schlong they had crossed a line.

He unzipped and pointed it at the toilet, giving it a cursory glance. 'Ain't fuck all wrong with it,' he said, more for his own assurance.

The bathroom was as dark as the rest of the

house. Sid didn't use the other rooms, and so there was no need for bulbs. Terry thought, as he began to piss, he would mention it to Sid when he returned to the table. What did the guy think was going to happen? Photosynthesis? The amount of money Sid had just relieved him of was enough to light the entire fucking house for the next century or so. Shit, it was enough to light the whole town for a few years.

Terry finished pissing and shook. The gentle *pitter-patter* of urine peppering the carpet didn't stop him from shaking his dick. 'Not so small now,' he mumbled, grinning.

He tucked himself in and turned to leave. But when he took a step forward, he met with an obstruction. At first he thought he'd lined up with the door wrong; it was easily done. The darkness was enough to disorientate anyone. He knew, though, that he was perfectly aligned with the door to the hall; there was somebody in the way, blocking his exit.

'Who *is* that?' he asked, trying not to sound like a complete pussy, which – given the circumstances – was a helluva lot more difficult than it sounded. 'Is that you, Sid? I said I was fuckin' sorry. You ain't been cheatin' me, *okay*.'

There came the sound of rustling clothes as the mystery intruder moved, ever-so-slightly, into the room. Terry raised his hand and began to paw at the space where the obstruction had been standing only a moment ago.

Nothing.

'This ain't funny, fools,' Terry said, wishing he could see who was in the bathroom with him. Shit, it was a small room – perhaps twelve feet square – so he knew that whoever it was, they were still within touching distance. 'Fuck this! Y'all just ruined this poker-night . . . crazy sonsofbitches.'

He took a step forward, hoping to reach the door, but a sharp pain in his lower back caused him to stop. At first, he thought it was just a muscle-spasm, the kind of thing you would get from making a sudden movement, but then he felt a blossoming stickiness, and then something warm trickling down his pants, pooling in and around his ass-crack.

'What the—' was all he managed. An arm choked the words off, and Terry's sentence finished with a high-pitched squeal and then the sound of choking. He dropped to his knees, slipping in the warm puddle that hadn't been there a few seconds ago.

Blood.

Terry dug his heels into the sodden carpet and pushed, hoping to unbalance the attacker, but the fucker just stepped aside and tightened his grip. It was a classic headlock, and Terry, being a major fan of wrestling, knew there was very little he could do to get out of it. The pain in his back suddenly heightened, almost as if the attacker was squeezing the blood down into the wounded area like a tube of toothpaste, trying to extract every last drop of life from him. He coughed, spluttered, wished it was Marcus who had needed a piss first, and then the attacker relented slightly, momentarily loosening his grasp.

In an ideal world, Terry would have taken this opportunity to smash back into the fucker, send him crashing into the pisser, but the energy he needed for such a move was absent and all he could do was flail around, trying to slap at the attacker with both hands.

Then came the pin-prick at his temple. His struggles only served to cut up the side of his face. Thin rivulets of blood dripped down his cheek.

A knife. The blade that had already stabbed him in the back and penetrated his kidney was now against his head. The helplessness washed over him, and he realised he was going to die, right there, on the bathroom floor in a puddle of his own blood and piss.

'Fuck you!' he gasped, and then the blade was pushed slowly through his head, separating his earlobe from the rest of him before continuing through to the other side.

*

'Oh, for *fuck's* sake, how long does it take to piss?' Sid growled. They had played one hand without Terry before deciding to wait. Poker just wasn't a game for two people.

'Ah, he's probably tryin' to find it,' Marcus laughed. Sid, however, felt the joke had run its course and didn't supply a laugh of his own. Marcus glanced across his shoulder, as if Terry would magically appear between the door-frame as a result. 'Terry! Y'all better hurry the fuck up!' He turned back to the table and, in a lowered voice, said, 'Sonofabitch drinks too much.'

Marcus picked up the cards and began to shuffle them, completely unaware that there was a third man in the room. Sid had watched him slowly – methodically – enter just as Marcus began to shuffle the deck. A tall guy, medium build, wearing a balaclava. The head that dangled from his clenched and bloodied fist was the reason why Sid had been unable to speak, or even make a sound, and he was paralysed, rooted to the spot like a fucking tree. It was Terry's head that the man was holding, and it was looking right at Sid, the tongue hanging listlessly from his dead lips. A slight noise finally fell from his mouth, but it was too late to warn Marcus of the newcomer.

The masked man slowly lowered the head in front of the unaware Marcus, who sighed, relaxed a little as he realised it was just Terry, and then panicked as he noticed the spinal-cord dangling from the stump, the blood dripping from the severed tendons. He tried to stand, but the knife came across so quickly that there was an audible *whoosh!* Before Marcus had time to fully swivel on his chair, the knife had slit his throat. Blood spurted from his neck in an arterial geyser; he dropped the deck of cards as he threw himself back into the chair. For a moment, Sid thought it had started to rain outside, but then he realised the terrible noise was Marcus's blood hitting the scattered deck, coating each and every one of them until you would do well to find a white spot.

Marcus's head fell back. The gaping wound in his throat seemed to smile across the table at Sid, opening and shutting slightly as if in speech. *You're next, Sid,* it was saying. *You're next.*

Suddenly, Sid was able to move again, and the only problem was: he didn't know what to do.

The masked man rounded the table. As he did, he reached down and grabbed it by its edge. With one almighty push, he tossed the table across the room where it landed in a pool of beer, glass, peanuts and bloody cards. The still-twitching body belonging to

Marcus was now sitting, openly, in the middle of the room, facing Sid as if they were about to embark upon some kind of interesting debate.

Sid cowered, shrinking into his chair, holding a placatory hand out, which trembled through absolute fear. 'Please, tell me what you want! Anything! Please, just don't hurt me!'

The man stopped moving three feet away from Sid. He even lowered the knife as he came to a halt. It was clear that he was thinking, trying to decide what to do next. He'd entered the room with intent, but he hadn't counted on someone *begging* him not to hurt them. Sid stared up into the eyes of the man behind the mask, and for a moment he almost recognised them.

'Please, I . . . I don't have much of worth, but I . . . just *take* what you want!' Sid was babbling like a little baby, and he knew it. If he lived through this, he would look back on it with shame and regret.

If he lived through this.

The masked man stood motionless, absorbing Sid's pleas with immense pleasure. He slowly reached for something, something that had thus far remained hidden behind his back. Sid watched; his terrified eyes bulged, threatening to drop from their sockets. His chest tightened, and he wondered if he was about to suffer a coronary. It wouldn't be the first, but it would certainly be the last.

When the hand emerged, something shiny was clenched tightly in it's white-knuckled fist. Sid's chest constricted some more as the realisation of what was about to happen hit home.

'*No! Please, no!*'

But the meat tenderiser was already mid-swing, and the masked man had closed the distance between them in a flash. If Sid had remained conscious for long enough, he would have seen teeth – his teeth – ping across the room and clatter against the refrigerator door. Thank heavens for small mercies; the darkness took him instantly.

*

'Wakey, wakey, you fucking prick!' Tom pulled the balaclava off. His face was dripping with sweat. He used the wooly mask to wipe the stinging perspiration from his eyes before screwing it up and tucking it into his back-pocket.

Sid came round slowly, blinking his eyes like a madman, rolling his head around as if he was warming up for exercise. Tom had panicked back there, and had clobbered the fucker a little harder than even he had anticipated. There were a few times, when Tom was tying him to his chair, that he believed he had killed him, accidentally gone in too hard and finished him with one swipe. He had checked for a pulse, and was relieved to find one, weak but present.

And now he was coming round; the fun could *really* start.

Tom paced across the room, being careful not to touch anything. He'd murdered two people, and was about to add to the tally; it was paramount that he didn't fuck up by leaving fingerprints all over the place. 'This is not a nice place you've got here, Sid,' he said as he carefully examined the magazines scattered in one corner of the room. They were the usual male-fodder; *Guns Magazine; Jeep World; Penthouse.* Tom toppled one of the stacks with his foot. 'I guess you can't buy the kind of stuff you're into, huh?'

He turned to find Sid trying to focus on him. His mouth was opening and closing – like a fish out of water – but the only sounds to emerge were croaks and groans.

'Ahh, never mind,' Tom said. 'It'll come to you in a minute.' He smiled, turned the knife over and over in his hand. The meat tenderiser had been useful, but it had almost killed the prick with one hit. Tom didn't want to make the same mistake again, so he'd reverted back to the blade.

'Tho . . .Thomash?' A thin string of bloody drool seeped from the corner of Sid's mouth. He gawked at

Tom with a mixture of sadness and confusion, and Tom didn't know whether the prick was shaking his head with dissent, or through uncontrollable fear. Secretly, he hoped it was a little of both.

'See, I *told* you it would come to you,' Tom said, traversing the room. 'And to think we haven't seen each other for what? Since Mom's funeral? Yeah, that's about right.'

Sid was trying to swallow, but he couldn't close his mouth in order to do so. The endless torrent of blood continued to fall from his lips; a crimson pool had formed in his lap.

'Whash . . . Sht—'

'That's a very good question, Sid,' Tom interjected. Sid flinched at the sound of his voice. 'After Mom died, you pretty much went about your shit, didn't you? There was no point keeping in touch with Jason and me. To be honest, Sid, I never liked you, and I knew what you used to do to Mom, hit her, make her dress how the fuck you wanted her to dress, but we never said anything, because we wanted her to be strong and stand up to you. In the end she wasn't strong enough. But guess what? It wasn't only Mom you were controlling, was it? You see, Jason died last week, Sid. I'll spare you the sordid details, not that you'd give a shit anyway, but Jason had cancer, and it got him in the end, the way we knew it would. So I was there just before he died, *Sidney,*' - he spat the name as if it offended his tongue – 'and Jason told me a little secret, something that had been killing him all these years. It wasn't the cancer – oh no, that was nothing compared to what he'd put up with.' Tom grimaced as Sid's expression altered.

The fucker knew *exactly* what he was talking about.

'I can see you're way ahead of me there, Sid,' Tom said, twisting the knife in his hand. Truth be told, he wanted to jam the fucking thing straight into the bound man's face, end it immediately, but there was no fun in that. Jason would have wanted the prick to suffer, the way he 'd made Jason suffer as a child. 'You never tried anything with me, though, did you? You knew damn well that Jason was the weakest and you . . . ' He trailed off; the thought of Jason being forced to do things against his will was too much, and it was all Tom could do not to ram the blade straight down into the top of Sid's evil fucking head.

Sid shifted nervously in his seat. If he hadn't been aware of the rope binding him before, he was now. 'I don't . . . *shit*, Thomash, I don't know what he told you—'

'You see,' Tom said. 'That's where you've gone wrong. This is your chance to own up, to *repent,* Sidney!' he pronounced it *Sid-neh* purposefully; he was pretty sure there had been a time, when they were children, that their mother had made the mistake of mispronouncing his name, and she'd suffered the brunt of his anger for it.

Sid lowered his head. If he was pretending to cry, he was a better actor than Tom remembered, though he had been acting all along, hadn't he? He had been smiling, playing at being a decent enough stepdad, and all along he was a beast masquerading as one. And somehow – Tom didn't know how – Sid had managed to convince Jason to keep it all to himself, to go about his days as if nothing was wrong. And Jason, against all odds and any urge he must have had to tell someone – *anyone* – had remained silent.

Tom moved slowly, deliberately, towards Sid. The knife no longer felt like a weapon in his hand; it was an extension of himself, an appendage all of its own. Sid whimpered; blood dripped from his chin.

'You know what pisses me off the most?' asked Tom. He was close enough to touch him now; close enough to cut the cunt's face or slit his throat from ear-to-ear, although even *that* wouldn't be enough. 'The fact that I never had a clue. I mean, I knew what you were doing to Mom, how you were beating her and making her explain herself every time she wanted to leave the fucking house, but not once did it cross my mind that you were nothing but a filthy, cunting pervert.'

Deep breaths, Tom, deeeeeep breaths . . .

'I shwear, Thom—'

'Don't you fucking call me that!' Tom spat. By the time the words left his mouth, a thin red slice had swelled up on Sid's forehead. Fresh blood oozed from it, thick and sublime. Tom didn't even recall lashing out, but that was anger for you. Sid hadn't seen it, either; he'd closed his eyes, expecting much worse than a gash to the head. The terror in his eyes, though, satisfied Tom somewhat.

Tom smiled before continuing. 'You humiliated him, then pretended everything was okay. I have no idea how anyone could do that, but people like you don't get second chances. Not where I come from. Not after what you did to Jason.'

Sid thought about objecting, saw his blood tainting the knife-edge, and decided it would do him no good to push his luck.

'So, Sid . . . *Dad*,' he said, callously barking the word at the man in the chair. 'I had to come see you one last time. There was one reason why you didn't try anything with me, wasn't there?' He didn't expect an answer, so when Sid opened his mouth to speak he waited with baited breath. The mouth shut; nothing. 'I'll tell you then, shall I? It was because I was always the stronger one. I wouldn't have let you pull any of that shit with me. I'd have cut your fucking dick off while you slept and rammed it down your throat.'

Sid flinched.

Tom didn't.

'I'm done,' Tom said, dropping the knife on the carpet. He glanced around at the mess, the blood, the dead man sitting in the chair opposite smiling through his neck. An *innocent*? Tom doubted it. There were no innocents, not in Sid's little gang. For all Tom knew, they were all part of some mass paedophile-ring, in which case he'd done the world a favour, and saved the tax-payers a lot of money in the process.

Sid watched as Tom reached into his back-pocket, retrieved the balaclava and proceeded to pull it over his head. Did he say he was *done*? Sid might have misheard as he could barely hear anything over the racing *hush-thump* of blood in his ears, but he thought – he *prayed* – he heard correctly. And Tom, after picking the knife back up from the carpet, backed slowly out of the room, his gaze darting from Sid, to the sitting corpse, then back to Sid.

And then he was gone.

Sid waited, listening. How long did he leave it before calling for help? Tom was, as far as Sid was aware, from the other side of the country, which meant that he'd drove a long fucking way to reach him. The noise of a car's engine starting up would be his cue to start screaming, though he doubted anyone would hear him; the nearest house was almost a mile down the road, and it was the middle of the night. There were hardly going to be joggers or dog-walkers at such an ungodly hour. He could be sitting there, pissing blood, for the next twelve hours.

The sound of an engine roaring to life never came, and Sid began to panic. There was a bang, one that he recognised as the sound of the front door slamming shut, and Sid frantically twisted and bucked in his seat, to no avail. He clenched his eyes shut, blinking away the blood from the seeping wound on his forehead, and when he opened them he saw the outline of Tom in the doorway, and then his vision cleared a little more, and that was when he spotted the chainsaw.

'After tonight,' Tom said, his lips curling into a grin between the wooly hole of the balaclava. 'I'm done.'

He yanked the starting pull-handle and the chainsaw roared into life. Sid found himself paralysed once again; a pool of warm urine blossomed on the front of his pants. And Tom came forward, still grinning, knowing that his brother would be watching from heaven, as proud as punch.

Tom began to dissect the prick, because that's what any good brother would do. And when it was done, he would take a piece to Jason's grave, and they would laugh one last time together.

Lythalia Calling

Jack sat staring through the window towards the woods at the rear of the garden, the way he had for twelve consecutive nights. Darkness had fallen; the sound of the wind rustling through the trees was the only thing he could hear. Courtenay House's garden was barely visible through the fog, and for a moment he panicked at the thought of not seeing *her* tonight.

The girl; the single-most terrifying – and yet resplendent – woman he had ever seen had visited him at the stroke of twelve for the last dozen nights. The first time she'd appeared – dancing amongst the cinquefoil – he'd been paralysed with both fear and fascination. Who was she, and what the hell was she doing in his garden? Part of his mind had screamed at him, urging him to go out and send her packing, or call the Bluebottles, who would no doubt cart her off to the cells for the night, or at least until she'd slept off whatever powerful elixir she'd imbibed to send her jigging through the undergrowth in the middle of the night. Another part of him – the more curious and adolescent half which cared nothing for consequences and even less for decorum – instructed him to quietly observe. She wasn't hurting anybody, was she? The plants would need replacing, but that was a small price to pay for the splendorous exhibition the girl was putting on.

Just for *him*?

That first night she'd danced for an hour, kicking through the garden like some mythical sprite. Jack couldn't recall blinking once during the whole performance. When she'd left – disappearing as clandestinely as she had appeared into the woods – he'd realised how sore his eyes were, and after applying drops he'd gone to bed and thought about her, about the way in which she sprang lithely from one foot to the next. He'd slept none that first night, not that he'd actively tried to switch off.

The second night he'd been tending to the dog – allowing it to shit, scratch, sniff around a little – when the girl appeared from the trees. He couldn't believe that she would return, and as he dragged the dog towards the house, so as not to startle the girl, he'd wondered whether she was really there, or if his wishful thinking from that day had manifested itself in a vision.

Charlie, his Red Fell Terrier, had run whimpering into the house, its business for the evening prematurely concluded, but Jack had watched from the shadows, mesmerised once again by her movements. She'd practically floated across the Amaryllis, her feet constantly shrouded with an emerald miasma.

Had that been there the previous night? Jack couldn't be sure.

The third, fourth and fifth nights she'd appeared and performed, and it was upon the sixth night that Jack had realised she wasn't human.

The word *Goddess* came to mind, though it wasn't the kind of word Jack liked to chuck around, willy-nilly. It conjured images of robed beauties playing chess with pieces carved from diamond and platinum. This girl *was* a Goddess, but not of that ilk. She was something else wholly, and Jack knew that somewhere along the line, their paths would inextricably cross and things would change forever.

But he'd kept his distance, watching from the sanctuary of the house or deep within the shadows provided by it. There was, he knew, a possibility that she might disapprove of his audience should she become aware of it, and that was something he wasn't willing to risk just yet.

He *had* to watch her; he had to see her dance, for if *he* didn't then it would all be for nothing. She might as well not exist.

Rain began to pepper the window. Jack watched as thin streaks dragged down to the sill, partially obscuring his view. It didn't worry him too much. The clock hanging upon the wall assured him that it was ten-fifteen; plenty of time for the rain to dissipate.

Once again he pondered the unimaginable, that she would not appear tonight. "Don't be a *fool*, Jack," he whispered, clouding the window with his exhalation. "She'll show."

The strangest thing was, he couldn't recall his life before two weeks ago. Everything that had come before had drifted into obscurity, as if nothing else mattered. His mother would have a coronary if she heard about it; that he was allowing a girl to frolic in the garden to which she so painstakingly tended. Edith Drummond was the epitome of old-fashioned, rendering her unapproachable as far as girls were concerned. Jack had never been able to discuss his romances with his mother, and this one – not that it was a romance, not even in the remotest sense of the word – would certainly be filed under S for *Secret*, and also N for *Never Tell Mother…*

With the rain gently pattering the glass, and the clock ticking behind him, Jack relaxed. Within three minutes he was drifting, weightless, his mind working overtime to placate him. She would be there when he woke up; he knew that her performances were all for him.

She must know, must feel my gaze upon her…

Panic washed over him as he bolted upright in his chair. He spun, allowed his eyes to adjust to the darkness of the room.

He sighed. The clock read one minute to midnight.

"I haven't missed her."

He turned his attention back to the garden, where a thick fog had descended while he slept, carpeting everything from the gravelled courtyard to the woods. The wind pushed it gently along the ground. Jack was just happy for the abeyance of the rain.

And there she was, right on time, hovering along on her viridian mist. Her long, brown hair flapped loosely around her face. Jack wanted nothing more than to bunch it up into his fists and inhale her scent.

She dance and gracefully cavorted; Jack watched and nervously hoped…hoped that she might look to the window and see him, beckon him down to her so that they might dance together, lose themselves in each other.

She looked stunning tonight. Ethereal yet tangible, and just beyond reach, though hadn't she always been?

"Not tonight," Jack whispered. He stood from the chair, unable to look away from the dancing girl. He knew he had to, though. Ten seconds was all it would take. Ten seconds and he would be outside with her, and they would dance together, becoming one.

He blinked, sighed, turned and rushed for the stairs. Taking them three at a time – and almost crippling himself in the process – it took less than three seconds to reach the ground-floor. He hurtled through the kitchen, grabbing for the keys which dangled from the locked door. As he fumbled erratically to unlock the door, Charlie whimpered from his basket. Did the dog know she was out there once again? Could it sense her, or hear her revelling in the copse? "It's okay, Charlie," Jack mumbled. "Daddy's just popping outside for a moment." Charlie settled, lowering his head. If Jack had turned in that moment and noticed the countenance of his pet, he might have considered calling the whole thing off, returning instead to the safety of his bedroom.

Finally the key turned. Jack spilled out into the inclemency of the night. He scanned the garden, fearing he'd made a mistake and that she had finished her routine and withdrawn, as was her wont, to the woods.

Then he saw her, cavorting by the pond. Was it possible that he could *love* her? It certainly felt like it, not that he had a basis of comparison. His mother would indubitably tell him it was nonsense; that it was impossible to fall for a girl who had done nothing more than trespass and drunkenly dance – and on her Clematis, nonetheless…

"Excuse me." The words leapt from his mouth. Had he been in control he might have continued to hide amongst the shadows, silently, but it was too late now.

She stopped, landing with a less-than-nimble thump upon the grass. Her neck arched as she glanced in his direction. Her expression was not of shock, but inevitability, as if she had expected to be caught.

Jack suddenly wished he'd remained upstairs; she would never return, not now, not after this. Her joyous midnight dancing was over, and Jack felt something tug at his heart – an emptiness – which he wished he could eliminate.

Then she did something he could never have anticipated. A smile, beautiful and impish, crept across her face. She wasn't disgusted, as Jack had first thought. She was happy. Perhaps this wasn't the end, after all.

Perhaps this was the beginning of something else.

Yeah, mother. Who's laughing now?...

Jack took a tentative step into the garden. Just because she was smiling didn't mean she wasn't frightened.

"I've watched you dance since the beginning," Jack said, hoping his honesty would somehow put her at ease. Although, now that he'd said it he couldn't help feeling that this admission portrayed him as creepy.

She smiled, took a step towards him, and said, "I know."

He'd expected a lot of ripostes, but not that one. That one was a game-changer.

"You know?"

She nodded, still smiling. As Jack cautiously approached, he noticed something he hadn't from the window. The emerald mist was dissipating, seeping away from her as if she no longer had a need for it.

And as the mist dissolved, he saw something that wasn't possible. It couldn't be possible.

Her legs didn't finish at her feet. In fact, her feet were nothing like human. They were covered with bark; an orange sap oozed out over her ankles and between her toes. Vegetation of some sort twisted up around her shins, stopping just shy of the hem of her dress. At first sight, one would imagine it as nothing more than a trick of the moonlight, but Jack was close enough to realise that the vines trailing off into the woods were as much a part of her as the hair on her head; hair that was a combination of slender twigs and rotting ivy.

"I don't—"was all he could manage, for something emerged from her mouth. Parting her lips and snapping her jaw in the process, a branch leapt out of her throat and coiled around his neck. Her wide eyes were now a luminous green, a hue similar to the fog which had shielded Jack from the truth. She gargled, though not in pain at the wooden protrusion, but in ecstasy. She flicked her head to the side and Jack stumbled to the ground, clawing at the tightening branch around his throat. He could breathe, but only just.

She headed for the woods at the back of the garden. Jack dragged along behind her, through the flowers that his mother – *Oh, mother, what have I done?* – would find dead at first light. And Jack hoped that this thing, this beautiful thing that had danced and frolicked with the innocence of a child, carried him far from Courtenay House so that his mother would only stumble upon the dead flowers in the garden, and not a dead son, as well.

The trees soon blocked out the moonlight, but Jack could see stars through the overhead branches; stars that were long deceased, ancient worlds that had been destroyed by impossible creatures and cosmic beings. And Lythalia – he knew her name, now, for he could feel it, hear it, resonating through the branch coiled around his neck – was a Goddess, after all. He just hadn't expected her to be Lythalia, *The Forest Goddess.*

Later that night, they danced together for the one and only time. If Jack had lived to tell the tale, he would have been lying if he said he hadn't enjoyed it.

Three Little Words

We sit atop our rotting caravan, emaciated, starving, watching the ink-blot clouds drift slowly across the scorched sky. Lydia grabs for my hand, realises it's not where it had been a moment before. She turns to face me, and I try to push the troubled expression from my face, though it's taken up permanent residence and there's very little I can do to make it go away.

"What is it?" she asks, her voice broken as if she is not my wife of forty years, but a girl yet to experience life.

I sigh, explore the heavens above as the acid rain once again begins to pepper our exposed flesh. I feel it burning, and Lydia's aggrieved expression suggests that she does, too. "It's nothing," I lie, reaching for the hand that had recently sought me out. In the distance – perhaps five miles away – jets take to the air in preparation for another battle. The dogfights seem to be lasting longer, now. It's as if the pilots know that everything is coming to a head. Neither Lydia nor I will be around to see the end; neither of us *wants* to be.

"Remember that time you fell in the lake?" she asks, feigning a giggle. This – these stupid reminiscences we constantly bombard each other with – is a game that we play, often late at night. It takes the edge off; partially drowns out the sound of explosions in the distance. It also helps us both remember how lucky we've been.

"I almost froze my ass off that day," I say, wiping burning rain from my eyes. "What year was that?"

She thinks for a moment; I can practically hear the cogs turning. "That would have to be…nineteeeeeeeeen…nineteen-eighty-seven," she says, suddenly pleased with herself. "It was the year after we went to Greece and you got that god-awful sunburn."

I laugh, though at the time I hadn't. Several of my blisters had been drained, such was the severity of the burn; the doctors said I was lucky not to have developed something more acute. "That's what happens when a redhead falls asleep in the sun," I say, though I'm not sure she hears the final part as an explosion tears through a city north of our position. In a few moments we'll see the smoke, rising towards the perpetually blackened sky.

If you were to ask me what I yearn for more than anything else, right now I would say: a glimpse of daylight. It is something none of us have seen for many years. Oil-slick skies, almost molten in appearance, are all we have to look forward to. The sulphurous atmosphere is, at times, unbearable. I coughed up so much blood yesterday that I took out my bible and made my peace with the Lord.

Lydia lies back in my arms just as the acid rain ceases to fleck us. The tinny drum of its patter upon the roof of the caravan leaves us, momentarily, in silence, though Lydia soon fills it.

"Were you happy, George?" she asks, and for once I wish the rain hadn't deserted us so easily. This wasn't part of our game; she'd never asked me anything like this, and it takes me a minute to fathom why she's asking me now.

"Not *all* of the time," I tell her. It's the truth; nobody is happy all of the time. That's not how life works. It's how you deal with the sadness that'll ultimately get you through the day. "But as much as I could wish for? Yeah, I'd say I've been pretty damn lucky."

South of our position, some asshole drops a nuke. It's a small yield, but it will be a few minutes before Lydia can respond. We wait, gazing into each other's eyes as the shockwave approaches. Her silver hair flies outwards, waving at something neither of us can see. My teeth – what remains of them – rattle inside my mouth, and I clench them, at least until I can speak once again. Sitting here like this, in complete silence, is something we didn't do enough of. It's taken an apocalypse to get us to this, but as I watch my wife's hair, floating horizontally, her face contorted as if in the throes of some intense pleasure (a face I haven't seen for quite some years), I realise that not everything has been lost.

"Phew," she says, smiling as the shockwave dissipates. "I thought we were a goner with that one."

Would that have been so bad? If that face shrivelled up with ecstasy was the last thing I saw before my flesh came apart?

"So yeah," I say, as if nothing has interrupted our conversation. "I've been happy, and *you've* made me that way."

She smiles; a tear escapes the corner of her eyes before clashing with the acid-rain already nestling upon her cheek. "I wouldn't change a thing about you, George."

I laugh. "I leave the toilet-seat up all the time. What, you wouldn't make it so I always remembered to put it down?"

"I'd have nothing to *complain* about then, would I?" she says.

Machine-gun fire drifts across on the wind, though neither of us is concerned. It would take a helluva shot to hit us way out here, and we've survived just fine like this for six months. In fact, we haven't seen another person for a year, maybe longer. At least, not a living person. There are bodies everywhere. Rotten, decaying cadavers; you can't move for 'em.

"I'm going to turn in for the night," Lydia says. She yawns as if to substantiate her comment. She leans across, kisses me once on the cheek, twice on the lips. It's been that combination for years. As she does it, I reach around and hold the back of her head, run my fingers through her now-lifeless hair, damp and smoking. I remember when that hair had been clean, silky, beautiful.

"I need to hear it," I say, allowing her movement but not enough to reach the ladder at the edge of the caravan's roof.

She sighs, rolls her eyes like a petulant child. "Do we have to do this every night?"

"Every night until it happens," I say. "C'mon, Lydia. It's just three little words. If I die in the night…" I begin for her.

Another explosion, this time to the east. We both ignore it; this is more important.

She conceded defeat. "I'll *eat* you," she says.

"Atta girl," I smile. "You eat me right up."

She nods and descends the ladder. I watch her go, still smiling a mouthful of popcorn teeth, before my gaze turns to the bones surrounding our home; remnants of our beloved children, never wasted, even in death.

If You Enjoyed This Collection, Please Visit

www.adam-millard.com

For News, Videos, Events & Future Releases

Acknowledgements

'The Marionnettiste of Versailles' copyright © 2012. Originally published in Rigorous Mortis: A Mortician's Tales.

'Your Cheatin' Heart' copyright © 2013

'Parasitic Embrace' copyright © 2012. Originally Published in Fading Light: An Anthology of the Monstrous.

'Benji' copyright © 2012. Originally Published in Satan's Toybox: Terrifying Teddies.

'Food of Love' copyright © 2013

'Sparrows' copyright © 2012. Originally Published in Sirens Call Ezine.

'Can You Read That Asteroid from Here?' copyright © 2013. Originally Published in Cosmic Vegetable.

'Hair' copyright © 2013. Originally Published in Serial Killers: Tres Tria.

'Phoenix Rising' copyright © 2013.

'Bug Boy' copyright © 2012.

'What's She Got That I Haven't?' copyright © 2013. Originally Published in Housewives Go Nuclear.

'Mad World' copyright © 2013 Originally Published in Carnage After the End: Volume One

'7:17 From Suicide Station' copyright © 2013. Originally Published in Miseria's Chorale

'A Small Matter of Transmutation' copyright © 2013. Originally Published in Shifters

FROM THE AUTHOR OF DEAD WEST
DEAD CELLS
ADAM MILLARD

DEAD FROST
adam millard

"This guy must be one of the best kept secrets in British horror." - Sean T. Page, Ministry Of Zombies, author of The Official Zombie Handbook
DEAD LINE
2011
ADAM MILLARD

From the author of The Susceptibles
DEATHDEALERS
AN ALEX WINTERBONE NOVEL
XIII
DEATH
ADAM MILLARD

ADAM MILLARD

THE SUSCEPTIBLES

The scary thing is, they could always see YOU...

The Secret Diary of
PETER CROMBIE
(Aged Deceased and 2/3)
Maisie Bruce smells
Zoms Rule
Another toof
RESTRICTED AREA
KEEP OUT
Z=oMbi3
Trevor + Maximus Sitting in a tree
ADAM MILLARD

Peter Crombie
TEENAGE
ZOMBIE
ADAM MILLARD

PETER CROMBIE VS
THE GRAMPIRES
ADAM MILLARD

a twisted reimagining
OLLY!
ADAM MILLARD

More from Crowded Quarantine

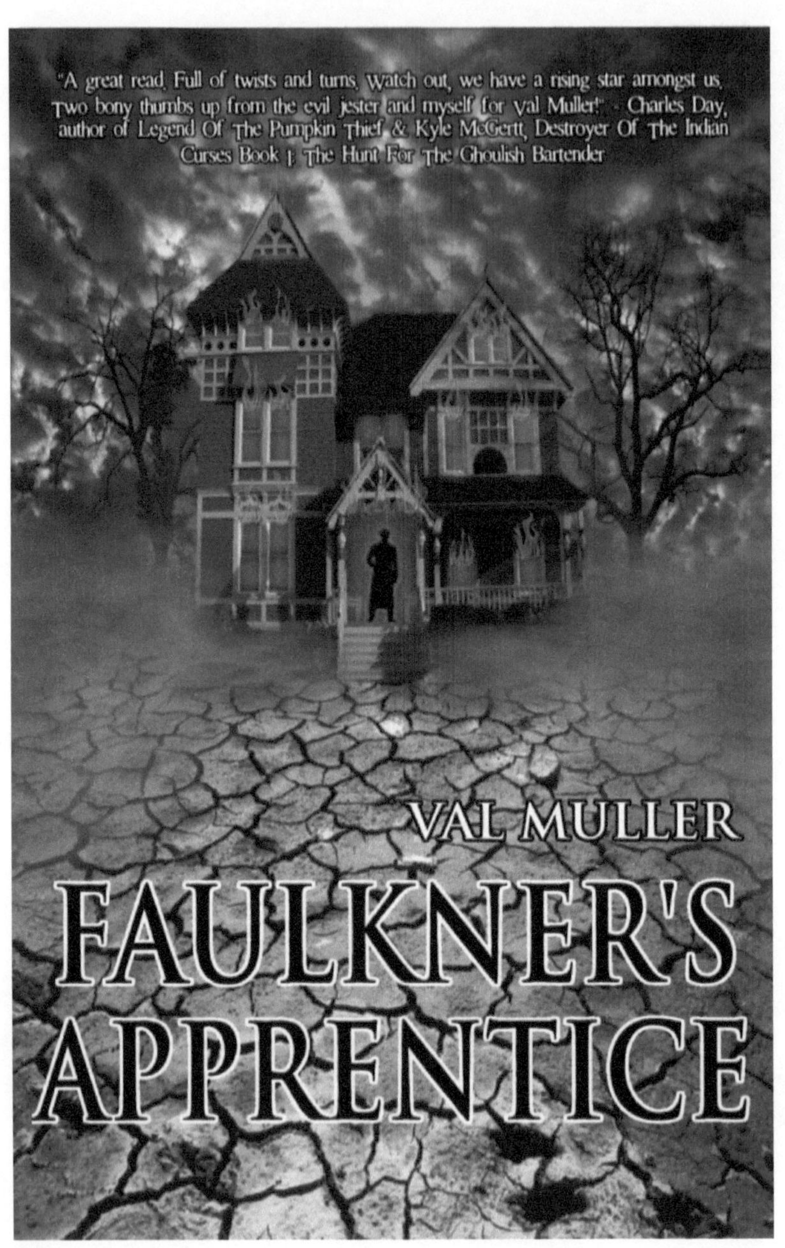
"A great read. Full of twists and turns. Watch out, we have a rising star amongst us.
Two bony thumbs up from the evil jester and myself for Val Muller!" - Charles Day,
author of Legend Of The Pumpkin Thief & Kyle McGertt, Destroyer Of The Indian
Curses Book 1: The Hunt For The Ghoulish Bartender
VAL MULLER
FAULKNER'S
APPRENTICE

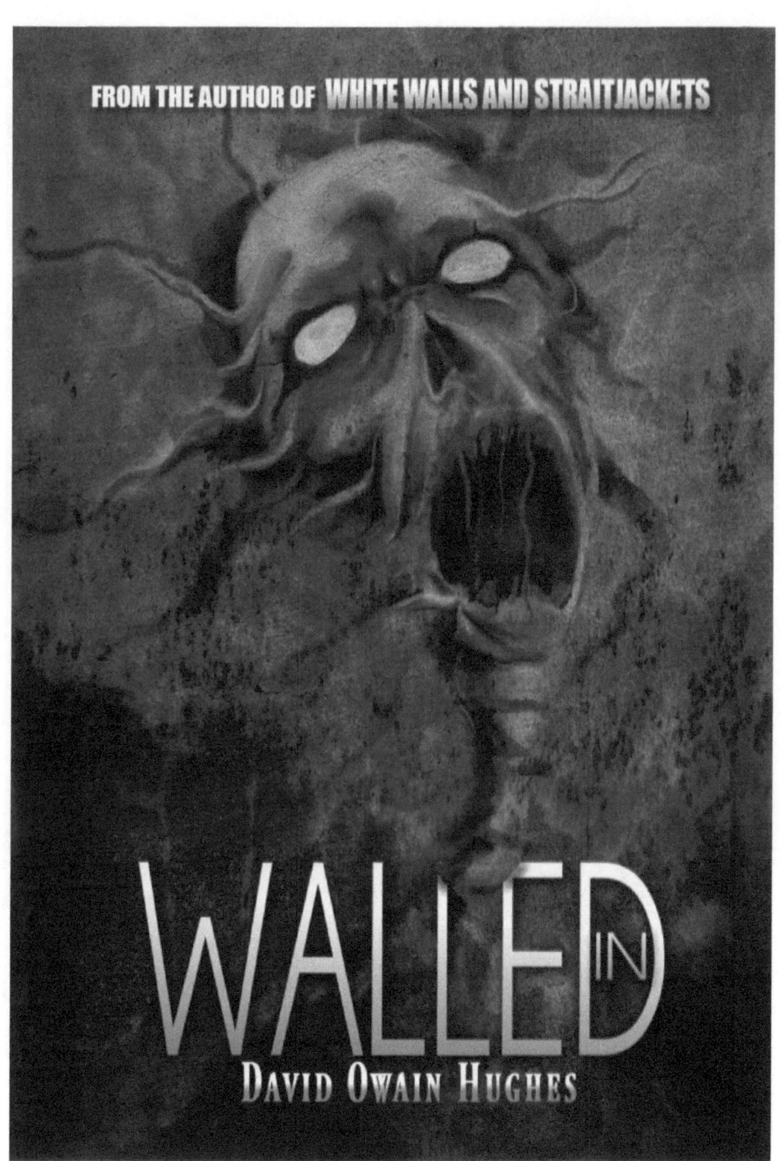
FROM THE AUTHOR OF WHITE WALLS AND STRAITJACKETS
WALLED IN
DAVID OWAIN HUGHES

"Chilling as an Arctic blast, Craig Saunders' bold and distinctive voice will haunt your dreams." - Bill Hussey, author of *Through A Glass, Darkly* and *The Abscence*
THE ESTATE
CRAIG SAUNDERS

"Schwamberger never fails to serve up the shocks." - Shroud Magazine
TY SCHWAMBERGER
THE TORCHLIGHT INN
last night out

MOONLIGHT MEDICINE:
ONSET
JEN HAEGER

DALE ELDON
REBECCA BESSER
RICH HAWKINS
WESLEY SOUTHARD
GRINDHOUSE
A CROWDED QUARANTINE PRODUCTION
Also Starring JASON RADAK - AIREKA SNEVE - DUSTIN WALKER
DUSTIN READE - JAY WILBURN - WAYNE C. ROGERS - INDY MCDANIEL
PATRICK MACADOO - JOSHUA DOBSON - PHILIP ROBERTS - ZOE ADAMS
HOLLY DAY - ALLEN JACOBY and NIKKI MCKENZIE
compiled and edited by ADAM MILLARD

Of Devils & Deviants

An Anthology of Erotic Horror

Graham Masterton
Taylor Grant
Maynard Sims
Ralph Robert Moore
Claude Lalumiere
Aaron J. French
Adam Howe
John McIlveen
C.W. LaSart
Lucy Taylor
Jeff Gardiner
Christian Larsen
Shaun Meeks
Mandy DeGeit
Cameron Trost
J. Daniel Stone
Kenzie Mathews
Eric LaRocca
Stacey Turner
Jenn Loring
Kenneth W. Cain
Ken MacGregor
Bear Wieter

Introduced by Bram Stoker Award-Winning Author, Lucy Taylor

Compiled and Edited by
Adam Millard & Zoe-Ray Millard

MEAT
SUITCASE
WOL-VRIEY

THE WAY OF ALL FLESH
KEVIN WALSH

THE
ETERNAL
WAR
Ashley Tia Long

www.ingramcontent.com/pod-product-compliance
Lightning Source LLC
Chambersburg PA
CBHW030540310726
48979CB00010B/1979/J